CONVERSATIONS WITH FRIENDS

SALLY ROONEY

LARGE
PRINT

First published in Great Britain 2017
by
Faber & Faber Ltd.

First Isis Edition
published 2018
by arrangement with
Faber & Faber Ltd.

Excerpts from *Meditations in an Emergency,*
copyright © 1957 by Frank O'Hara. Used by permission of
Grove/Atlantic, Inc. Any third party use of this material,
outside of this publication, is prohibited.

Conversations with Friends receives financial assistance
from the Arts Council.

A catalogue record for this book is available
from the British Library.

ISBN 978–1–78541–477–0 (hb)
ISBN 978–1–78541–483–1 (pb)

Published by
F. A. Thorpe (Publishing)
Anstey, Leicestershire

Set by Words & Graphics Ltd.
Anstey, Leicestershire
Printed and bound in Great Britain by
T. J. International Ltd., Padstow, Cornwall

This book is printed on acid-free paper

In times of crisis, we must all decide again and again whom we love.

FRANK O'HARA

PART ONE

CHAPTER
ONE

Bobbi and I first met Melissa at a poetry night in town, where we were performing together. Melissa took our photograph outside, with Bobbi smoking and me self-consciously holding my left wrist in my right hand, as if I was afraid the wrist was going to get away from me. Melissa used a big professional camera and kept lots of different lenses in a special camera pouch. She chatted and smoked while taking the pictures. She talked about our performance and we talked about her work, which we'd come across on the internet. Around midnight the bar closed. It was starting to rain then, and Melissa told us we were welcome to come back to her house for a drink.

We all got into the back of a taxi together and started fixing up our seat belts. Bobbi sat in the middle, with her head turned to speak to Melissa, so I could see the back of her neck and her little spoon-like ear. Melissa gave the driver an address in Monkstown and I turned to look out the window. A voice came on the radio to say the words: eighties . . . pop . . . classics. Then a jingle played. I felt excited, ready for the challenge of visiting a stranger's home, already preparing compliments and certain facial expressions to make myself seem charming.

The house was a semi-detached red-brick, with a sycamore tree outside. Under the streetlight the leaves looked orange and artificial. I was a big fan of seeing the insides of other people's houses, especially people who were slightly famous like Melissa. Right away I decided to remember everything about her home, so I could describe it to our other friends later and Bobbi could agree.

When Melissa let us in, a little red spaniel came racing up the hall and started barking at us. The hallway was warm and the lights were on. Next to the door was a low table where someone had left a stack of change, a hairbrush and an open tube of lipstick. There was a Modigliani print hanging over the staircase, a nude woman reclining. I thought: this is a whole house. A family could live here.

We have guests, Melissa called down the corridor.

No one appeared so we followed her into the kitchen. I remember seeing a dark wooden bowl filled with ripe fruit, and noticing the glass conservatory. Rich people, I thought. I was always thinking about rich people then. The dog had followed us to the kitchen and was snuffling around at our feet, but Melissa didn't mention the dog so neither did we.

Wine? Melissa said. White or red?

She poured huge, bowl-sized glasses and we all sat around a low table. Melissa asked us how we'd started out performing spoken word poetry together. We had both just finished our third year of university at the

4

time, but we'd been performing together since we were in school. Exams were over by then. It was late May.

Melissa had her camera on the table and occasionally lifted it to take a photograph, laughing self-deprecatingly about being a "work addict". She lit a cigarette and tipped the ash into a kitschy-looking glass ashtray. The house didn't smell of smoke at all and I wondered if she usually smoked in there or not.

I made some new friends, she said.

Her husband was in the kitchen doorway. He held up his hand to acknowledge us and the dog started yelping and whining and running around in circles.

This is Frances, said Melissa. And this is Bobbi. They're poets.

He took a bottle of beer out of the fridge and opened it on the countertop.

Come and sit with us, Melissa said.

Yeah, I'd love to, he said, but I should try and get some sleep before this flight.

The dog jumped up on a kitchen chair near where he was standing and he reached out absently to touch its head. He asked Melissa if she had fed the dog, she said no. He lifted the dog into his arms and let the dog lick his neck and jaw. He said he would feed her, and he went back out the kitchen door again.

Nick's filming tomorrow morning in Cardiff, said Melissa.

We already knew that the husband was an actor. He and Melissa were frequently photographed together at events, and we had friends of friends who had met them. He had a big, handsome face and looked like he could comfortably pick Melissa up under one arm and fend off interlopers with the other.

He's very tall, Bobbi said.

Melissa smiled as if "tall" was a euphemism for something, but not necessarily something flattering. The conversation moved on. We got into a short discussion about the government and the Catholic Church. Melissa asked us if we were religious and we said no. She said she found religious occasions, like funerals or weddings, "comforting in a kind of sedative way". They're communal, she said. There's something nice about that for the neurotic individualist. And I went to a convent school so I still know most of the prayers.

We went to a convent school, said Bobbi. It posed issues.

Melissa grinned and said: like what?

Well, I'm gay, said Bobbi. And Frances is a communist.

I also don't think I remember any of the prayers, I said.

We sat there talking and drinking for a long time. I remember that we talked about the poet Patricia Lockwood, who we admired, and also about what Bobbi disparagingly called "pay gap feminism". I started to get tired and a little drunk. I couldn't think of anything witty to say and it was hard to arrange my face in a way that would convey my sense of humour. I think I laughed and nodded a lot. Melissa told us she was working on a new book of essays. Bobbi had read her first one, but I hadn't.

It's not very good, Melissa told me. Wait till the next one comes out.

At about three o'clock, she showed us to the spare room and told us how great it was to meet us and how glad she was that we were staying. When we got into bed I stared up at the ceiling and felt very drunk. The room was spinning repetitively in short, consecutive spins. Once I adjusted my eyes to one rotation, another would begin immediately. I asked Bobbi if she was also having a problem with that but she said no.

She's amazing, isn't she? said Bobbi. Melissa.

I like her, I said.

We could hear her voice in the corridor and her footsteps taking her from room to room. Once when the dog barked we could hear her yell something, and then her husband's voice. But after that we fell asleep. We didn't hear him leave.

Bobbi and I had first met in secondary school. Back then Bobbi was very opinionated and frequently spent time in detention for a behavioural offence our school called "disrupting teaching and learning". When we were sixteen she got her nose pierced and took up smoking. Nobody liked her. She got temporarily suspended once for writing "fuck the patriarchy" on the wall beside a plaster cast of the crucifixion. There was no feeling of solidarity around this incident. Bobbi was considered a show-off. Even I had to admit that teaching and learning went a lot more smoothly during the week she was gone.

When we were seventeen we had to attend a fundraising dance in the school assembly hall, with a partially broken disco ball casting lights on the ceiling and the barred-up windows. Bobbi wore a flimsy summer dress and looked like she hadn't brushed her hair. She was radiantly attractive, which meant everyone had to work hard not to pay her any attention. I told her I liked her dress. She gave me some of the vodka she was drinking from a Coke bottle and asked if the rest of the school was locked up. We checked the door up to the back staircase and found it was open. All the lights were off and no one else was up there. We could hear the music buzzing through the floorboards, like a ringtone belonging to someone else. Bobbi gave me some more of her vodka and asked me if I liked girls. It was very easy to act unfazed around her. I just said: sure.

I wasn't betraying anyone's loyalties by being Bobbi's girlfriend. I didn't have close friends and at lunchtime I read textbooks alone in the school library. I liked the other girls, I let them copy my homework, but I was lonely and felt unworthy of real friendship. I made lists of the things I had to improve about myself. After Bobbi and I started seeing each other, everything changed. No one asked for my homework any more. At lunchtime we walked along the car park holding hands and people looked away from us maliciously. It was fun, the first real fun I'd ever had.

After school we used to lie in her room listening to music and talking about why we liked each other. These were long and intense conversations, and felt so momentous to me that I secretly transcribed parts of them from memory in the evenings. When Bobbi talked about me it felt like seeing myself in a mirror for the first time. I also looked in actual mirrors more often. I started taking a close interest in my face and body, which I'd never done before. I asked Bobbi questions like: do I have long legs? Or short?

At our school graduation ceremony we performed a spoken word piece together. Some of the parents cried, but our classmates just looked out the assembly-room windows or talked quietly amongst themselves. Several months later, after more than a year together, Bobbi and I broke up.

Melissa wanted to write a profile about us. She sent us an email asking if we were interested, and attached some of the photographs she had taken outside the bar. Alone in my room, I downloaded one of the files and opened it up to fullscreen. Bobbi looked back at me, mischievous, holding a cigarette in her right hand and pulling on her fur stole with the other. Beside her, I looked bored and interesting. I tried to imagine my name appearing in a profile piece, in a serif font with thick stems. I decided I would try harder to impress Melissa next time we met.

Bobbi called me almost immediately after the email arrived.

Have you seen the photographs? she said. I think I'm in love with her.

I held my phone in one hand and zoomed in on Bobbi's face with the other. It was a high-quality image but I zoomed until I could see the pixellation.

Maybe you're just in love with your own face, I said.

Just because I have a beautiful face doesn't mean I'm a narcissist.

I let that one go. I was involved in the zooming process still. I knew that Melissa wrote for several big literary websites, and her work circulated widely online. She had written a famous essay about the Oscars which everyone reposted every year during awards season. Sometimes she also wrote local profiles, about artists who sold their work on Grafton Street or buskers in London; these were always accompanied by beautiful photographs of her subjects, looking human and full of "character". I zoomed back out and tried to look at my own face as if I were a stranger on the internet seeing it for the first time. It looked round and white, the eyebrows like overturned parentheses, my eyes averted from the lens, almost shut. Even I could see I had character.

We emailed her back saying we'd be delighted, and she invited us over for dinner to talk about our work and get some additional photographs. She asked me if I could forward some copies of our poetry and I sent her three or four of the best pieces. Bobbi and I discussed at length what Bobbi would wear to the dinner, under the guise of talking about what we should both wear. I lay in my room watching her look at herself in the mirror, moving pieces of her hair back and forth critically.

So when you say you're in love with Melissa, I said.

I mean I have a crush on her.

You know she's married.

You don't think she likes me? said Bobbi.

She was holding up one of my white brushed-cotton shirts in front of the mirror.

What do you mean likes you? I said. Are we being serious or just joking?

I am partly being serious. I think she does like me.

In an extramarital affair kind of way?

Bobbi just laughed at that. With other people I generally had a sense of what to take seriously and what not to, but with Bobbi it was impossible. She never seemed to be either fully serious or fully joking. As a result I had learned to adopt a kind of Zen acceptance of the weird things she said. I watched her take her blouse off and pull on the white shirt. She rolled up the sleeves carefully.

Good? she said. Or terrible?

Good. It looks good.

CHAPTER
TWO

It rained all day before we went for dinner at Melissa's. I sat in bed in the morning writing poetry, hitting the return key whenever I wanted. Eventually I opened my blinds, read the news online and showered. My apartment had a door out into the courtyard of the building, which was lavish with greenery and featured a cherry blossom tree in the far corner. It was almost June now, but in April the blossoms were bright and silky like confetti. The couple next door had a little baby who cried sometimes at night. I liked living there.

Bobbi and I met in town that evening and got a bus to Monkstown. Finding our way back to the house felt like unwrapping something in a game of pass the parcel. I mentioned this to Bobbi on the way and she said: is it the prize, or just another layer of wrapping?

We'll catch up on that after dinner, I said.

When we rang the bell, Melissa answered the door with her camera slung over one shoulder. She thanked us for coming. She had an expressive, conspiratorial smile, which I thought she probably gave to all of her subjects, as if to say: you're no ordinary subject to me, you're a special favourite. I knew I would enviously practise this smile later in a mirror. The spaniel yapped in the kitchen doorway while we hung up our jackets.

In the kitchen her husband was chopping vegetables. The dog was really excited by this gathering. It leapt onto a kitchen chair and barked for ten or twenty seconds before he told it to stop.

Can we get you both a glass of wine? Melissa said.

We said sure, and Nick poured the glasses. I had looked him up online since the first time we met him, partly because I didn't know any other actors in real life. He had mainly worked in theatre, but he'd also done some TV and film. He had once, several years previously, been nominated for a major award, which he didn't win. I'd happened on a whole selection of shirtless photographs, most of which showed him looking younger, coming out of a swimming pool or showering on a TV show that had long ago been cancelled. I sent Bobbi a link to one of these photographs with the message: trophy husband.

Melissa didn't appear in many photographs on the internet, though her collection of essays had generated a lot of publicity. I didn't know how long she had been married to Nick. Neither of them was famous enough for that kind of information to be online.

So you guys write everything together? Melissa said.

Oh God, no, said Bobbi. Frances writes everything. I don't even help.

That's not true, I said. That's not true, you do help. She's just saying that.

Melissa cocked her head to the side and gave a kind of laugh.

All right, so, which one of you is lying? she said.

I was lying. Except in the sense of enriching my life, Bobbi didn't help me write the poetry. As far as I knew she had never written creatively at all. She liked to perform dramatic monologues and sing anti-war ballads. Onstage she was the superior performer and I often glanced at her anxiously to remind myself what to do.

For dinner we had spaghetti in a thick white-wine sauce, and lots of garlic bread. Mostly Nick stayed quiet while Melissa asked us questions. She made us all laugh a lot, but in the same way you might make someone eat something when they don't fully want to eat it. I didn't know if I liked this sort of cheery forcefulness, but it was obvious how much Bobbi was enjoying it. She was laughing even more than she really had to, I could tell.

Although I couldn't specify why exactly, I felt certain that Melissa was less interested in our writing process now that she knew I wrote the material alone. I knew the subtlety of this change would be enough for Bobbi to deny it later, which irritated me as if it had already happened. I was starting to feel adrift from the whole set-up, like the dynamic that had eventually revealed itself didn't interest me, or even involve me. I could have tried harder to engage myself, but I probably resented having to make an effort to be noticed.

After dinner Nick cleared all the plates up and Melissa took photographs. Bobbi sat on the windowsill looking at a lit candle, laughing and making cute faces.

14

I sat at the dinner table without moving, finishing my third glass of wine.

I love the window thing, Melissa said. Can we do a similar one, but in the conservatory?

The conservatory opened out from the kitchen through a pair of double doors. Bobbi followed Melissa, who shut the doors behind them. I could see Bobbi sit on the windowsill, laughing, but I couldn't hear her laughter. Nick started to fill the sink with hot water. I told him again how good the food was and he looked up and said: oh, thanks.

Through the glass I watched Bobbi remove a dab of makeup from under her eye. Her wrists were slender and she had long, elegant hands. Sometimes when I was doing something dull, like walking home from work or hanging up laundry, I liked to imagine that I looked like Bobbi. She had better posture than I did, and a memorably beautiful face. The pretence was so real to me that when I accidentally caught sight of my reflection and saw my own appearance, I felt a strange, depersonalising shock. It was harder to do it now when Bobbi was sitting right in my eyeline, but I tried it anyway. I felt like saying something provocative and stupid.

I guess I'm kind of surplus to requirements, I said.

Nick looked out at the conservatory, where Bobbi was doing something with her hair.

Do you think Melissa's playing favourites? he said. I'll have a word with her if you want.

It's okay. Bobbi is everyone's favourite.

Really? I warmed to you more, I have to say.

We looked at each other. I could see he was playing along with me so I smiled.

Yes, I felt we had a natural rapport, I said.

I'm drawn to the poetic types.

Oh, well. I have a rich inner life, believe me.

He laughed when I said that. I knew I was being a little inappropriate, but I didn't feel too badly about it. Outside in the conservatory Melissa had lit a cigarette and put her camera down on a glass coffee table. Bobbi was nodding at something intently.

I thought tonight was going to be a nightmare, but it was actually fine, he said.

He sat back down at the table with me. I liked his sudden candour. I was conscious that I had looked at shirtless photographs of him on the internet without him knowing, and in the moment I found this knowledge very amusing and almost wanted to tell him about it.

I'm not the most dinner party person either, I said.

I think you were pretty good.

You were very good. You were great.

He smiled at me. I tried to remember everything he had said so I could play it over for Bobbi later on, but in my head it didn't sound quite as funny.

The doors opened and Melissa came back in, carrying her camera in both hands. She took a photograph of us sitting at the table, Nick holding his glass in one hand, me staring into the lens vacantly. Then she sat down opposite us and looked at her camera screen. Bobbi came back and refilled her own wine glass without asking. She had a beatific expression

16

on her face and I could see she was drunk. Nick watched her but didn't say anything.

I suggested that we should head off in time for the last bus and Melissa promised to send on the photographs. Bobbi's smile dropped a little but it was too late to suggest we should stay any longer. We were already being handed our jackets. I felt giddy, and now that Bobbi had gone quiet, I kept laughing at nothing on my own.

We had a ten-minute walk to the bus stop. Bobbi was subdued at first, so I gathered she was upset or annoyed.

Did you have a good time? I said.

I'm worried about Melissa.

You're what?

I don't think she's happy, said Bobbi.

In what sense not happy? Was she talking to you about this?

I don't think she and Nick are very happy together.

Really? I said.

It's sad.

I didn't point out that Bobbi had only met Melissa twice, though maybe I should have. Admittedly it didn't seem like Nick and Melissa were crazy about each other. He had told me, apropos of nothing, that he'd expected a dinner party she'd arranged to be "a nightmare".

I thought he was funny, I said.

He hardly opened his mouth.

Yeah, he had a humorous silence about him.

Bobbi didn't laugh. I dropped it. We hardly spoke on the bus, since I could see she wasn't going to be interested in the effortless rapport I had established with Melissa's trophy husband, and I couldn't think of anything else to talk about.

When I got back to my apartment I felt drunker than I had been at the house. Bobbi had gone home and I was on my own. I turned all the lights on before I went to bed. Sometimes that was something I did.

Bobbi's parents were going through an acrimonious breakup that summer. Bobbi's mother Eleanor had always been emotionally fragile and given to long periods of unspecified illness, which made her father Jerry the favoured parent in the split. Bobbi always called them by their first names. This had probably originated as an act of rebellion but now just seemed collegial, like their family was a small business they ran cooperatively. Bobbi's sister Lydia was fourteen and didn't seem to be handling the whole thing with Bobbi's composure.

My parents had separated when I was twelve and my father had moved back to Ballina, where they'd met. I lived in Dublin with my mother until I finished school, and then she moved back to Ballina too. When college started I moved into an apartment in the Liberties belonging to my father's brother. During term time, he let out the second bedroom to another student, and I had to keep quiet in the evenings and say hi politely when I saw my room-mate in the kitchen. But in the summer when the room-mate went home, I was allowed to live there all on my own and make coffee whenever I wanted and leave books splayed open on all the surfaces.

I had an internship in a literary agency at the time. There was one other intern, called Philip, who I knew from college. Our job was to read stacks of manuscripts and write one-page reports on their literary value. The value was almost always nil. Sometimes Philip would sardonically read bad sentences aloud to me, which made me laugh, but we didn't do that in front of the adults who worked there. We worked three days a week and were both paid "a stipend" which meant we basically weren't paid at all. All I needed was food, and Philip lived at home, so it didn't matter much to us.

This is how privilege gets perpetuated, Philip told me in the office one day. Rich assholes like us taking unpaid internships and getting jobs off the back of them.

Speak for yourself, I said. I'm never going to get a job.

CHAPTER
THREE

Bobbi and I often performed at spoken word events and open mic nights that summer. When we were outside smoking and male performers tried to talk to us, Bobbi would always pointedly exhale and say nothing, so I had to act as our representative. This meant a lot of smiling and remembering details about their work. I enjoyed playing this kind of character, the smiling girl who remembered things. Bobbi told me she thought I didn't have a "real personality", but she said she meant it as a compliment. Mostly I agreed with her assessment. At any time I felt I could do or say anything at all, and only afterwards think: oh, so that's the kind of person I am.

Melissa sent us the image files from the dinner party a few days later. I'd expected Bobbi to dominate the photo set, along with maybe one or two token photographs of me, blurry behind a lit candle, holding a forkful of spaghetti. In fact, for every picture of Bobbi, I appeared too, always lit perfectly, always beautifully framed. Nick was in the photographs also, which I hadn't expected. He looked luminously attractive, even more so than he had in real life. I wondered if that was why he was a successful actor. It was difficult to look at the photo set and not feel that he was the primary presence in the room, which I definitely hadn't felt at the time.

Melissa herself didn't appear in any of the images. As a result, the dinner party depicted in the photographs bore only an oblique relationship to the one we had actually attended. In reality, all our conversation had orbited around Melissa. She had prompted our various expressions of uncertainty or admiration. She was the one whose jokes we were always laughing at. Without her in the images, the dinner seemed to take on a different character, to go spinning off in subtle and strange directions. The relationships of the people who appeared in the photographs, without Melissa, became unclear.

In my favourite picture, I was looking straight into the lens with a dreamy expression, and Nick was looking at me as if waiting for me to say something. His mouth was a little open. It looked like he hadn't seen the camera. It was a good photograph, but of course I had really been looking up at Melissa at the time, and Nick simply hadn't seen her come through the doorway. It captured something intimate that had never really happened, something elliptical and somehow fraught. I saved it to my Downloads folder to look at later on.

Bobbi messaged me about an hour after the photographs arrived.

Bobbi: how good do we look though?

Bobbi: i wonder if we can use these as facebook
    profilers.
me: no
Bobbi: she says the piece won't be out till september
    apparently?
me: who says
Bobbi: melissa
Bobbi: do you want to hang out tonight?
Bobbi: and watch a film or something

Bobbi wanted me to know that she had been in touch with Melissa when I hadn't. It did impress me, which she wanted it to, but I also felt bad. I knew Melissa liked Bobbi more than she liked me, and I didn't know how to join in their new friendship without debasing myself for their attention. I had wanted Melissa to take an interest in me, because we were both writers, but instead she didn't seem to like me and I wasn't even sure I liked her. I didn't have the option not to take her seriously, because she had published a book, which proved that lots of other people took her seriously even if I didn't. At twenty-one, I had no achievements or possessions that proved I was a serious person.

I'd told Nick that everyone preferred Bobbi to me, but that wasn't really true. Bobbi could be abrasive and unrestrained in a way that made people uncomfortable, while I tended to be encouragingly polite. Mothers always liked me a lot, for example. And because Bobbi mostly treated men with amusement or contempt, men usually ended up liking me better too. Of course, Bobbi made fun of me about this. She once emailed me a picture of Angela Lansbury with the subject heading: your core demographic.

Bobbi did come over that night, though she didn't mention Melissa at all. I knew that she was being strategic, and that she wanted me to ask, so I didn't. This sounds more passive-aggressive than it really was. Actually we had a nice evening. We stayed up talking and Bobbi went to sleep on the mattress in my room.

That night I woke up sweating underneath the duvet. At first it felt like a dream or maybe a film. I found the orientation of my room confusing, as if I was further from the window and door than I should have been. I tried to sit up and then felt a strange, wrenching pain in my pelvis, which made me gasp out loud.

Bobbi? I said.

She rolled over. I tried to reach out of the bed to shake her shoulder, but I couldn't, and I felt exhausted by the effort. At the same time I was exhilarated by the seriousness of my pain, like it might change my life in an unforeseen way.

Bobbi, I said. Bobbi, wake up.

She didn't wake up. I moved my legs off the bed and managed to stand. The pain was more bearable if I hunched my body over and held onto my abdomen tightly. I went around her mattress and out to the bathroom. It was raining loudly onto the glazed plastic wall vent. I sat on the side of the bath. I was bleeding. It was just period pain. I put my face in my hands. My fingers were trembling. Then I got down onto the floor and put my face onto the cool rim of the bath.

After a while Bobbi knocked on the door.

What's up? she said from outside. Are you okay?

Just period pain.

Oh. You have painkillers in there?

No, I said.

I'll get you some.

Her footsteps went away. I hit my forehead against the side of the bath to distract myself from the pain in my pelvis. It was a hot pain, like all my insides were contracting into one little knot. The footsteps came back and the bathroom door opened an inch. She slid through a packet of ibuprofen. I crawled over and took them, and she went away.

Eventually it got light outside. Bobbi woke up and came in to help me onto the couch in the living room. She made me a cup of peppermint tea and I sat slouched holding the cup against my T-shirt, just above my pubic bone, until it started to scald me.

You suffer, she said.

Everybody suffers.

Ah, Bobbi said. Profound.

I hadn't been kidding with Philip about not wanting a job. I didn't want one. I had no plans as to my future financial sustainability: I never wanted to earn money for doing anything. I'd had various minimum-wage jobs in previous summers — sending emails, making cold calls, things like that — and I expected to have more of them after I graduated. Though I knew that I would eventually have to enter full-time employment, I certainly never fantasised about a radiant future where I was paid to perform an economic role. Sometimes this felt like a failure to take an interest in my own life, which depressed me. On the other hand, I felt that my disinterest in wealth was ideologically healthy. I'd checked what the average yearly income would be if the gross world product were divided evenly among everyone, and according to Wikipedia it would be $16,100. I saw no reason, political or financial, ever to make more money than that.

Our boss at the literary agency was a woman named Sunny. Both Philip and I really liked Sunny, but Sunny preferred me. Philip was sanguine about this. He said he preferred me too. I think deep down Sunny knew that I didn't want a job as a literary agent, and it may even have been this fact that distinguished me in her eyes. Philip was plainly pretty enthused about working for the agency, and though I didn't judge him for making life plans, I felt like I was more discerning with my enthusiasms.

Sunny was interested in the question of my career. She was a very candid person who was always making refreshingly candid remarks, that was one of the things Philip and I liked most about her.

What about journalism? she asked me.

I was handing her back a pile of completed manuscripts.

You're interested in the world, she said. You're knowledgeable. You like politics.

Do I?

She laughed and shook her head.

You're bright, she said. You're going to have to do something.

Maybe I'll marry for money.

She waved me away.

Go and do some work, she said.

We were performing at a reading in the centre of town that Friday. I could perform each poem for a period of about six months after I'd written it, after which point I couldn't stand to look at it, never mind read it aloud in public. I didn't know what caused this process, but I was glad the poems were only ever performed and never published. They floated away ethereally to the sound of applause. Real writers, and also painters, had to keep on looking at the ugly things they had done for good. I hated that everything I did was so ugly, but also that I lacked the courage to confront how ugly it was. I had explained that theory to Philip but he'd just said: don't be down on yourself, you're a real writer.

Bobbi and I were applying make-up in the venue bathrooms and talking about the newest poems I had written.

What I like about your male characters, Bobbi said, is they're all horrible.

They're not all horrible.

At best they're very morally ambiguous.

Aren't we all? I said.

You should write about Philip, he's not problematic. He's "nice".

She did air quotes around the word nice, even though she did really think that about Philip. Bobbi would never describe anyone as nice without quotation marks.

Melissa had said she would come along that night, but we didn't see her until afterwards, at maybe half ten or eleven o'clock. She and Nick were sitting together, and Nick was wearing a suit. Melissa congratulated us and told us she'd really enjoyed our performance. Bobbi looked at Nick as if waiting for him to compliment us, which made him laugh.

I didn't see your set, he said. I just got here.

Nick's in the Royal this month, Melissa said. He's doing *Cat on a Hot Tin Roof*.

But I'm sure you were great, though, he said.

Let me get you both drinks, said Melissa.

Bobbi went with her to the bar, so Nick and I were left alone at the table. He didn't have a tie on and his suit looked expensive. I felt too hot, and worried I was sweating.

How was the play? I said.

Oh, what, tonight? It was okay, thanks.

He was taking his cufflinks off. He placed them on the table, beside his glass, and I noticed they were coloured enamel, art deco-looking. I thought about admiring them aloud, but then felt unable to. Instead I pretended to look for Melissa and Bobbi over my shoulder. When I turned back he had taken out his phone.

I'd like to see it, I said. I like the play.

You should come along, I can hold tickets for you.

He didn't look up when he spoke, so I felt certain he was being insincere or would at least forget the conversation quickly. I just said something affirmative and non-committal. Now that he wasn't paying attention to me, I could watch him more closely. He really was exceptionally handsome. I wondered if people just got used to being so good-looking and eventually found it boring, but it was hard to imagine. I thought if I was as good-looking as Nick I would probably have fun all the time.

Sorry I'm being rude, Frances, he said. This is my mother on the phone. She texts now. I should tell her I'm talking to a poet, she'd be very impressed.

Well, you don't know. I could be a terrible poet.

He smiled and slipped his phone back in his inside pocket. I looked at his hand and looked away.

That's not what I've heard, he said. But maybe next time I'll get to decide for myself.

Melissa and Bobbi came back with the drinks. I noticed that Nick had dropped my name into conversation, as if to show that he remembered me from last time we talked. Of course, I remembered his name too, but he was older and somewhat famous, so I found his attention very flattering. It transpired that Melissa had taken their car into town, and so Nick had been forced to join us after his show to get a lift home. This arrangement did not seem to have been drawn up with his convenience in mind, and he looked tired and bored for most of our conversation.

Melissa sent me an email the next day saying they had put two theatre tickets aside for us next Thursday but that we shouldn't feel bad about it if we had made other plans. She included Nick's email address and wrote: in case you need to get in touch.

CHAPTER
FOUR

Bobbi was going out to dinner with her father on Thursday, so we offered Philip the spare ticket to the play. Philip kept asking if we were going to have to talk to Nick afterwards, and I didn't know. I doubted if he would come out especially to talk to us, so I said I was sure we could just leave as usual. Philip had never met Nick but had seen him on TV and considered his looks "intimidating". He asked me a lot of questions about what Nick was like in real life, none of which I felt qualified to answer. When we bought the programme, Philip leafed straight to the actor bios and showed me Nick's photograph. In the dim light it was really just an outline of a face.

Look at his jaw, he said.

Yeah, I see it.

The lights came up onstage, and the actress playing Maggie came on and started yelling in a Southern accent. It wasn't a bad accent, but it still felt like an actor's accent. She got out of her dress and stood there in a white slip, like Elizabeth Taylor's white slip in the film, though this actress looked both less artificial and also somehow less convincing. I could see a care label bunched inside the seam of the slip she was wearing,

30

which destroyed the effect of reality for me, although the slip and its care label were undoubtedly themselves real. I concluded that some kinds of reality have an unrealistic effect, which made me think of the theorist Jean Baudrillard, though I had never read his books and these were probably not the issues his writing addressed.

Finally Nick appeared, out of a door on stage left, buttoning up a shirt. I felt a sting of self-consciousness, as if the audience had all turned at this moment to observe my reaction. He looked very different onstage, and spoke in an unrecognisably different voice. His manner was cool and detached in a way that suggested sexual brutality. I breathed in and out through my mouth several times, and wet my lips repeatedly with my tongue. The production in general was not very good. The other actors had off-key accents and everything onstage looked like a prop waiting to be handled. In a way this just emphasised how spectacularly beautiful Nick was, and made his misery seem more authentic.

When we came out of the theatre it was raining again. I felt pure and tiny like a newborn baby. Philip put up his umbrella and we walked toward his bus stop while I sort of grinned manically at nothing and touched my own hair a lot.

That was interesting, Philip said.

I thought Nick was probably a lot better than the other actors.

Yeah, it was stressful, wasn't it? But he was pretty good.

I laughed much too loudly at this remark and then stopped when I realised nothing about it was funny. A light, cool rain feathered the umbrella and I tried to think of something interesting to say about the weather.

He is handsome, I heard myself saying.

To an almost off-putting extent.

We reached Philip's bus stop and had a short discussion about which of us should take the umbrella. In the end I took it. It was raining heavily and getting dark. I wanted to talk more about the play but I could see Philip's bus was about to pull in. I knew he wouldn't want to talk much more about the play anyway, but I still felt disappointed. He started counting out his fare and said he'd see me tomorrow. I walked back to my apartment on my own.

When I got inside I left the umbrella by the courtyard door and opened up my laptop to look at Nick's email address. I felt I should send him a short thank-you message for the tickets, but I kept getting distracted by items in the room, like a Toulouse-Lautrec poster I had hanging above the fireplace and a particular smudge on the patio window. I got up and walked around for a while to think about it. I cleaned the smudge with a damp cloth and then made a cup of tea. I considered calling Bobbi to talk about whether it would be normal to send an email or not, but I remembered she was with her father. I wrote a sample message, and then deleted the draft in case I might accidentally hit send. Then I wrote the same thing over again.

I sat staring at my laptop screen until it went black. Things matter to me more than they do to normal people, I thought. I need to relax and let things go. I should experiment with drugs. These thoughts were not unusual for me. I put *Astral Weeks* on the stereo in the living room and slumped right onto the floor to listen. Though I was trying not to dwell on the play, I found myself thinking about Nick onstage yelling: I don't want to lean on your shoulder, I want my crutch. I wondered if Philip was similarly preoccupied, or was this more private. I need to be fun and likeable, I thought. A fun person would send a thank-you email.

I got up and typed a brief message congratulating Nick on his performance and expressing gratitude for the tickets. I moved the sentences here and there, and then seemingly at random I hit the send button. Afterwards I shut my laptop and went back to sitting on the floor.

I was expecting to hear from Bobbi about her dinner with Jerry and eventually, after the album was finished, she did call. I was still sitting slumped against the wall when I answered the phone. Bobbi's father was a high-ranking civil servant in the Department of Health. She did not apply her otherwise rigorous anti-establishment principles to her relationship with Jerry, or at least not with any consistency. He'd taken her to a very expensive restaurant for dinner and they'd had three courses with wine.

He's just trying to emphasise that I'm an adult member of the family now, Bobbi said. And he takes me seriously, blah blah blah.

How's your mother holding up?

Oh, it's migraine season again. We're all tiptoeing around like fucking Trappist monks. How was the play?

Nick was really good, actually, I said.

Oh, that's a relief. I felt like it might be terrible.

No, it was. Sorry, I remember your question now. The play was bad.

Bobbi hummed a kind of tuneless piece of music to herself and offered no further remark.

Remember last time we visited their house, and afterwards you said you thought they were like, unhappily married? I said. What made you say that?

I just thought Melissa seemed depressed.

But why, because of their marriage?

Well, don't you find Nick sort of hostile toward her? said Bobbi.

No. Do you?

The first time we went over there, remember he went around scowling at us and then he yelled at her about feeding the dog? And we could hear them arguing when we went to bed?

Now that she said that, I did remember perceiving a certain animosity between them on that occasion, though I didn't accept that he had yelled.

Was she there? Bobbi said. At the play?

No. Well, I don't know, we didn't see her.

She doesn't like Tennessee Williams anyway. She finds him mannered.

I could hear that Bobbi said this with an ironic smile, because she was aware that she was showing off. I was jealous, but I also felt that because I had seen the play

I was party to something Bobbi didn't know about. She still saw Nick as a background figure, with no significance other than as Melissa's husband. If I told her that I had just sent him an email thanking him for the tickets, she wouldn't understand that I was showing off too, because to her Nick was just a function of Melissa's unhappiness, and uninteresting in his own right. It seemed unlikely she would see the play now, and I couldn't think of any other way to impress her with Nick's personal significance. When I mentioned that he was planning to come and see us perform sometime soon, she just asked if that meant Melissa would come too.

Nick replied to my email the next afternoon in all lower case, thanking me for coming to the play and asking when Bobbi and I were next performing. He said they were running a show in the Royal every night and matinees at weekends so he would almost certainly miss our set unless it started sometime after half ten. I told him I would see what I could do, but not to worry if he couldn't make it. He replied saying: oh well, it wouldn't be very reciprocal then, would it?

CHAPTER
FIVE

Over the summer I missed the periods of intense academic concentration which helped to relax me during term time. I liked to sit in the library to write essays, allowing my sense of time and personal identity to dissolve as the light dimmed outside the windows. I would open fifteen tabs on my web browser while producing phrases like "epistemic rearticulation" and "operant discursive practices". I mostly forgot to eat on days like this and emerged in the evening with a fine, shrill headache. Physical sensations reintroduced themselves to me with a feeling of genuine novelty: breeze felt new, and the sound of birds outside the Long Room. Food tasted impossibly good, as did soft drinks. Afterwards I'd print the essay out without even looking over it. When I went to get my feedback, the notes in the margins always said things like "well argued" and sometimes "brilliant". Whenever I got a "brilliant" I took a little photograph of it on my phone and sent it to Bobbi. She would send back: congrats, your ego is staggering.

My ego had always been an issue. I knew that intellectual attainment was morally neutral at best, but when bad things happened to me I made myself feel better by thinking about how smart I was. When I couldn't make friends as a child, I fantasised that I was smarter than all my teachers, smarter than any other student who had been in the school before, a genius hidden among normal people. It made me feel like a spy. As a teenager I started using internet messageboards and developed a friendship with a twenty-six-year-old American grad student. He had very white teeth in his photographs and told me he thought I had the brain of a physicist. I sent him messages late at night confessing that I was lonely in school, that the other girls didn't seem to understand me. I wish I had a boyfriend, I wrote. One night he sent me a picture of his genitals. It was a flash photograph, zoomed right in on the erect penis, as if for medical examination. For days afterwards I felt guilty and terrified, like I had committed a sick internet crime which other people could discover at any moment. I deleted my account and abandoned the associated email address. I told no one, I had no one to tell.

On Saturday I talked to the venue organiser and got our set pushed back until half ten. I didn't mention to Bobbi that I had done that, or why. We had smuggled in a bottle of white wine which we shared from plastic cups in the downstairs bathrooms. We liked to have one or two glasses of wine before performing, but no more than that. We sat on the sinks refilling our cups and talking about the new stuff we were going to perform.

I didn't want to tell Bobbi I was nervous, but I was. Even looking in the mirror made me nervous. I didn't think I looked awful. My face was plain, but I was so extremely thin as to look interesting, and I chose my clothing to emphasise this effect. I wore a lot of dark colours and severe necklines. That night I was wearing a reddish-brown lipstick and in the weird bathroom light I looked sick and faint. Eventually the features of my face seemed to come apart from one another or at least lose their ordinary relationships to each other, like a word you read so many times it makes no sense any more. I wondered if I was having an anxiety attack. Then Bobbi told me to stop staring at myself and I stopped.

When we went upstairs we could see Melissa sitting alone with a glass of wine and her camera. The seat beside her was empty. I cast around but it was clear to me, from something about the shape or the noise of the room, that Nick was not there. I thought this would calm me down, but it didn't. I licked my teeth several times and waited for the man to say our names into the microphone.

Onstage, Bobbi was always precise. All I had to do was try and tune in to her particular rhythm and as long as I could do that, I would be fine too. Sometimes I was good, sometimes I was just okay. But Bobbi was exact. That night she made everyone laugh and got a lot of applause. For a few moments we stood there in the light, being applauded and gesturing to each other, like: it's all her. It was at this point I saw Nick enter from the door at the back. He looked slightly breathless, like he had taken the stairs too quickly. Instantly I looked away and pretended I hadn't noticed him. I could see that he was trying to catch my eye and that if I returned his gaze he would give me a kind of apologetic expression. I found this idea too intense to think about, like the glare of a bare lightbulb. The audience continued to applaud and I could feel Nick watching us as we left the stage.

At the bar afterwards Philip bought us a round of drinks and said the new poem was his favourite. I had forgotten to bring his umbrella.

See, and people say I hate men, Bobbi said. But I actually really like you, Philip.

I swallowed half my glass of gin and tonic in two mouthfuls. I was thinking about leaving without saying hello to anyone. I could leave, I thought, and it felt good to think about it, as if I was in control of my own life again.

Let's go find Melissa, Bobbi said. We can introduce you.

By then Nick was sitting beside Melissa and already drinking from a bottle of beer. I felt very awkward about approaching them. The last time I had seen him he'd had a fake accent and different clothes, and I wasn't sure I was ready to hear his real accent again. But Melissa had spotted us already anyway. She asked us to sit down.

Bobbi introduced Melissa and Nick to Philip, and Philip shook their hands. Melissa said she remembered them meeting before, which delighted him. Nick said something about being sorry he'd missed our performance, though I still wasn't looking at him. I drained the rest of my gin and tonic and then knocked the ice from side to side in the glass. Philip congratulated Nick on the play and they talked about Tennessee Williams. Melissa called him "mannered" again and I pretended not to know she had made the observation before.

After we bought a new round of drinks, Melissa suggested we go out for a cigarette. The smoking area was a little walled garden downstairs and it wasn't particularly full, since it was raining. I hadn't seen Nick smoking before, and I took a cigarette too although I didn't want one. Bobbi was doing an impression of one of the men who had performed before us at the reading. It was a very funny though also cruel impression. We all laughed. It was starting to rain harder then, so we gathered underneath the shallow ledge projecting from the window. We talked for a while, Bobbi mostly.

It's cool you're playing a gay character, Bobbi was saying to Nick.

Is Brick gay? he said. I think maybe he's just bisexual.

Don't say "just bisexual", she said. Frances is bisexual, you know.

I didn't know that, Melissa said.

I chose to drag on my cigarette for a long time before saying anything. I knew that everyone was waiting for me to speak.

Well, I said. Yeah, I'm kind of an omnivore.

Melissa laughed at that. Nick looked at me and gave an amused smile, which I looked away from quickly and pretended to take an interest in my glass.

Me too, Melissa said.

I could tell Bobbi was enthralled by this remark. She asked Melissa something I didn't listen to. Philip said he was going to the bathroom and left his drink on the windowsill. I stroked the chain of my necklace, feeling the alcohol warm inside my stomach.

Sorry I was late, Nick said.

He was speaking to me. In fact it seemed that he had waited for Philip to leave us alone so he could address this sentence to me. I told him I didn't mind. He held the cigarette between his index and middle fingers, where it looked miniature compared to the breadth of his hand. I was aware of the fact that he could pretend to be anyone he wanted to be, and I wondered if he also lacked a "real personality" the same way I did.

I arrived in time for the wild applause, he said. So I can only assume good things. I've read your work actually, is that a terrible thing to say? Melissa forwarded it on to me, she thinks I like literature.

At this point I felt a weird lack of self-recognition, and I realised that I couldn't visualise my own face or body at all. It was like someone had lifted the end of an invisible pencil and just gently erased my entire appearance. This was curious and actually not unpleasant, though I was also aware that I was cold and might have been shivering.

She didn't tell me she was going to forward it to people, I said.

Not people, just me. I'll send you an email about it. If I compliment you now you'll think I'm just saying it, but the email will be very flattering.

Oh, that's nice. I like getting compliments where I don't have to make eye contact with the person.

He laughed at that, which gratified me. It had started raining harder and Philip had come back from the bathroom to shelter under the ledge with us again. My arm was touching Nick's and I felt a pleasant sense of illicit physical closeness.

It's weird knowing someone just casually, he said, and then later finding out they're observing things all the time. It's like, God, what has this person noticed about me?

We looked at one another. Nick's face was handsome in the most generic way: clear skin, pronounced bone structure, the mouth a little soft-looking. But his expressions seemed to pass over it with a certain subtlety and intelligence, which gave his eye contact a charismatic quality. When he looked at me, I felt vulnerable to him, but I also felt strongly that he was letting himself be observed, that he had noticed how interested I was in forming an impression of him, and he was curious about what it might be.

Yeah, I said. All kinds of bad things.

And you're what, like, twenty-four?

I'm twenty-one.

For a second he looked at me like he thought I was kidding, eyes widened, eyebrows raised, and then he shook his head. Actors learn to communicate things without feeling them, I thought. He already knew I was twenty-one. Maybe what he really wanted to communicate was an exaggerated awareness of our age difference, or a mild disapproval or disappointment about it. I knew from the internet that he was thirty-two.

But don't let that get in the way of our natural rapport, I said.

He looked at me for a moment and then he smiled, an ambivalent smile, which I liked so much that I became very conscious of my own mouth. It was open slightly.

No, I couldn't possibly, he said.

Philip told us he was going to get the last bus, and Melissa said she had a meeting the next morning and she was planning to head off too. Quickly after that the whole group dispersed. Bobbi got the DART back to Sandymount, and I walked back along the quays. The Liffey was swollen up and looked irritated. A school of taxis and cars swam past and a drunk man walking on the other side of the street yelled that he loved me.

While I let myself into the apartment I thought about Nick entering the room while everybody applauded. This now felt perfect to me, so perfect that I was glad he had missed the performance. Maybe having him witness how much others approved of me, without taking any of the risks necessary to earn Nick's personal approval, made me feel capable of speaking to him again, as if I also was an important person with lots of admirers like he was, as if there was nothing inferior about me. But the acclaim also felt like part of the performance itself, the best part, and the most pure expression of what I was trying to do, which was to make myself into this kind of person: someone worthy of praise, worthy of love.

CHAPTER
SIX

After that we saw Melissa sporadically and she sent us occasional email updates about the profile piece. We didn't visit her at home again, but we ran into her now and then at literary events. I usually speculated in advance about whether she or Nick might attend a particular thing, because I liked them, and I liked having other people observe their warmth toward me. They introduced me to editors and agents who acted very charmed to meet me and who asked interested questions about my work. Nick was always friendly, and even praised me to other people sometimes, but he never seemed particularly eager to engage me in conversation again, and I got used to meeting his eye without feeling startled.

Bobbi and I went along to these events together, but for Bobbi it was really only Melissa's attention that mattered. At a book launch on Dawson Street she told Nick she had "nothing against actors", and he was like, oh thanks Bobbi, that's so generous of you. When he attended on his own once, Bobbi said: just you? Where's your beautiful wife?

Do I get the sense you don't like me? said Nick.

It's nothing personal, I said. She hates men.

If it makes you feel better, I do also personally dislike you, said Bobbi.

Nick and I had started to exchange emails after the night he missed our performance. In the message he'd promised to send about my work, he described a particular image as "beautiful". It was probably true to say that I had found Nick's performance in the play "beautiful", though I wouldn't have written that in an email. Then again his performance was related to the physicality of his existence in a way that a poem, typed in a standard font and forwarded on by someone else, was not. At a certain level of abstraction, anyone could have written the poem, but that didn't feel true either. It seemed as though what he was really saying was: there's something beautiful about the way you think and feel, or the way that you experience the world is beautiful in some way. This remark returned to me repeatedly for days after the email arrived. I smiled involuntarily when I thought of it, like I was remembering a private joke.

It was easy to write to Nick, but also competitive and thrilling, like a game of table tennis. We were always being flippant with each other. When he found out my parents lived in Mayo, he wrote:

we used to have a holiday home in Achill (like every other wealthy South Dublin family I'm sure).

I replied:

I'm glad my ancestral homeland could help nourish your class identity. P.S. It should be illegal to have a holiday home anywhere.

He was the first person I had met since Bobbi who made me enjoy conversation, in the same irrational and sensuous way I enjoyed coffee or loud music. He made me laugh. Once, he mentioned that he and Melissa slept in separate rooms. I didn't tell Bobbi about that, but I thought about it a lot. I wondered if they still "loved" one another, although it was hard to imagine Nick being that unironic about anything.

He never seemed to go to bed until the early morning, and we increasingly emailed one another late at night. He told me he had studied English and French at Trinity, so we had even had some of the same lecturers. He'd majored in English and had written his final-year dissertation on Caryl Churchill. Sometimes while we talked I typed his name into Google and looked at photographs of him, to remind me what he looked like. I read everything about him on the internet and often emailed him quotes from his own interviews, even after he asked me to stop. He said he found it "super embarrassing". I said: stop emailing me at 3.34a.m. then (don't actually). He replied: me email a 21 year old in the middle of the night? i don't know what you're talking about. i would never do that.

One night at the launch of a new poetry anthology, Melissa and I were left alone in a conversation with a male novelist whose books I had never read. The others had gone to get drinks. We were in a bar somewhere off

Dame Street and my feet hurt because I was wearing shoes that I knew were too small. The novelist asked me who I liked to read and I shrugged. I wondered if I could just remain silent until he left me alone, or if this would be a mistake, since I didn't know how acclaimed his books were.

You have a real coolness about you, he said to me. Doesn't she?

Melissa nodded but not enthusiastically. My coolness, if I had any, had never moved her.

Thanks, I said.

And you can take a compliment, that's good, he said. A lot of people will try to run themselves down, you've got the right attitude.

Yes, I'm quite the compliment-taker, I said.

At this point I could see him try to exchange a look with Melissa, who remained disinterested. He seemed almost on the point of winking at her but he didn't. Then he turned back to me with a smirking expression.

Well, don't get cocky, he said.

Nick and Bobbi rejoined us then. The novelist said something to Nick, and Nick replied with the word "man", like: oh, sorry about that, man. I would later make fun of this affectation in an email. Bobbi leaned her head on Melissa's shoulder.

When the novelist left the conversation, Melissa drained her wine glass and grinned at me.

You really charmed him, she said.

Is that sarcastic? I asked.

He was trying to flirt with you. He said you were cool.

I was very aware of Nick standing at my elbow, though I couldn't see his expression. I knew how badly I wanted to remain in control of the conversation.

Yeah, men love telling me I'm cool, I said. They just want me to act like I've never heard it before.

Melissa really did laugh then. I was surprised I could make her laugh like that. I felt for a moment that I'd misjudged her and, in particular, her attitude toward me. Then I realised Nick was laughing also, and I lost interest in what Melissa felt.

Cruel, he said.

Don't think you're exempt, said Bobbi.

Oh, I'm definitely a bad guy, Nick said. That's not why I'm laughing.

At the end of June I went to Ballina for a couple of days to visit my parents. My mother didn't enforce these visits, but lately when we spoke on the phone she'd started saying things like: oh you're alive, are you? Am I going to recognise you next time you come home, or will you have to put a flower in your lapel? Eventually I booked a train ticket. I sent her a text telling her when to expect me and signed off: in the spirit of filial duty, your loyal daughter.

Bobbi and my mother got along famously. Bobbi studied History and Politics, subjects my mother considered serious. Real subjects, she would say, with an eyebrow lifted at me. My mother was a kind of social democrat, and at this time I believe Bobbi identified herself as a communitarian anarchist. When my mother visited Dublin, they took mutual enjoyment in having minor arguments about the Spanish Civil War. Sometimes Bobbi would turn to me and say: Frances, you're a communist, back me up. And my mother would laugh and say: that one! You may as well ask the teapot. She had never taken much interest in my social or personal life, an arrangement which suited us both, but when I broke up with Bobbi she described it as "a real shame".

After she picked me up from the train on Saturday, we spent the afternoon in the garden. The grass had been cut and gave off a warm, allergenic smell. The sky was soft like cloth and birds ran over it in long threads. My mother was weeding and I was pretending to weed but actually just talking. I discovered an unforeseen enthusiasm for talking about all the editors and writers I had met in Dublin. I took my gloves off to wipe my forehead at one point and didn't put them back on. I asked my mother if she wanted tea and she ignored me. Then I sat under the fuchsia bush plucking little fuchsias off the branches and talking about famous people again. The words just flew out of my mouth deliciously. I had no idea I had so much to say, or that I would enjoy saying it so much.

Eventually my mother stripped her gloves off and sat on a lawn chair. I was sitting with my legs crossed, examining the tips of my sneakers.

You seem very impressed with this woman Melissa, she said.

Do I?

She certainly introduces you to a lot of people.

She likes Bobbi more than she likes me, I said.

But her husband likes you.

I shrugged and said I didn't know. Then I licked my thumb and started scrubbing at a little fleck of dirt on my sneaker.

And they're rich, are they? said my mother.

I think so. The husband is from a wealthy background. And their house is really nice.

It's not like you to get carried away with posh houses.

This comment stung me. I continued scrubbing my shoe as if I hadn't noticed her tone.

I'm not getting carried away, I said. I'm just reporting what their house is like.

I have to say, it all sounds very odd to me. I don't know what this woman is doing hanging around with college students at her age.

She's thirty-seven, not fifty. And she's writing a profile about us, I told you that.

My mother got up from the lawn chair and wiped her hands on her linen gardening trousers.

Well, she said. It's far from nice houses in Monkstown you were reared.

I laughed, and she offered her hand to help me up. Her hands were large and sallow, not at all like mine. They were full of the practicality I lacked, and my hand fit into them like something that needed fixing.

Will you see your father this evening? she said.

I withdrew my hand and pocketed it.

Maybe, I said.

★　★　★

It had been obvious to me from a young age that my parents didn't like one another. Couples in films and on television performed household tasks together and talked fondly about their shared memories. I couldn't remember seeing my mother and father in the same room unless they were eating. My father had "moods". Sometimes during his moods my mother would take me to stay with her sister Bernie in Clontarf, and they would sit in the kitchen talking and shaking their heads while I watched my cousin Alan play *Ocarina of Time*. I was aware that alcohol played a role in these incidents, but its precise workings remained mysterious to me.

I enjoyed our visits to Bernie's house. While we were there I was allowed to eat as many digestive biscuits as I wanted, and when we returned, my father was either gone out or else feeling very contrite. I liked it when he was gone out. During his periods of contrition he tried to make conversation with me about school and I had to choose between humouring and ignoring him. Humouring him made me feel dishonest and weak, a soft target. Ignoring him made my heart beat very hard and afterwards I couldn't look at myself in the mirror. Also it made my mother cry.

It was hard to be specific about what my father's moods consisted of. Sometimes he would go out for a couple of days and when he came back in we'd find him taking money out of my Bank of Ireland savings jar, or our television would be gone. Other times he would bump into a piece of furniture and then lose his

51

temper. He hurled one of my school shoes right at my face once after he tripped on it. It missed and went in the fireplace and I watched it smouldering like it was my own face smouldering. I learned not to display fear, it only provoked him. I was cold like a fish. Afterwards my mother said: why didn't you lift it out of the fire? Can't you at least make an effort? I shrugged. I would have let my real face burn in the fire too.

When he came home from work in the evening I used to freeze entirely still, and after a few seconds I would know with complete certainty if he was in one of the moods or not. Something about the way he closed the door or handled his keys would let me know, as clearly as if he yelled the house down. I'd say to my mother: he's in a mood now. And she'd say: stop that. But she knew as well as I did. One day, when I was twelve, he turned up unexpectedly after school to pick me up. Instead of going home, we drove away from town, toward Blackrock. The DART went past on our left and I could see the Poolbeg towers out the car window. Your mother wants to break up our family, my father said. Instantly I replied: please let me out of the car. This remark later became evidence in my father's theory that my mother had poisoned me against him.

After he moved to Ballina, I visited every second weekend. He was usually on good behaviour then, and we got takeaway for dinner and sometimes went to the cinema. I watched constantly for the flicker that meant his good mood was over and bad things would happen. It could be anything. But when we went to McCarthy's in the afternoons, my father's friends would ask: this is your little prodigy, is it, Dennis? And they asked me crossword clues from the back of the paper, or how to spell very long words. When I was right, they clapped me on the back and bought me red lemonade.

She'll go off and work for NASA, his friend Paul said. You'll be made up for life.

She'll do whatever she likes, my father said.

Bobbi had only met him once, at our school graduation. He came up to Dublin for the ceremony, wearing a shirt and a purple tie. My mother had told him about Bobbi, and when he met her after the ceremony he shook her hand and said: that was a grand performance. We were in the school library eating triangular sandwiches and drinking glasses of cola. You look like Frances, Bobbi said. My father and I looked at each other and he gave a sheepish laugh. I don't know about that, he said. Afterwards he told me she was a "pretty girl" and kissed my cheek goodbye.

In college I stopped visiting so often. I went to Ballina once a month instead, and stayed with my mother when I was there. After he retired, my father's moods became more erratic. I started to realise how much time I spent appeasing him, being falsely cheerful, and picking up things he'd knocked over. My jaw started to feel stiff, and I noticed myself flinching at small noises. Our conversations became strained, and more than once he accused me of changing my accent. You look down on me, he said during an argument. Don't be so stupid, I replied. He laughed and said: oh, there we have it. The truth is out now.

After dinner I told my mother I would visit him. She kneaded my shoulder and told me she thought it was a good idea. It's a great idea, she said. Good woman.

I walked through town with my hands in my jacket pockets. The sun was setting and I wondered what would be on television. I could feel a headache developing, like it was coming down from the sky directly into my brain. I tried stamping my feet as loudly as I could to distract myself from bad thoughts, but people gave me curious looks and I felt cowed. I knew that was weak of me. Bobbi was never cowed by strangers.

My father lived in a little terraced house near the petrol station. I rang the doorbell and put my hands back in my pockets. Nothing happened. I rang again and then I tried the handle, which felt greasy. The door opened up and I stepped in.

Dad? I said. Hello?

The house smelled of chip oil and vinegar. The carpet in the hallway, which had been patterned when he first moved in, was now walked flat and brown. A family photo taken on holiday in Majorca was hanging above the telephone, depicting me at age four in a yellow T-shirt. The T-shirt said BE HAPPY.

Hello? I said.

My father appeared out of the kitchen doorway.

Is it yourself, Frances? he said.

Yeah.

Come on inside, I was just eating.

The kitchen had a high mottled window onto a concrete yard. Unwashed dishes were stacked up by the sink and the bin was spilling small items over the lip of the plastic and onto the floor: receipts, potato peelings. My father walked right over them like he didn't notice. He was eating from a brown bag propped on a small blue plate.

You've had dinner, have you? he said.

I have, yeah.

Tell us the news from Dublin.

Nothing much, I'm afraid, I said.

After he was finished eating I boiled a kettle and filled the sink with hot water and lemon-scented washing liquid. My father went into the other room to look at the television. The water was too hot, and I could see when I lifted my hands they had turned a glaring pink colour. I washed the glasses and cutlery first, then the dishes, then the pots and pans. When everything was clean, I emptied the sink, wiped down the kitchen surfaces and swept the peelings back into the bin. Watching the soap bubbles slide silently down the blades of the kitchen knives, I had a sudden desire to harm myself. Instead I put away the salt and pepper shakers and went into the living room.

I'm off, I said.

You're away, are you?

That bin needs taking out.

See you again, my father said.

CHAPTER
SEVEN

Melissa invited us to her birthday party in July. We hadn't seen her for a while and Bobbi started worrying about what to buy her, and whether we should get her separate gifts or just one from both of us. I said I was only going to get her a bottle of wine anyway so that was the end of the discussion as far as I cared about it. When we saw one another at events Melissa and I increasingly avoided making eye contact. She and Bobbi whispered in each other's ears and laughed, like they were in school. I didn't have the courage to really dislike her, but I knew I wanted to.

Bobbi wore a tight cropped T-shirt and black jeans to the party. I wore a summer dress with tiny, fiddly shoulder straps. It was a warm evening, and the sky was only beginning to darken as we reached the house. The clouds were green and the stars reminded me of sugar. We could hear the dog barking in the back garden. I hadn't seen Nick in real life for what seemed like a long time, and I felt a little nervous about it, because of how droll and indifferent I had pretended to be in all our emails.

Melissa answered the door herself. She embraced us in turn and placed a powdery kiss on my left cheekbone. She smelled of a perfume I recognised.

No gifts necessary! she said. You're too generous! Come on in, get yourselves a drink. It's great to see you.

We followed her into the kitchen, which was dim and full of music and people wearing long necklaces. Everything looked clean and spacious. For a few seconds I imagined that this was my house, that I had grown up here, and the things in it belonged to me.

There's wine on the counter, and spirits are in the utility room at the back, Melissa said. Help yourselves.

Bobbi poured herself a huge glass of red wine and followed Melissa into the conservatory. I didn't want to tag along so I pretended I wanted spirits instead.

The utility room was a cupboard-sized space through a door at the back of the kitchen. Inside were maybe five people, smoking a joint and laughing loudly about something. One of the people was Nick. When I came in someone said: oh no, it's the cops! Then they laughed again. I stood there feeling younger than them, and thinking about how low my dress was cut at the back. Nick was sitting on the washing machine drinking from a beer bottle. He was wearing a white shirt open at the collar and I noticed that he seemed flushed. It was very hot and smoky in the room, much hotter than in the kitchen.

Melissa said the spirits were in here, I said.

Yeah, Nick said. What can I get you?

I said I would have a glass of gin while everyone stared at me in a peaceable, stoned-looking way. Other than Nick there were two women and two men. The women weren't looking at one another. I glanced at my own fingernails to reassure myself they were clean.

Are you another actress? someone asked.

She's a writer, Nick said.

He introduced me to the other people then, and I immediately forgot their names. He was pouring a large measure of gin into a big glass tumbler and he said there was tonic water somewhere so I waited for him to find it.

I'm not being offensive, the guy said, there are a lot of actresses.

Yeah, Nick has to be careful where he looks, said someone else.

Nick looked at me, though it was difficult to tell if he was embarrassed or just high. The remark definitely had sexual connotations, though it wasn't clear to me precisely what they were.

No, I don't, he said.

Melissa must have gotten pretty open-minded then, someone else said.

They all laughed at that, except Nick. I knew at this point that I was being interpreted as some kind of vaguely disruptive sexual presence for the sake of their joke. It didn't bother me, and in fact I thought about how funny I could make it sound in an email. Nick handed me the glass of gin and tonic and I smiled without showing my teeth. I didn't know whether he expected me to leave now that I had the drink, or if that would be rude.

How was the visit home? he said.

Oh, good, I said. Parents well. Thank you for asking.

Whereabouts are you from, Frances? said one of the men.

I'm from Dublin, but my parents live in Ballina.

So you're a culchie, the man said. I didn't think Nick had culchie friends.

Well, I grew up in Sandymount, I said.

Which county do you support in the All Ireland? someone asked.

I inhaled the second-hand smoke through my mouth, the sweet rancid taste of it. As a woman I have no county, I said. It felt good to belittle Nick's friends, although they seemed harmless. Nick laughed, as if to himself at something he had just remembered.

Someone out in the kitchen yelled something about cake then and everyone left the utility room except for us two. The dog came in and Nick pushed her out with his foot and closed the door. He looked shy to me suddenly, but maybe only because he was still very flushed from the heat. That James Blake song "Retrograde" was playing outside in the kitchen. Nick had mentioned in an email how much he liked the album, and I wondered if he had chosen the music for the party.

I'm sorry, he said. I'm so high I can't really see straight.

I'm jealous.

I rested my back against the fridge and fanned my face a little with my hand. He held up his beer bottle and touched it to my cheek. The glass felt fantastically cold and wet, so much that I exhaled quickly without meaning to.

Is that good? he said.

Yeah, that's incredible. What about here?

I shifted aside one of the shoulder straps of my dress and he rested the bottle against my collarbone. A bead of cold condensation rolled down my skin and I shivered.

That's so good, I said.

He didn't say anything. His ears were red, I noticed that.

Do the back of my leg, I said.

He moved the bottle to his other hand and held it against the back of my thigh. His fingertips felt cold brushing my skin.

Like that? he said.

But come closer.

Are we flirting now?

I kissed him. He let me. The inside of his mouth was hot and he put his free hand on my waist, like he wanted to touch me. I wanted him so much that I felt completely stupid, and incapable of saying or doing anything at all.

He drew away from me after a few seconds and wiped his mouth, but tenderly, as if he was trying to make sure it was still there.

We probably shouldn't do that in here, he said.

I swallowed. I said: I should go. Then I left the utility room, pinching my bottom lip with my fingers and trying not to make any expression with my face.

Out in the conservatory Bobbi was sitting on a windowsill talking to Melissa. She waved me over and I felt I had to join them although I didn't want to. They were eating clean little slices of cake, with two thin lines of cream and jam that looked like toothpaste. Bobbi was eating hers with her fingers, Melissa had a fork. I smiled and touched my mouth again compulsively. Even while I did it I knew it was a bad idea, but I couldn't stop.

I'm just telling Melissa how much we idolise her, Bobbi said.

Melissa gave me a levelling glance and took out a packet of cigarettes.

I don't think Frances idolises anyone, she said.

I shrugged, helplessly. I finished my gin and tonic and poured myself a glass of white wine. I wanted Nick to come back into the room, so I could look at him across the countertop. Instead I looked at Melissa and thought: I hate you. This idea just came from nowhere, like a joke or an exclamation. I didn't even know if I really hated her, but the words felt and sounded right, like the lyrics to a song I had just remembered.

Hours passed and I didn't see Nick again at all. Bobbi and I had planned to stay the night in their spare room but most of the guests didn't leave until four or five that morning. By that time I didn't know where Bobbi was. I went up to the spare room to look for her but it was empty. I lay on the bed in my clothes and wondered if I was going to start feeling some particular emotion, like sadness or regret. Instead I just felt a lot of things I didn't know how to identify. In the end I fell asleep and when I woke up Bobbi wasn't there. It was a grey morning outside and I left the house on my own, without seeing anybody, to get the bus back to town.

CHAPTER
EIGHT

That afternoon I lay on my bed smoking with the window open, dressed in a vest and my underwear. I was hungover and still hadn't heard from Bobbi. Through the window I could see the breeze rearranging the foliage and two children appearing and disappearing from behind a tree, one of them carrying a plastic lightsaber. I found this relaxing, or at least it distracted me from feeling terrible. I was a little chilly, but I didn't want to break the spell by getting dressed.

Eventually, at three or four in the afternoon, I got out of bed. I didn't feel like writing anything. In fact I felt that if I tried to write, what I produced would be ugly and pretentious. I wasn't the kind of person I pretended to be. I thought of myself trying to be witty in front of Nick's friends in the utility room and felt sick. I didn't belong in rich people's houses. I was only ever invited to places like that because of Bobbi, who belonged everywhere and had a quality about her that made me invisible by comparison.

I got an email from Nick that evening.

hi frances, i'm really sorry about what happened last night. it was fucking stupid of me and i feel awful. i

don't want to be that person and i don't want you to
think of me as that person either. i feel really bad
about it. i should never have put you in that situation.
i hope you're feeling ok today.

I made myself take an hour before responding. I watched some cartoons on the internet and made a cup of coffee. Then I read his email again several times. I was relieved he had put the whole thing in lower case like he always did. It would have been dramatic to introduce capitalisation at such a moment of tension. Eventually I wrote my reply, saying that it was my fault for kissing him, and that I was sorry.

He emailed back promptly.

no, it wasn't your fault. i'm like 11 years older than
you and it was also my wife's birthday. i behaved terribly, i really don't want you to feel guilty about it.

It was getting dark out. I felt dizzy and restless. I thought about going for a walk but it was raining and I'd had too much coffee. My heart was beating too quickly for my body. I hit reply.

Do you often kiss girls at parties?

He responded within about twenty minutes.

since i got married, never. although i think that might
make it worse.

My phone rang and I picked up, still looking at the email.

Do you want to hang out and watch *Brazil*? Bobbi said. What?

Do you want to watch *Brazil* together? Hello? The dystopian film with the Monty Python guy. You said you wanted to see it.

What? I said. Yeah, okay. Tonight?

Are you sleeping or something? You sound weird.

I'm not sleeping. Sorry. I was looking at the internet. Sure, let's hang out.

It took her about half an hour to get to my apartment. When she did, she asked if she could stay over. I said yes. We sat on my bed smoking and talking about the party the night before. I felt my heart beating hard in the knowledge that I was being deceitful, but outwardly I was a capable liar, even a competitive one.

Your hair is getting really long, Bobbi said.

Do you think we should cut it?

We decided to cut it. I sat on a chair in front of the living-room mirror, surrounded by old pages of newspaper. Bobbi used the same scissors I used to cut open kitchen items, but she washed them with boiled water and Fairy liquid first.

Do you still think Melissa likes you? I said.

Bobbi gave me a little indulgent smile, as if she had never actually ventured that theory.

Everyone likes me, she said.

But I mean, do you think she feels a particular connection with you, in comparison to other people. You know what I mean.

I don't know, she's difficult to get a read on.

I find that too, I said. Sometimes I feel like she loathes me.

No, she definitely likes you as a person. I think you remind her of her.

I felt even more dishonest then, and a sensation of heat crawled up into my ears. Maybe knowing that I'd betrayed Melissa's trust made me feel like a liar, or maybe this imaginative connection between us suggested something else. I knew I was the one who had kissed Nick and not the other way around, but I also believed that he'd wanted me to. If I reminded Melissa of herself, was it possible I reminded Nick of Melissa also?

We could give you a fringe, said Bobbi.

No, people mix us up too much already.

It's offensive to me how offensive that is to you.

After she cut my hair we made a pot of coffee and sat on the couch talking about the college feminist society. Bobbi had left the society the previous year, after they invited a British guest speaker who had supported the invasion of Iraq. The society president had described Bobbi's objection to the invitation as "aggressive" and "sectarian" on the group's Facebook page, which privately we all agreed was total bullshit, but because the speaker had never actually accepted the invite, Philip and I had not gone so far as to formally renounce our membership. Bobbi's attitude toward this decision varied greatly, and tended to be an indicator of how well she and I were getting along at a given time. When things were good, she considered it a sign of my tolerance and even self-sacrifice to the cause of gender revolution. When we were having a minor dispute over something, she sometimes referred to it as an example of my disloyalty and ideological spinelessness.

Do they have a stance on sexism these days? she said. Or are there two sides to that as well?

They definitely want more women CEOs.

You know, there's a distinct lack of female arms dealers, I've always thought.

We put on the film eventually, but Bobbi fell asleep while we were watching it. I wondered if she preferred sleeping in my apartment because being near to her parents caused her anxiety. She hadn't mentioned it, and she was usually pretty free with the details of her emotional life, but family things were different. I didn't feel like watching the film on my own so I switched it off and just read the internet instead. Eventually Bobbi woke up and then went to bed properly, on the mattress in my room. I liked having her sleeping there while I was awake, it felt reassuring.

That night while she was in bed I opened up my laptop and replied to Nick's last email.

After that I went back and forth on the question of whether to tell Bobbi that I had kissed Nick. I had, regardless of my ultimate decision, meticulously rehearsed the way I would tell her about it, which details I would emphasise and which I would leave out.

It just kind of happened, I would say.

That's crazy, Bobbi would reply. But I've always kind of thought he liked you.

I don't know. He was really high, it was stupid.

But in the email he definitely implied it was his fault, didn't he?

I could tell that I was using the Bobbi character mainly to reassure myself that Nick was interested in me, and I knew in real life Bobbi wouldn't react that way at all, so I stopped. I did feel an urge to tell someone who would understand the situation, but I also didn't want to risk Bobbi telling Melissa, which I thought she might do, not as a conscious betrayal but in an effort to weave herself further into Melissa's life.

I decided not to tell her, which meant I couldn't tell anyone, or no one who would understand. I mentioned to Philip that I had kissed someone I shouldn't have kissed, but he didn't know what I was talking about.

Is it Bobbi? he said.

No, it's not Bobbi.

Worse or better than if you had kissed Bobbi?

Worse, I said. A lot worse. Just forget about it.

Jesus, I didn't think anything could be worse than that.

There wasn't any point in trying to tell him anyway.

I once kissed an ex at a party, he said. Weeks of drama. Ruined my focus.

Is that so.

She had a boyfriend, though, which complicated things.

I bet, I said.

The next day there was a book launch in Hodges Figgis and Bobbi wanted to go and get a copy of the book signed. It was a very warm afternoon in July and I sat inside for the hour before the launch pulling knots out of my hair with my fingers, pulling them so hard that little broken strands of hair tangled and snapped out. I thought: probably they won't even be there, and I'll have to come home and sweep up all these strands of hair and feel terrible. Probably nothing of import will happen in my life again and I'll just have to sweep things up until I die.

I met Bobbi in the door of the bookshop and she waved at me. She had a row of bangles on her left wrist, which rattled elegantly down her arm with the waving gesture. Often I found myself believing that if I looked like Bobbi, nothing bad would happen to me. It wouldn't be like waking up with a new, strange face: it would be like waking up with a face I already knew, the face I already imagined was mine, and so it would feel natural.

On our way up to the launch I saw Nick and Melissa through the staircase railings. They were standing next to a display of books. Melissa's calves were bare and very pale and she was wearing flat shoes with an ankle strap. I stopped walking and touched my collarbone.

Bobbi, I said. Does my face look shiny?

Bobbi glanced back and scrunched up her eyes to inspect me.

Yeah, a little, she said.

I let the air out of my lungs quietly. There wasn't anything I could do now anyway since I was on the stairs already. I wished I hadn't asked.

Not in a bad way, she said. You look cute, why?

I shook my head and we continued up the stairs. The reading hadn't started yet, so everyone was still milling around holding wine glasses expectantly. The room was very hot, though they had opened the windows out over the street, and a cool mouthful of breeze touched my left arm and made me shiver. I was sweating. Bobbi was talking about something in my ear, and I nodded and pretended to listen.

Eventually Nick looked over and I looked back. I felt a key turning hard inside my body, turning so forcefully that I could do nothing to stop it. His lips parted like he was about to say something, but he just inhaled and then seemed to swallow. Neither of us gestured or waved, we just looked at one another, as if we were already having a private conversation that couldn't be overheard.

After a few seconds I was conscious that Bobbi had stopped talking, and when I turned to see her she was looking over at Nick too, with her bottom lip pushed out a little, like: oh, now I see who you're staring at. I wanted a glass to hold against my face.

Well, at least he can dress himself, she said.

I didn't pretend to be confused. He was wearing a white T-shirt and he had suede shoes on, the kind everyone wore then, desert boots. Even I wore desert boots. He only looked handsome because he was handsome, though Bobbi wasn't sensitive to the effects of beauty like I was.

Or maybe Melissa dresses him, said Bobbi.

She was smiling to herself as if concealing a mystery, though her behaviour wasn't in the least mysterious. I ran my hand through my hair and looked away. A white square of sunlight lay on the carpet like snow.

They don't even sleep together, I said.

Our eyes met then and Bobbi lifted her chin just barely.

I know, she said.

During the reading we didn't whisper in each other's ears like we usually did. It was a book of short stories by a female writer. I glanced at Bobbi but she kept looking forward, so I knew I was being punished for something.

We saw Nick and Melissa after the reading was over. Bobbi went to meet them and I followed her, cooling my face against the back of my hand. They were standing near the refreshments table and Melissa reached over to get us both a glass of wine. White or red? she said.

White, I said. Always white.

Bobbi said: when she drinks red her mouth goes like, and she gestured to her own mouth in a little circle. Melissa handed me a glass and said: oh I get that. It's not so bad, I think. There's something appealingly evil about it. Bobbi agreed with her. Like you've been drinking blood, she said. And Melissa laughed and said: yes, sacrificing virgins.

I looked into the wine, which was clear and almost greenish-yellow, the colour of cut grass. When I glanced back at Nick he was looking at me. The light from the window felt hot on the back of my neck. I was wondering if you'd be here, he said. It's nice to see you. And he slipped his hand into his pocket as if he was afraid of what else he might do with it. Melissa and Bobbi were talking still. No one was paying us any attention. Yeah, I said. You too.

CHAPTER
NINE

Melissa was working in London the following week. It was the hottest week of the year, and Bobbi and I sat in the empty college campus together eating ice cream and trying to get a tan. One afternoon I emailed Nick asking him if I could come over so we could talk. He said sure. I didn't tell Bobbi. I brought my toothbrush in my bag.

When I arrived at the house all the windows and doors were open. I rang the doorbell anyway and heard him saying come in from the kitchen, he didn't even check who it was. I closed the door behind me anyway. When I got inside he was drying his hands on a tea towel, like he'd just finished washing up. He smiled and told me he'd been feeling nervous about seeing me again. The dog was lying on the sofa. I hadn't seen her on the sofa before and wondered if maybe Melissa wouldn't let her sleep there. I asked Nick why he was nervous and he laughed and made a little shrugging gesture, though one that seemed more relaxed than anxious. I leaned my back against the countertop while he folded the towel away.

So, you're married, I said.

Yeah, it looks like it. Do you want a drink?

I accepted a small bottle of beer, though only because I wanted something to hold in my hand. I felt restless, the way you feel when you've already done the wrong thing and you're anxious about what the outcome is going to be. I told him I didn't want to be a homewrecker or whatever. He laughed at that.

That's funny, he said. What does that mean?

I mean, you've never had an affair before. I don't want to wreck your marriage.

Oh, well, the marriage has actually survived several affairs, I just haven't been involved in any of them.

He said this amusingly, and it made me laugh, though it also had the effect, which I guess was intended, of making me relax about the morality side of things. I hadn't really wanted to feel sympathetic to Melissa, and now I felt her moving outside my frame of sympathy entirely, as if she belonged to a different story with different characters.

When we went upstairs I told Nick I had never had sex with a man before. He asked if that was a big deal and I said I didn't think it was, but it might be weird if he only found out later. While we undressed I tried to seem casual by keeping my limbs still and not trembling violently. I was afraid of undressing in front of him, but I didn't know how to shield my body in a way that wouldn't look awkward and unattractive. He had a very imposing upper body, like a piece of statuary. I missed the distance between us when he'd watched me being applauded, which now seemed protective, even necessary. But when he asked me if I was sure I wanted to do all this, I heard myself say: I didn't really come over just to talk, you know.

In bed he asked me what felt good a lot. I said everything felt good. I felt very flushed and I could hear myself making a lot of noise, but only syllables, no real words. I closed my eyes. The inside of my body was hot like oil. I was possessed by an overwhelming and intense energy which seemed to threaten me. Please, I was saying. Please, please. Eventually Nick sat up to take a box of condoms from his bedside locker and I thought: I might never be able to speak again after this. But I surrendered without struggle. Nick murmured the word "sorry", as if the several seconds I had been lying there waiting constituted a minor wrong on his part.

When it was over I lay on my back shivering. I had been so terribly noisy and theatrical all the way through that it was impossible now to act indifferent like I did in the emails.

That felt kind of okay, I said.

Did it?

I think I liked it more than you did.

Nick laughed and lifted his arm to place a hand behind his head.

No, he said, you really didn't.

You were very nice to me.

Was I?

Seriously, I really do appreciate how nice you were, I said.

Wait. Hey. Are you all right?

74

Little tears had started slipping out of my eyes and down onto the pillow. I wasn't sad, I didn't know why I was crying. I'd had this problem before, with Bobbi, who believed it was an expression of my repressed feelings. I couldn't stop the tears so I just laughed self-effacingly instead, to show that I wasn't invested in the crying. I knew I was embarrassing myself badly, but there was nothing I could do about it.

This happens, I said. It wasn't anything you did.

Nick touched his hand to my body then, just under my breast. I felt soothed like I was an animal, and I cried harder.

Are you sure? he said.

Yeah. You can ask Bobbi. I mean, don't.

He smiled and said: yeah, I won't. He was stroking me with the tips of his fingers, like the way he petted his dog. I wiped at my face roughly.

You're really handsome, you know, I said.

He laughed then.

Is that all I get? he said. I thought you liked my personality.

Do you have one?

He turned over on his back, looking up at the ceiling with a bemused expression. I can't believe we did this, he said. I knew then that the crying was over. I felt good about everything I could think of. I touched the inside of his wrist and said: yes, you can.

I woke up late the next morning. Nick made French toast for breakfast and I got the bus back into town. I sat at the back, near a window, where the sun bore down on my face like a drill and the cloth of the seat felt sensationally tactile against my bare skin.

That evening Bobbi said she needed somewhere to stay to get away from the "domestic situation". Apparently Eleanor had thrown away some of Jerry's possessions over the weekend, and at the height of the ensuing argument Lydia had locked herself in the bathroom and screamed that she wanted to die.

Deeply uncool, Bobbi said.

I told her she could stay with me. I didn't know what else to say. She knew I had an empty apartment. That evening she played around with my electric piano using my laptop for sheet music and I checked my email on my phone. No one had been in touch. I picked up a book but didn't feel like reading. I hadn't done any writing that morning, or the morning before. I had started reading long interviews with famous writers and noticing how unlike them I was.

You've got a notification on your instant message thing, said Bobbi.

Don't read it. Let me see it.

Why are you saying don't read it?

I don't want you to read it, I said. Give me the laptop.

She handed me the laptop, but I could see she wasn't going back to the piano. The message was from Nick.

Nick: i know, i'm a bad person
Nick: do you want to come over again some time this
   week?

Who's it from? Bobbi said.

Can you relax about it?

Why did you go "don't read it"?

Because I didn't want you to read it, I said.

She bit on her thumbnail coquettishly and then got onto the bed beside me. I shut my laptop screen, which made her laugh.

I didn't open it, she said. But I did see who it was from.

Okay, good for you.

You really like him, don't you?

I don't know what you're talking about, I said.

Melissa's husband. You have a serious thing for him.

I rolled my eyes. Bobbi lay back on the bed and grinned. I hated her then and even wanted to harm her.

Why, are you jealous? I said.

She smiled, but absently, as if she was thinking of something else. I didn't know what else to say to her. She went back to the piano for a while and then she wanted to go to bed. When I woke up the next morning she was already gone.

I stayed with Nick most nights that week. He wasn't working, so he went to the gym for a couple of hours in the morning and I went into the agency or just wandered around the shops. Then in the evening he made dinner and I played with the spaniel. I told Nick I didn't think I'd eaten so much food in my life, which was true. At home my parents had never cooked with chorizo or aubergine. I had also never tasted fresh avocado before, though I didn't tell Nick about that.

One night I asked him if he was afraid of Melissa finding out about us and he said he didn't think she would find out.

But you found out, I said. When she had affairs.

No, she told me.

What, really? Out of the blue?

The first time, yeah, he said. It was very surreal. She was away at one of these book festivals, and she called me at like five in the morning and said she had something to tell me, that was it.

Fuck.

But it was just a one-off thing, they didn't keep seeing each other after that. The other time was a lot more involved. I probably shouldn't be telling you all these secrets, should I? I'm not trying to make her look bad. Or at least I don't think I am, I don't know.

Over dinner we exchanged some of the details about our lives. I explained that I wanted to destroy capitalism and that I considered masculinity personally oppressive. Nick told me he was "basically" a Marxist, and he didn't want me to judge him for owning a house. It's this or paying rent forever, he said. But I acknowledge it's troubling. It sounded to me like his family was very wealthy, but I was wary of probing the issue, since I already felt self-conscious about never paying for anything. His parents were still married and he had two siblings.

During these discussions, Nick laughed at all my jokes. I told him I was easily seduced by people who laughed at my jokes and he said he was easily seduced by people who were smarter than he was.

I guess you just don't meet them very often, I said. See, isn't it nice to flatter each other?

The sex was so good that I often cried while it was happening. Nick liked me to go on top, so he could sit back against the headboard, and we could talk quietly. I could tell that he liked it when I talked to him about how good it felt. It was very easy to make him come if I talked about that too much. Sometimes I liked to do that just to feel powerful over him, and afterwards he would say: God, I'm sorry, that's so embarrassing. I liked him saying that even more than I liked the sex itself.

I became infatuated with the house he lived in: how immaculate everything was, and the coolness of the floorboards in the morning. They had an electric coffee grinder in the kitchen and Nick bought whole-bean coffee and then put small portions in the grinder before breakfast. I wasn't sure if this was pretentious or not, though the coffee tasted incredibly good. I told him it was pretentious anyway and he said, what do you drink? Fucking Nescafé? You're a student, don't act like you've got taste. Of course I secretly liked all the expensive utensils they had in their kitchen, the same way I liked to watch Nick press the coffee so slowly that a film of dark cream formed on its surface.

He talked to Melissa pretty much every day during the week. Usually she would call in the evenings, and he'd take the phone into another room while I lay on the couch watching TV or went outside to smoke. These conversations often took twenty minutes or more. Once I watched an entire episode of *Arrested*

Development before he came back in the room, it was the one where they burn down the banana stand. I never heard anything Nick said on the phone. I asked once: she's not suspicious or anything, is she? And he just shook his head and said, no, it's okay. Nick wasn't physically affectionate toward me outside of his room. We watched TV together the way we would have done if we were just waiting for Melissa to get home from work. He let me kiss him if I wanted to, but I always had to initiate it.

It was hard to figure out how Nick really felt. In bed he never put any pressure on me to do anything, and he was always very sensitive to what I wanted. Still, there was something blank and withholding about him. He never said anything nice about my appearance. He never touched or kissed me spontaneously. I still felt nervous whenever we undressed, and the first time I gave him head he was so quiet that I stopped to ask if I was hurting him. He said no, but when I started again, he stayed completely silent. He didn't touch me, I didn't even know if he was looking at me. When it was finished I felt awful, like I had made him endure something neither of us enjoyed.

After I left the agency on Thursday that week, I walked past him in town. I was with Philip, going from work to get coffee, and we saw Nick with a tall woman who was directing a pushchair with one hand and talking on the phone with the other. Nick was holding an infant. The infant was wearing a red hat. Nick waved hello as they walked by us, we even looked at one another quickly, but they didn't stop and talk. That morning he had watched me get dressed, lying with his hands behind his head.

That's not his baby, is it? Philip said.

I felt like I was playing a video game without knowing any of the controls. I just shrugged and said, I don't think he has children, does he? I got a text from Nick shortly afterwards saying: my sister Laura and her daughter. Sorry for walking on, they were kind of in a rush. I texted back: cute baby. Can I come over tonight?

That night at dinner he asked me, so did you really think the baby was cute? I told him I didn't get a good look at her, but from a distance she seemed like a cute one. Oh, she's the best, Nick said. Rachel. I don't love many things in life, but I really love that baby. The first time I saw her I just started crying, she was so small. This was by far the most emotion I'd ever heard Nick express, and I was jealous. I thought about making a joke of how jealous I was, but it felt creepy to be jealous of a baby, and I doubted Nick would appreciate it. That's sweet, I said. He seemed to sense my lack of enthusiasm and said awkwardly: you're probably too young to care about babies anyway. I felt hurt and raked my fork over the dish of risotto silently. Then I said, no, I really thought you were being sweet. Uncharacteristically.

What, like I'm usually gruff and aggressive? he said.

I shrugged. We went on eating. I knew I was starting to make him nervous, I could see him watching me across the table. He wasn't in the least gruff or aggressive, and I saved the question in my mind for later, feeling that he had unintentionally revealed some private fear.

When we undressed that night his bedsheets felt icy against my skin, and I mentioned how cold it was. The house? he said. Do you find it cold at night?

No, I mean just now, I said.

I went to kiss him and he allowed me to, but absently, and without real feeling. Then he pulled away and said: because if you're cold at night, I can put the heating on.

I'm not, I said. The sheets felt cold just now, that's all.

Right.

We had sex, it was nice, and afterwards we lay there looking up at the ceiling. Air hauled itself into my lungs, I felt peaceful. Nick touched my hand and said: are you warm now? I'm warm, I said. Your concern for my temperature is quite touching. Oh well, he said. It would look bad for me if you froze to death. But he was stroking my hand when he said it. The police might have some questions, I said. He laughed. Yeah, he said. Like, what's this beautiful corpse doing in bed with you, Nick? It was just a joke, he would never really call me beautiful. But I liked the joke anyway.

On Friday night, before Melissa came home from London, we watched *North by Northwest* and shared a bottle of wine. Nick was leaving the country the following week to film something in Edinburgh, so I wouldn't see him again for a short time. I can't remember most of what we said that night. I remember the scene on the train where Cary Grant's character is flirting with the blonde woman, and that for some reason I repeated one of her lines out loud in a clipped American accent. I said: and I don't *particularly* like the book I've started. This made Nick laugh a lot, for no real reason, or maybe because my accent was so bad.

Now you do Cary Grant, I said.

In a mid-Atlantic cinema voice Nick said: the moment I meet an attractive woman, I have to start pretending I have no desire to make love to her.

Do you typically pretend for long? I said.

You tell me, Nick said in his normal voice.

I think I figured it out pretty quickly. But I was concerned I was just deluding myself.

Oh, I felt the same way about you.

He had picked up the bottle and was refilling our glasses.

So is this just sex, I said, or do you actually like me?

Frances, you're drunk.

You can tell me, I won't be offended.

No, I know you won't, he said. I think you want me to say it's just sex.

I laughed. I was happy he said that, because it was what I wanted him to think, and because I thought he really knew that and was just kidding around.

Don't feel bad, I said. It's terribly enjoyable. I may have mentioned that before.

Only a couple of times. But I'd like it in writing if possible. Just something permanent that I can look at on my deathbed.

He slipped his hand between my knees then. I was wearing a striped dress and my legs were bare; the moment he touched me I felt hot and passive as if I were asleep. Any strength I had seemed to leave me completely and when I tried to speak I stammered.

What happens when your wife gets home? I said.

Yeah. We'll work something out.

CHAPTER
TEN

I hadn't spoken to Bobbi since the night she'd stayed over in the apartment. Because I was staying with Nick and not thinking about anything else, I hadn't tried to get in touch with her or put much thought into the question of why she hadn't called. Then after Melissa came back to Dublin, I got an email from Bobbi with the subject heading "jealous???"

look, i don't care if you have a crush on nick, and i wasn't trying to embarrass you or whatever. sorry if it came across that way. (and i'm not going to be moralistic about him being married either, i'm pretty sure melissa has affairs anyway). BUT it was really fucked up of you to accuse me of being jealous of him. it is just so stereotypically homophobic to accuse a gay woman of being secretly jealous of men, which i know you know. but even more than that it's really devaluing to our friendship to make out like i'm competing with a man for your attention. what does that say about how you see me? do you really rank our relationship below your passing sexual interest in some middle aged married guy? it hurt my fucking feelings actually.

I was in work when I received the email, but none of the other people who worked there were around. I read the message several times. For some reason I deleted it briefly, and then went into my trash folder to retrieve it almost straight away. Then I marked it as unread and opened it to read it again as if for the first time. Of course Bobbi was right. I had called her jealous to try and hurt her. I just hadn't known that it had actually worked, or that it was even possible to hurt her no matter how hard I tried. Realising not only that hurting Bobbi's feelings was within my power but that I had done it practically offhandedly and without noticing, made me uncomfortable. I wandered around the office and poured some water from the cooler into a plastic cup though I wasn't thirsty. Then eventually I sat back down.

It took me several drafts to finish writing my reply.

Hey, you're right, it was a weird and wrong thing to say and I shouldn't have said it. I felt defensive and I just wanted to make you angry. I feel guilty for hurting your feelings over something so stupid. I'm sorry.

I sent it and then logged out of my email for a while to get some work done.

Philip came in around eleven and we talked a little. I told him I hadn't written anything in a week and he raised his eyebrows.

I thought you were all about discipline, he said.

I was.

86

Are you having a weird month? You seem like you are.

On my lunch break I logged back into my email. Bobbi had replied.

ok i forgive you. but really, nick? is that your thing now? i just feel like he probably unironically reads articles called "one weird trick for perfect abs"

if it absolutely had to be a man i assumed it would be someone wussy and effeminate like philip, this is so unexpected.

I didn't reply to that. Bobbi and I had always shared a contempt for the cultish pursuit of male physical dominance. Even very recently we had been asked to leave Tesco for reading aloud inane passages from men's magazines on the shop floor. But Bobbi was wrong about Nick. That wasn't what he was like. Really he was the kind of person who would laugh at Bobbi's cruel impression of him and not try to correct her. But I couldn't explain that to her. I certainly couldn't tell her what I found most endearing about him, which was that he was attracted to plain and emotionally cold women like me.

By the time I finished work I was tired and I had a headache, a bad one. I walked home and decided to lie in bed for a while. It was five o'clock. I didn't wake up until midnight.

I didn't see Nick again before he left for Scotland. Because he was on set from early in the morning, the only way we could talk was online, late at night. He was usually tired by then and seemed withdrawn, and I started writing only terse responses to his messages, or not responding at all. Online he talked about trivial things, like how much he hated his co-workers. He never said that he missed me, or thought about me at all. When I made any reference to the time we'd spent in his house together he tended to skip over it and talk about something else. In response I felt myself becoming cold and sarcastic.

Nick: the only reasonable person on set is stephanie
me: why don't you have an affair with her then.
Nick: well i think that could only harm our working relationship
me: is that a hint
Nick: also she is at least 60
me: and you're what like.. 63?
Nick: funny
Nick: i'll run it by her if you want
me: oh please do

At home I watched YouTube clips of his film and TV appearances. He had once played the young father of a kidnap victim in an episode of a long-running crime drama, and in one scene he broke down and cried in the police station. That was the clip I watched most often. He cried exactly the way I imagined he would in real life: hating himself for crying, but hating himself so much that it only made him cry harder. I found that if I watched this clip before we spoke at night, I tended to be more sympathetic toward him. He had a very basic HTML fansite online that hadn't been updated since 2011, which I looked at sometimes while we were talking.

I was sick at the time, I had cystitis. For a while the persistent discomfort and mild fever felt psychologically appropriate and I did nothing about them, but eventually I went to see the college doctor and she gave me antibiotics and a painkiller that made me drowsy. I spent the evenings looking at my own hands or trying to focus on a laptop screen. I felt disgusting, like my body was full of evil bacteria. I knew that Nick was suffering no similar after-effects. There was nothing equivalent about us. He had screwed me up in his hand like paper and tossed me away.

I tried to start writing again, but everything I produced was full of a bitterness that made me ashamed. Some of it I deleted, some I hid in folders I never looked inside. I was taking things too seriously again. I fixated on perceived wrongs Nick had done to me, callous things he had said or implied, so that I could hate him and therefore justify the intensity of my feelings for him as pure hatred. But I recognised that the only thing he had done to hurt me was to withdraw his affection, which he had every right to do. In every other way he had been courteous and thoughtful. At times I thought this was the worst misery I had experienced in my life, but it was also a very shallow misery, which at any time could have been relieved completely by a word from him and transformed into idiotic happiness.

One night online I asked him if he had sadistic tendencies.

Nick: not that i know of
Nick: why do you ask?
me: you seem like someone who does
Nick: hm
Nick: that's worrying

Some time passed. I stared at the screen but didn't type anything. I was one day away from finishing my antibiotics.

Nick: is there an example you're thinking of?
me: no
Nick: ok
Nick: i think when i hurt people it tends to be through selfishness
Nick: rather than being an end in itself
Nick: have i done something to hurt you?
me: no
Nick: are you sure?

I let more time go by. With the pad of my finger I covered his name on my laptop screen.

Nick: are you still there?
me: yeah
Nick: oh
Nick: i guess you don't feel like talking then
Nick: that's ok, i should go to bed anyway

The next morning he sent me an email that read:

i can see you don't really feel like keeping in touch at the moment, so i'm going to stop sending you messages, ok? i'll see you when i'm back.

I considered writing a spiteful email in response but instead I didn't reply at all.

The following night Bobbi suggested we watch one of Nick's films.

That would be weird, I said.

He's our friend, why would it be weird?

She was on my laptop, searching Netflix. I had made a pot of peppermint tea and we were waiting for it to brew.

It's on here, she said. I saw it on here. It's the one about the bridesmaid marrying her boss.

Why are you even looking for his films?

It's a pretty minor part but he does take his shirt off at one point. You're into that, right?

Genuinely, please stop, I said.

She stopped. She was sitting cross-legged on the floor and she reached to pour herself a splash of tea to see if it was ready.

Do you like him as a person? she said. Or is it just like, he's good-looking and married to someone interesting?

I could tell she was still hurt by the jealousy remark, but I had apologised already. I didn't want to indulge her hostility toward Nick, especially since I wasn't talking to him then. It was obvious to me that Bobbi's feelings were not sincerely hurt anymore, if they ever had been, and that she just liked to make fun of me whenever I experienced romantic feelings. I looked at her like she was something very far away from me, a friend I used to have, or someone whose name I didn't remember.

Melissa's not that interesting, I said.

When Bobbi went home I looked up the film she was talking about. It had been released six years previously, when I was fifteen. Nick appeared in it as a character with whom the protagonist has a regrettable one-night stand. I found a video link and skipped ahead to the scene where he was getting out of her shower the next morning. He looked younger, and his face was different, although even in this video he was older than me. I watched the scene twice. After he left, the protagonist called her friend and they laughed hysterically about what a jerk Nick's character was, which was a bonding moment for their friendship.

I sent him an email after I watched it. I wrote:

Sure, if that's what you want. I hope the filming is going okay.

He replied at about 1a.m.

i should have told you before, but i'm going to be in the north of france for most of august with melissa and various other people. it's a huge villa type place in a village called etables. people are always coming and going, so you're welcome to come and stay for a while if you want, though i can see why that might not appeal.

I was sitting cross-legged in bed trying to work on a spoken word thing when the email notification came through. I replied:

So are we still having an affair or is that over now?

He didn't reply for a while. I guessed he had gone to bed, but the possibility that he hadn't yet made me not want to work any more. I made myself a cup of instant coffee and watched some YouTube videos of other spoken word performers.

Eventually a notification came through on instant messenger.

Nick: are you awake
me: yes
Nick: so yeah look
Nick: i don't know what you want
Nick: obviously we can't see each other very often
Nick: and having an affair is reasonably stressful
me: haha
me: are you breaking up with me
Nick: if we never actually see one another
Nick: then the affair just consists of like
Nick: worrying about the affair
Nick: do you see what i mean
me: I can't believe you're breaking up with me over
    instant messenger

me: I thought you were going to leave your wife so we
   could run away together
Nick: you don't need to be defensive
me: how do you know what I need
me: maybe I'm actually really upset
Nick: are you
Nick: i never have any idea what you feel about
   anything
me: well it doesn't really matter now, does it

He had to be back on set early that morning so he
went to bed. I kept thinking about the time I gave him
head and he just lay there quietly letting me do it. I had
never done that before, I wanted to explain. You could
have told me what was so bad about it instead of just
letting me carry on. It wasn't kind. I felt so foolish. But
I knew he had done nothing wrong really. I considered
calling Bobbi and telling her everything, in the hope
that she would tell Melissa and then Nick's life would
be ruined. But I decided it would be too humiliating a
story to relate.

CHAPTER
ELEVEN

I missed work the next day because I slept in. I sent Sunny a grovelling email and she responded: we survived. It was noon by the time I showered. I put on a black T-shirt dress and went out for a walk, though it was too hot to enjoy walking. The air felt helpless and trapped on the streets. Shop windows reflected blinding flares of sunlight and my skin was damp. I sat on the campus cricket pitch on my own and smoked two cigarettes, one after another. I had a headache, I hadn't eaten. My body felt used up and worthless to me. I didn't want to put food or medicine into it any more.

That afternoon when I got back, I had a new email from Nick.

so i feel like our conversation last night was kind of awkward. it's obviously hard for me to tell what you actually want and i don't really know if you were joking about being hurt. you're a very stressful person to talk to online. i hope you're not upset or anything.

I wrote back:

Forget about it. See you in September, I hope the weather is good in France.

He didn't email me again after that.

Three days later, Melissa invited Bobbi and me to come stay in the villa in Étables for a few days in August. Bobbi kept sending me links to the Ryanair website and saying we should go for just a week, or even just five days. I could afford the flights and Sunny didn't mind me taking time off.

Eventually I said: fine. Let's go.

Bobbi and I had been on several foreign trips together before. We always took the cheapest flights, early in the morning or late at night, and as a consequence we usually spent the first day of the trip feeling irritable and trying to find free WiFi. The only day I had ever spent in Budapest we'd sat in a coffee shop with our luggage while Bobbi drank espressos and engaged in a heated online argument about drone strikes, which she relayed to me aloud. When I told her I wasn't particularly interested in hearing the discussion, she said: children are dying, Frances. We didn't speak for several hours after that.

In the days preceding our trip, Bobbi sent me frequent text messages about items I should remember to pack. It was in my nature to remember what I needed, and very much in Bobbi's nature not to. One evening she called around to the apartment with a list, and when I answered the door she was holding her phone between her shoulder and ear.

Hey, I'm just at Frances's place now, she said. Do you mind if I put you on speakerphone?

Bobbi closed the door and followed me into the living room, where she dropped her phone unceremoniously onto the table, with the speakerphone enabled.

Hi Frances, said Melissa's voice.

I said hello, though what I meant was: I hope you haven't found out about me sleeping with your husband.

So whose is the house exactly? Bobbi said.

It belongs to a friend of mine called Valerie, said Melissa.

I mean, I say friend, she's in her sixties. More like a mentor. She was very helpful with getting the book published, and all that. Anyway, old old money. And she likes to have people staying in her various properties when she's not around.

I said that she sounded interesting.

You'd like her, Melissa said. You might get to meet her, she does spend a day or two in the house sometimes. She lives in Paris usually.

Wealthy people sicken me, said Bobbi. But yeah, I'm sure she's great.

How have you been keeping, Frances? Melissa said. It feels like an age since I've seen you.

I paused, and then said: I've been well, thank you. And you? Melissa also paused and then replied: good.

How was London? I asked. You were over there last month, were you?

Was that last month? she said. Time is so funny.

She said she had better be getting back to dinner and hung up. I didn't think there was anything remotely funny about time, certainly not "so funny".

After Bobbi left that night I wrote for an hour and a half, poetry in which I figured my own body as an item of garbage, an empty wrapper or a half-eaten and discarded piece of fruit. Putting my self-loathing to work in this way didn't make me feel better as such, but it tired me out. Afterwards I lay on my side with *A Critique of Postcolonial Reason* propped half-open on the pillow beside me. Occasionally I lifted a finger to turn the page and allowed the heavy and confusing syntax to drift down through my eyes and into my brain like fluid. I'm bettering myself, I thought. I'm going to become so smart that no one will understand me.

Before we left the country, I sent Nick an email telling him we were coming to stay. I said: I'm sure Melissa told you already, I just want to assure you I'm not planning on making a scene. He replied saying: cool, it'll be nice to see you. I stared at that message repeatedly, often reopening it to stare at it again. It was so devoid of tone or meaning that it infuriated me. It was as if, our relationship having come to an end, he had demoted me right back to my previous status as an acquaintance. The affair might be over, I thought, but something being over is not the same as something never having happened. In my anger I even began searching my emails and texts for "evidence" of our affair, which consisted of a few boring logistical messages about when he would be back in the house and what time I might arrive. There were no passionate

98

declarations of love or sexually graphic text messages. This made sense, because the affair was conducted in real life and not online, but I felt robbed of something anyway.

On the plane I shared my headphones with Bobbi, who had forgotten hers. We had to turn the volume way up to be able to hear anything over the engines. Bobbi was a nervous flyer, or she said she was, but I thought she played it up to an extent just for fun. When we flew together she made me hold hands. I wished I could ask her what she thought I should do, but I was sure if she knew what had happened she'd be appalled at the idea of me even going to Étables. In a way I was appalled too, but also fascinated. Before that summer I'd had no idea I was the kind of person who would accept an invitation like this from a woman whose husband I'd repeatedly slept with. This information was morbidly interesting to me.

Bobbi fell asleep for most of the flight and only woke up when we landed. She squeezed my hand while the other passengers got up to get their luggage, and said: flying with you is so relaxing. You have a very stoic disposition. The airport smelled of artificial air freshener, and Bobbi bought us two black coffees while I figured out which bus we had to catch. Bobbi had studied German in school and spoke no French, but wherever we went she managed to communicate effectively with her hands and face. I saw the man behind the coffee counter smiling at her like a beloved cousin, while I desperately repeated the names of towns and bus services to the woman at the ticket desk.

Bobbi had a way of belonging everywhere. Though she said she hated the rich, her family was rich, and other wealthy people recognised her as one of their own. They took her radical politics as a kind of bourgeois self-deprecation, nothing very serious, and talked to her about restaurants or where to stay in Rome. I felt out of place in these situations, ignorant and bitter, but also fearful of being discovered as a moderately poor person and a communist. Equally, I struggled to make conversation with people of my own parents' background, afraid that my vowels sounded pretentious or my large flea-market coat made me look rich. Philip also suffered from looking rich, though in his case because he really was. We two often fell silent while Bobbi chatted effortlessly with taxi drivers about current affairs.

It was six in the morning by the time we boarded the bus to Étables. I was exhausted, and a headache had settled behind my eyes so I had to squint at the tickets to read them. The bus took us through verdant countryside, which a white mist had settled over, shot through with sunlight. On the bus radio, voices chatted lightly in French, laughing sometimes, and then there was music. We passed farmland on either side, vineyards with hand-painted signs and immaculate drive-through bakeries advertised in neat sans-serif lettering. Very few cars were on the roads, it was early.

By seven the sky had thinned out into a soft, lipless blue. Bobbi was asleep on my shoulder. I fell asleep too and dreamt that I had a problem with my teeth. My mother was sitting very far away from me, at the end of the room, and she said: it's expensive to get those things fixed, you know. Obediently, I worked my tongue down underneath my tooth, until the tooth came loose into my mouth and I spat it into my hand. Is that it? my mother said, but I couldn't answer because the hole in my mouth was pumping blood. The blood tasted thick, clotted and salty. I could feel it, vividly, running back down my throat. Well, spit it out, my mother said. I spat helplessly onto the floor. My blood was the colour of blackberries. When I woke up the bus driver was saying: Étables. And Bobbi was pulling gently on my hair.

CHAPTER
TWELVE

Melissa was waiting for us at the bus stop, right by the harbour. She was wearing a red wrap dress, low-cut and gathered with a ribbon at her waist. She had large breasts, a generous figure, not at all like mine. She was leaning on the railings gazing out onto the sea, which looked flat like a sheet of plastic. She offered to help us with our bags but we said we'd carry them ourselves and she shrugged. The skin on her nose was peeling. She looked pretty.

When we got to the house, the dog ran outside and started yelping and jumping up on its back feet like a little circus animal. Melissa ignored that and opened the gate. The house had a huge stonework façade, with blue-painted shutters on the windows and white stairs running up to the front door. Inside, everything was pristinely tidy and smelled faintly of cleaning agents and suncream. The walls were papered with a pattern of sailboats, and I saw the shelves were full of French-language novels. Our rooms were downstairs, on the basement floor: Bobbi's looked out over the yard, while mine faced the sea. We left our luggage inside and Melissa said the others were having breakfast out the back.

In the garden, they had a large white tent covering a table and chairs, with the canvas doors rolled up and tied with ribbon. The dog followed at my ankles and shrieked for my attention. Melissa introduced us to her friends, a couple called Evelyn and Derek. They looked the same age Melissa did, or maybe a little older. They were laying out cutlery on the table. The dog barked at me again and Melissa said: oh, she must like you. You know she needs a passport to travel overseas? It's like having a toddler. I laughed at nothing, while the dog butted her head against my shins and whimpered.

Nick came out of the house, carrying plates. I felt myself swallow, hard. He looked thin and very tired. The sun was in his eyes and he squinted over at us as if he hadn't seen that we'd arrived. Then he did see us. He said, oh hi, how was the trip? He glanced away from me and the dog howled. Uneventful, said Bobbi. Nick put the plates down and wiped his hand against his forehead as if it was wet, though it didn't look to be.

Were you always this skinny? Bobbi said. I remembered you bigger.

He's been sick, said Derek. He had bronchitis, he's very sensitive about it.

It was pneumonia, Nick said.

Are you okay now? I asked.

Nick looked in the direction of my shoes and nodded. He said Yeah, sure, I'm fine. He did look different, his face was thinner and he had damp circles below his eyes. He said he'd finished the antibiotics. I pinched hard on my earlobe to distract myself.

Melissa laid the table and I sat beside Bobbi, who said funny things and laughed a lot. Everyone seemed charmed by her. There was a plastic, slightly sticky tablecloth covering the table, and lots of fresh croissants and various preserves and hot coffee. I could think of nothing to say that wouldn't make me feel unwelcome. I stayed quiet and refilled my coffee cup three times. In a small bowl next to my elbow was a stack of glittering white sugar cubes, which I sank into my cup and stirred one by one.

At one point, Bobbi said something about Dublin airport, and Derek said: ah, Nick's old haunt.

Do you have a particular love of the airport? Bobbi said.

He's a jetsetter, said Evelyn. He practically lives there.

He's even had a wild affair with a stewardess, Derek said.

My chest tightened but I didn't look up. Though my coffee was already too sweet, I lifted another sugar cube and placed it on my saucer.

She wasn't a stewardess, said Melissa. She worked in the Starbucks.

Stop that, Nick said. They're going to think you're serious.

What was her name again? said Evelyn. Lola?

Louisa, Nick said.

Finally I looked at him, but he wasn't looking at me. He was smiling with one half of his mouth.

Nick went on a date with a girl he met in the airport, Evelyn said to us.

104

Unwittingly, said Nick.

Well, a bit wittingly, Derek said.

Nick looked at Bobbi then, with an expression of feigned exasperation, like: okay, here we go. But truly he didn't seem to mind telling the story.

This is like three years ago, said Nick. I was in the airport constantly at the time, so I knew this girl to see, we sometimes talked while I was waiting for my order. Anyway one week she asked me to meet her for coffee in town. I thought . . .

At this, the others all started talking again, laughing and making remarks all at once.

I thought, Nick repeated, that she actually just wanted coffee.

What happened? said Bobbi.

Well, when I got there, I realised it was supposed to be a date, Nick said. And I completely panicked, I felt terrible.

The others started to interject again, Evelyn laughing, Derek saying he doubted Nick felt all that terrible. Without looking up from her plate, Melissa said something I couldn't hear.

So I told her I was married, Nick said.

You must have known at some level, said Derek. What she was after.

Honestly, Nick said. People have coffee together all the time, it just didn't occur to me.

It's a great cover story, Evelyn said. If you did have an affair with her.

Was she attractive? said Bobbi.

Nick laughed and lifted a hand palm-up like, what do you think? Ravishingly, he said.

Melissa laughed at that and he smiled down at his lap, like he was pleased with himself for making her laugh. Under the table I stepped on my own toes with the heel of my sandal.

And she was stupidly young, wasn't she? said Derek. Twenty-three or something.

Maybe she knew you were married, Evelyn said. Some women like married men, it's a challenge.

I stepped on my foot so hard the pain shot up my leg and I had to bite down on my lip to stay quiet. Releasing my heel, I could feel my toes throbbing.

I don't really believe that, said Nick. She also seemed pretty disappointed when I mentioned it.

Evelyn and Derek went down to the beach after breakfast, while Bobbi and I stayed to unpack our things. We could hear Melissa and Nick talking upstairs, but only the cadence of their voices, not the actual words. A bumblebee flew through the open window and cast a comma of shadow on the wallpaper before flying out again. When I finished unpacking I showered and changed into a sleeveless grey cotton dress, listening to Bobbi singing a Françoise Hardy song in the next room.

It was two or three o'clock when we all left the house together. The route to the beach was down a little paved hill, past two white houses, and then a zig-zag of steps set into the cliff rock. The beach was full of young families lying out on coloured towels, applying sun lotion on each other's backs. The tide had receded out past a crust of dried green seaweed and a group of teenagers were playing volleyball down by the rocks. We could hear them shouting in foreign accents. The sun was beating onto the sand and I was starting to sweat. We saw Evelyn and Derek waving to us, Evelyn in a brown one-piece swimsuit, her thighs pocked like the texture of whipped cream.

We laid our towels out and Melissa put some sun lotion on the back of Bobbi's neck. Derek told Nick the water was "refreshing". The smell of salt stung my throat. Bobbi undressed down to her bikini. I averted my eyes from Nick and Melissa while they undressed together. She asked him something and I heard him say: no, I'm fine. Evelyn said, you'll burn.

Aren't you getting in the water, Frances? Derek said.

Everyone turned to look at me then. I touched the side of my sunglasses and lifted one shoulder, not even a full shrug.

I'd rather lie in the sun, I said.

The truth was that I didn't want to change into my swimsuit in front of them. I felt I owed it to my own body not to. Nobody minded, they left me where I was. When they were gone I took off my sunglasses to make sure I didn't get tan lines on my face. There were children playing with plastic toys nearby and yelling at one another in French, which sounded urbane and sophisticated to me because I couldn't understand it. I was lying on my front, so I couldn't see the children's faces, but occasionally in my peripheral vision I caught a blur of primary colour, a spade or bucket, or a flash of ankle. A weight had settled in my joints like sand. I thought about the heat on the bus that morning.

After I turned to lie on my back, Bobbi came up from the water, shivering and looking very white. She wrapped herself in a huge beach towel, with another light blue towel draped over her head like the Virgin Mary.

It's Baltic, she said. I thought I was going to go into cardiac arrest.

You should have stayed here. I'm a little too warm if anything.

She removed the towel from her head and shook her hair like a dog, until a shower of droplets hit my bare skin and I swore. You deserved it, she said. She sat down then and opened up her book, her body still swaddled in the big towel, which had a picture of Super Mario on it.

On the way down to the water everyone was talking about you, she said.

What?

Yeah, there was a little group conversation about you. Apparently you're very impressive. It's news to me, obviously.

Who says so? I said.

Can we smoke on the beach or not?

I told her I didn't think we were allowed to smoke on the beach. She sighed performatively and squeezed out some remaining seawater from her hair. Because Bobbi would not tell me who had complimented me, I felt certain it had actually been Bobbi herself.

108

Nick didn't really say anything, she said. About whether you're impressive. I was watching him, though, he seemed very awkward.

Maybe because you were watching him.

Or maybe because Melissa was.

I coughed and said nothing. Bobbi took a cereal bar out of the bottom of her handbag and started chewing on it.

So how bad is this crush, from one to ten? she said. Ten being the kind of crush you had on me in school.

And one being a really serious crush?

She laughed, even though her mouth was full of cereal bar.

Whatever, she said. Is it like, you have fun talking to him online, or like, you want to tear him open and drink his blood?

I don't want to drink his blood.

I landed a little heavily on the final word of this sentence without meaning to, which made Bobbi snort. I'm not ready to think about what else you want to drink, she said. That's fucked up. I thought about telling her what had happened between me and Nick then, because it could be framed in the format of a joke, and anyway it was over now. For some reason though, I didn't say anything, and she just said: sex with men, how weird.

CHAPTER
THIRTEEN

The next day we were clearing up the breakfast dishes and Melissa asked Nick if he would take the car to some shopping complex outside town to get new deckchairs. She said she had planned to go the day before but she forgot about it. Nick didn't seem wild about the suggestion, although he said he would go. He said something like: oh, that place is fucking miles away. But not with any particular conviction. He was washing up the dishes in the sink and I was drying them and handing them to Melissa to put back in the cupboard. Standing between them I felt clumsy and unwanted, and I was sure Bobbi could see I was flushed. She was sitting on the kitchen table swinging her legs and eating a piece of fruit.

Take the girls with you then, Melissa said.

Don't call us girls, Melissa, please, said Bobbi.

Melissa gave her a look and Bobbi bit into her nectarine innocently.

Take the young women with you then, Melissa said.

What, like for my amusement? said Nick. I'm sure they'd rather go to the beach.

You could take them to the lake, Melissa said. Or you could go to Châtelaudren.

Is that place there still open? he said.

They discussed whether the place in Châtelaudren was still open. Then Nick turned to look at Bobbi. His hands and wrists were wet.

How do you feel about long car journeys? he said.

Don't listen to him, it's not that long, said Melissa. It'll be fun.

She laughed when she said this, as if to signal that she knew perfectly well it would not be fun. She gave us a box of pastries and a bottle of rosé wine to take in the car in case we wanted to have a picnic. And she pressed Nick's hand quickly when she thanked him.

The car had been sitting in the sun all morning and we had to roll the windows down before we could even get in. Inside it smelled like dust and heated plastic. I sat in the back and Bobbi leaned her little face out the passenger window like a terrier. Nick switched on the radio and Bobbi withdrew her face from the window and said, do you not have a CD player? Can we listen to music? Nick said: sure, okay. Bobbi started looking through the CDs then and saying whether she thought they were his or Melissa's.

Who likes Animal Collective, you or Melissa? she said.

I think we both like them.

But who bought the CD?

I don't remember, he said. You know, we share those things, I don't remember whose is whose.

Bobbi glanced at me over the back of her seat. I ignored her.

Frances? she said. Did you know that Nick appeared on a Channel 4 documentary about gifted children in 1992?

I looked up at her then and said: what? Nick was already saying: where did you hear about that? Bobbi had taken one of the pastries out of the box, something with whipped cream on top, and she was spooning the cream into her mouth with an index finger.

Melissa told me, she said. Frances was also a gifted child so I thought she'd be interested. She wasn't on any documentaries though. She also wasn't alive in 1992.

I went downhill from then, he said. Why is Melissa telling you this stuff?

She looked up at him, sucking the whipped cream off her finger in a gesture that seemed more insolent than seductive.

She confides in me, she said.

I looked at Nick in the rear-view mirror, but he was watching the road.

I'm a big hit with her, said Bobbi. I'm not sure it'll go anywhere though, I think she's married.

Just to some actor, said Nick.

It took Bobbi three or four bites to finish the pastry. Then she put on the Animal Collective CD and turned the music up really loud. When we got to the home supplies store Bobbi and I just smoked in the car park while Nick went inside to get the deckchairs. He came back out carrying them under one arm, looking very masculine. I crushed my cigarette under the toe of my sandal while he opened the boot and said, I'm afraid this lake is going to be a major disappointment.

Twenty minutes later Nick parked the car and we all went down a little lane, surrounded by trees. The lake lay blue and flat, reflecting the sky. There wasn't anyone else around. We sat on the grass by the water, in the shade of a willow tree, and ate cream pastries. Bobbi and I took turns drinking from the bottle of wine, which was warm and sweet.

Can you swim in it? Bobbi said. The lake.

Yeah, I think so, said Nick.

She stretched out her legs on the grass. She said she wanted to swim.

You don't have your swimsuit, I said.

So? she said. There's no one here anyway.

I'm here, I said.

Bobbi laughed at that. She threw back her head and laughed up into the trees. She was wearing a sleeveless cotton blouse, printed with tiny flowers, and her arms looked slender and dark in the shade. She started unbuttoning the blouse. Bobbi, I said. You're not really.

He can take his shirt off, but I can't? she said.

I threw up my hands. Nick coughed, like an amused little cough.

I actually wasn't planning to take my shirt off, Nick said.

I'm going to be offended if you try to object, said Bobbi.

Frances is the one objecting, not me.

Oh, her, said Bobbi. She'll live.

Then she left her clothes folded up on the grass and walked down to the lake. The muscles of her back moved smoothly under her skin, and in the glare of sunlight her tan lines were almost invisible, so she appeared whole and completely perfect. The only sound after that was the sound of her limbs moving through the water. It was very hot, and we had finished the pastries. The light had moved and we were no longer in the shade. I drank some more wine and looked out for Bobbi's figure.

She's literally shameless, I said. I wish I was more like that.

Nick and I were sitting quite close together, so that if I inclined my head I could touch it to his shoulder. The sunlight was inordinately bright. I closed my eyes and let strange patterns form behind my eyelids. The heat poured down over my hair and little insects purred in the undergrowth. I could smell the laundered scent of Nick's clothing, and the orange-oil shower gel I had used when I stayed in his house.

That was awkward yesterday, he said. About the girl at the airport.

I tried to give a cute, impartial smile, but his tone made it hard for me to breathe evenly. It sounded like he had been waiting for an opportunity to speak to me alone, and immediately I was in his confidence again.

Some girls just like married men, I said.

He laughed, I heard him. I kept my eyes closed and let the red shapes in my eyelids unfold themselves like kaleidoscopes.

I said I didn't think that was true, he said.

114

Loyal of you.

I was afraid you'd think they were being serious.

You didn't like her? I said.

Louisa? Oh, you know. She was nice. I didn't dream about her at night.

Nick had definitely never told me that he dreamed about me at night, or even that he especially liked me. In terms of verbal declarations, "I didn't dream about her at night" was the first thing I could remember him saying that implied I had any special status to him at all.

So are you seeing anyone at the moment? he said.

I opened my eyes then. He wasn't looking at me, he was inspecting a dandelion between his thumb and forefinger. He didn't seem to be joking. I held my legs together very tightly.

Well, I was for a while, I said. But I'm afraid he ended it.

He twisted the flower stem back and forth, smiling a reluctant smile.

He did? Nick said. What was he thinking?

You know, I have no idea.

He looked at me and I was afraid of what expression my face was making.

I'm very happy you're here, he said. It's good to see you again.

I raised an eyebrow and then turned my face away. I could see Bobbi's head dipping and rising in the silver water like a seal.

And I am sorry, he said.

I smiled mechanically, and said: oh, for hurting my feelings? Nick sighed as if placing down something heavy. He relaxed, I could feel his posture changing. I lay back and let the blades of grass touch my shoulders.

Sure, if you have any, he said.

Have you ever said one sincere thing in your life?

I said I was sorry, that was sincere. I tried to tell you how nice it is to see you again. What do you want? I could grovel but I don't think you're the kind of person it would appeal to.

How well do you think you know me? I said.

He gave me a look then, like he was finally dropping some long pretence. It was a good look, but I knew that he could practise it just as well as any of the others.

Well, I'd like to get to know you better, he said.

We saw that Bobbi was coming out of the water then, but I stayed lying in Nick's shade, and he didn't move his arm from where it nearly brushed my cheek. Bobbi came up the bank shivering and wringing her hair out. When she put her clothes back on her blouse soaked through on her skin until it was almost sheer. We looked up at her and asked how the water was and she said: so cold, it felt incredible.

On the way back in the car I rode in the front seat and Bobbi lay with her legs stretched out in the back. When Nick and I looked at one another we looked away quickly, but not quickly enough to stop us from smiling. From the back seat Bobbi said: what's funny? But she asked only lazily, and didn't press for an answer. I put a Joni Mitchell album in the CD player and looked out the window to feel the cool air on my face. It was early evening by the time we got back to the house.

That night Nick and I sat together at dinner. After the food was finished Melissa opened another bottle of wine and Nick leaned over to light my cigarette. When he shook the match out he placed his arm on the back of my chair quite casually. Nobody seemed to notice, actually it probably looked perfectly normal, but I found it impossible to concentrate while he was doing it. The others were talking about refugees. Evelyn kept saying: some of these people have degrees, these are doctors and professors we're talking about. I had noticed before this tendency of people to emphasise the qualifications of refugees. Derek said: whatever about the others, imagine turning doctors away. It's insane.

What does that mean? said Bobbi. Don't let them in unless they've got a medical degree?

Evelyn said that wasn't what Derek meant, and Derek interrupted Evelyn to say something about Western value systems and cultural relativism. Bobbi said that the universal right to asylum was a constituent part of the "Western value system" if any such thing existed. She did the air quotes.

The naive dream of multiculturalism, Derek said. Žižek is very good on this. Borders do exist for a reason, you know.

You don't know how right you are, said Bobbi. But I bet we disagree about what the reason is.

Nick started laughing then. Melissa just looked away as if she wasn't paying attention to the conversation. I

117

pulled my shoulders back fractionally to feel Nick's arm against my skin.

We're all on the same side here, Derek said. Nick, you're an oppressive white male, you back me up.

I actually agree with Bobbi, said Nick. Oppressive though I certainly am.

Oh, God save us, Derek said. Who needs liberal democracy? Maybe we should just burn down Government Buildings and see where that gets us.

I know you're exaggerating, said Nick, but increasingly it's hard to see why not.

When did you get so radical? Evelyn said. You're spending too much time around college students, they're putting ideas in your head.

Melissa tipped some ash off her cigarette into a tray she was holding in her left hand. She was smiling then, a comical little smile.

Yeah, Nick, you used to love the police state, Melissa said. What happened?

You invited all these college students on holiday with us, he said. I was powerless to resist.

She sat back and looked at him, through the glimmer of smoke. He lifted his arm off the back of my chair and put his cigarette out in the ashtray. The temperature seemed to drop perceptibly, and I saw everything in dimmer colours.

Did you stop by the lake earlier? she said.

On the way back, yeah, said Nick.

Frances got sunburnt, Bobbi said.

Actually I wasn't really burnt, but my face and arms were a little pink, and warm to the touch. I shrugged.

118

Well, Bobbi insisted on taking her clothes off and getting into the water, I said.

You snitch, said Bobbi. I'm ashamed of you.

Melissa was still looking over at Nick. He didn't seem at all unsettled by this; he looked back at her and smiled, a relaxed and spontaneous smile, which made him look handsome. She shook her head in a gesture of amusement or exasperation, and finally looked away.

We all went to bed late that night, at about two in the morning. For ten or twenty minutes I lay on my bed in the dark hearing the quiet complaint of floorboards above me, and doors clicking shut. No voices. Bobbi's room next door was entirely silent. I sat up and then lay down again. I felt myself developing a plan to go upstairs for a glass of water, though I wasn't really thirsty. I could even hear myself justifying my thirst with reference to the wine I'd had at dinner, as if I would later be subject to interview about what I was doing upstairs. I sat up again, feeling my own forehead, which was normal temperature. Quietly I crept out of bed and up the stairs, wearing my white nightdress with the pattern of tiny rosebuds. The light in the kitchen was on. My heart started to beat very hard.

Inside the kitchen Nick was putting the clean wine glasses away in the cabinet. He looked up at me and said: oh, hello. Instantly, like I was reciting something, I replied: I felt like a glass of water. He made a humorous face, like he didn't really believe me, but he handed me a glass anyway. I poured the water and then stood against the fridge door to drink it. It was lukewarm and tasted chlorinated. Eventually Nick stood in front of me and said, there aren't any more wine glasses, so. We were looking at each other. I told him he was a total embarrassment and he said he was "extremely aware" of that. He put his hand on my waist and I felt my whole body lift toward him. I touched the buckle of his belt and said: we can sleep together if you want, but you should know I'm only doing it ironically.

Nick's room was on the same floor as the kitchen. It was the only bedroom on that floor of the house; the others were upstairs or else down in the basement like mine. His window was open onto the sea, so he pulled the shutters over quietly and closed it while I got onto the bed. When he was inside me I pressed my face into his shoulder and said: does it feel okay?

I keep wanting to say thank you, he said. That's weird, isn't it?

I told him to say it and he did. Then I told him I was coming and he shut his eyes and said, oh. Afterwards I sat with my back against the wall, looking down at him, where he was lying on his back and breathing.

I've had a rough couple of weeks, he said. I'm sorry about the thing on the internet.

I know I was being cold toward you. I didn't realise you had pneumonia.

He smiled, he touched the soft underside of my knee with his fingers.

I thought you wanted me to leave you alone, he said. I was really sick and lonely, you know. It just seemed like you wanted nothing to do with me.

I thought about saying: no, I wanted you to tell me that you dreamt about me at night.

120

I was having a bad time too, I said. Let's forget about it.

Well, that's generous. I think I could have handled it a lot better.

But I forgive you, so it's okay now.

He sat up on his elbows then and looked at me.

Yeah, but I mean you've forgiven me very quickly, he said. Considering I tried to break up with you. You could have dragged it out a lot more if you wanted.

No, I just wanted to get back into bed with you.

He laughed, as if this delighted him. He lay back down with his face turned away from the light, his eyes closed.

I didn't think I was that good, he said.

You're okay.

I thought I was a total embarrassment.

You are, but I take pity on you, I said. And the sex is very nice.

He said nothing. I couldn't sleep in his room that night anyway, in case someone saw me leaving in the morning. Instead I went back down to my own bed and lay on my own, curled up as small as I could go.

CHAPTER
FOURTEEN

The next day I felt warm and sleepy, like a child. I ate four slices of bread at breakfast and drank two whole bowls of coffee, with cream and sugar. Bobbi called me a little pig, though she said she meant this "in a cute way". And I brushed Nick's leg under the table and watched him trying not to laugh. I was filled with an exuberant, practically spiteful sense of joy.

Three whole days passed this way in Étables. At mealtimes out in the garden, Nick and Bobbi and I sat together at one end of the table and interrupted one another a lot. Nick and I both found Bobbi screamingly funny and we always laughed at everything she said. Once Nick cried at breakfast when Bobbi did an impersonation of a friend of theirs called David. We had only met David briefly, at literary things in Dublin, but Bobbi had his voice down perfectly. Nick also helped us to improve our language skills by speaking to us in French and repeatedly pronouncing the "r" noise on request. Bobbi told him I could already speak French and that I was faking it to get his lessons. We could see it made him blush, and she flashed her eyes at me across the room.

On the beach in the afternoons, Melissa sat under a parasol reading the newspaper while we lay in the sun and drank from water bottles and reapplied sun lotion on each other's shoulders. Nick liked to go swimming and then come back out of the water glistening wet and looking like an advertisement for cologne. Derek said he found it emasculating. I turned a page in my Robert Fisk book and pretended not to listen. Derek said: Melissa, does he spend a lot of time preening? Melissa didn't look up from her newspaper. She said, no, he's just naturally gorgeous, I'm afraid. That's what you get when you marry for looks. Nick laughed. I turned another page in the book although I hadn't read the previous one.

For two nights in a row, I went to bed on my own until I heard the house go quiet, and then I went up to Nick's room. I didn't feel too tired to stay up late, though during the day I often fell asleep at the beach or in the garden. We couldn't have been getting more than four or five hours' sleep, but he didn't complain of feeling tired, or hurry me out of his room even when it was very late. After the first night, he stopped drinking wine with dinner. I don't think he had anything to drink again at all. Derek pointed this out frequently, and I noticed Melissa offering him wine even after he said he didn't want any.

Once when we were coming up from the sea together after swimming, I asked him: you don't think they know, do you? We were waist deep in the water still. He shielded his eyes with the flat of his hand and looked at me. The others were back on the shore, with the towels, we could see them. In the sunlight my own arms looked lilac-white and dimpled with goosebumps.

No, he said. I don't think so.

They might hear things at night.

I think we're pretty quiet.

It seems insanely risky what we're doing, I said.

Yeah, of course it is. Did that just occur to you now?

I dipped my hands in the water and it stung of salt. I lifted a handful and let it fall back onto the surface from my palm.

Why are you doing it then? I said.

He dropped his hand from his eyes and started to shake his head. He was all white like marble. There was something so austere about the way he looked.

Are you flirting with me? he said.

Come on. Tell me you crave me.

He slapped a handful of water at my bare skin. It splashed my face and felt so cold it almost hurt. I looked up at the spotless blue lid of sky.

Fuck off, he said.

I liked him, but he didn't need to know that.

After dinner on the fourth night we all went for a walk into the village together. Over the harbour the sky was a pale coral colour, and the ocean looked dark like lead. Rows of yachts nodded in the dockyard and good-looking people in bare feet carried bottles of wine along the decking. Melissa had her camera on a shoulder strap and occasionally took photographs. I was wearing a navy linen dress, with buttons.

124

Outside the ice-cream shop my phone started to ring. It was my father calling. I turned away from the others instinctively as I picked up, as if I were shielding myself. His voice was muffled, and there seemed to be some noise in the background. I started biting on my thumbnail while he spoke, feeling the grain of it with my teeth.

Is everything okay? I said.

Oh, very nice. Am I not allowed to give my only daughter a ring now and then?

His voice wandered up and down the tonal scale when he spoke. His drunkenness made me feel unclean. I wanted to shower or eat a fresh piece of fruit. I wandered a little away from the others then, but I didn't want to leave them behind completely. Instead I lingered near a lamp-post while everyone else discussed whether to get ice cream or not.

No, obviously you can, I said.

So how are things? How is work?

You know I'm in France, right?

What's that? he said.

I'm in France.

I was self-conscious about repeating such a simple sentence, even though I didn't think anyone else was listening.

Oh, you're in France, are you? he said. That's right, sorry. How's it going out there?

It's been very nice, thanks.

Great stuff. Listen, your mother is going to give you the allowance next month, okay? For college.

Okay, fine, I said. That's fine.

Bobbi signalled to me that they were going inside the ice-cream shop and I smiled what I felt was probably a manic-looking smile and waved them away.

You're not stuck for money, are you? said my father.

What? No.

The old saving, you know? It's a great habit to get into.

Yeah, I said.

Through the windows of the shop I could see a long display of ice-cream flavours beneath the glass, and Evelyn's silhouette at the counter, gesticulating.

How much do you have saved now? he said.

I don't know. Not a lot.

A great habit, Frances. Hm? That's it. Saving.

The phone call ended shortly after that. When the others came out of the shop, Bobbi was holding two ice-cream cones, one of which she gave to me. I felt a terrible gratitude that she had bought me an ice cream. I took the cone and thanked her, and she scanned my face and said, are you okay? Who was that on the phone? I blinked and said, just Dad. No news. She grinned and said, oh, okay. Well, you're welcome for the ice cream. I'll have it if you don't want it. In the corner of my eye I could see Melissa lift her camera and I turned away irritably, as if Melissa had wronged me by lifting her camera, or by doing something else a longer time ago. I knew it was a petulant gesture, but I'm not sure Melissa noticed.

We smoked a lot that night, and Nick was still kind of high when I got to his room, after everyone else had gone to sleep. He was fully dressed, sitting on the side of his bed and reading something on his MacBook, but he was squinting like he couldn't see the text that well, or it was just confusing. He looked good like that. He was maybe a little sunburnt. I guess I was probably high too. I sat on the floor at his feet and let my head rest against his calf.

Why are you on the floor? he said.

I like it down here.

Oh hey, who was that on the phone earlier?

I closed my eyes and leaned my head harder against him until he said, stop that.

It was my dad on the phone, I said.

He didn't know you were here?

I got up on the bed then and sat behind Nick, with my arms around his waist. I could see what he was reading, it was a long article about the Camp David Accords. I laughed and said, is this what you do when you get high, read essays about the Middle East?

It's interesting, he said. So hey, your dad didn't know you were over here, or what?

I told him, he's just not a very good listener.

I rubbed my nose slightly and then put my forehead on Nick's back, against the white cloth of his T-shirt. He smelled clean, like soap, and also faintly of seawater.

He has some issues with alcohol, I said.

Your dad does? You never told me about that.

He closed his MacBook and looked around at me.

I've never told anyone about it, I said.

Nick sat back against the headboard then and said: what kind of issues?

127

He just seems to be drunk when he calls me a lot of the time, I said. We've never talked about it in depth or anything. We're not close.

I got into Nick's lap then, so we were facing one another, and he ran his hand over my hair automatically like he thought I was somebody else. He never touched me like that usually. But he was looking at me, so I guess he must have known who I was.

Does your mother know about it? Nick said. I mean, I know they're not together.

I shrugged and said he had always been the same way. I'm a pretty horrible daughter, I said. I never really talk to my dad. But he gives me an allowance when I'm in college, that's bad, isn't it?

Is it? he said. You mean you think you're enabling him, because you take the allowance but you don't hassle him about the drinking.

I looked at Nick and he looked back up at me, with a slightly glassy, earnest expression. I realised he really was being earnest, and he really did mean to touch my hair like that, affectionately. Yeah, I said. I guess so.

But what are you supposed to do instead? he said. The whole financial dependency thing is so fucked up. Everything definitely improved for me when I stopped having to borrow money from my parents.

You like your parents, though. You get along with them.

He laughed and said, oh God, no I don't. Are you kidding? Bear in mind these are the people who made me go on TV when I was ten wearing a fucking blazer and talking about Plato.

Did they make you do that? I said. I assumed it was your idea.

Oh no. I was very troubled at the time. Ask my psychiatrist.

Do you really see a psychiatrist, or is that part of the joke?

He made a noise like hmm, and he touched my hand sort of curiously. He was definitely still high.

No, I have these depressive episodes, he said. I'm on medication and everything.

Really?

Yeah, I was pretty sick for a while last year. And, uh. I had a bad week or two over in Edinburgh, with the pneumonia and all that. This is probably a very uninteresting thing to tell you about. But I'm feeling okay now anyway.

It's not uninteresting, I said.

I knew Bobbi would know what to say in this situation, because she had a lot of opinions about mental health in public discourse. Out loud I said: Bobbi thinks depression is a humane response to the conditions of late capitalism. That made him smile. I asked him if he wanted to talk about being sick and he said no, not desperately. He had his fingers in my hair, at the back of my neck, and his touch made me want to be quiet.

For a little while we kissed and didn't talk at all, except occasionally I would say something like: I want it so much. He was breathing hard then and saying things like hm, and oh, good, like he always did. He put his hand under my dress and stroked the inside of my

129

thigh. I held his wrist on a sudden impulse and he looked at me. Is this what you want? I said. He looked confused, like I was posing a riddle which I might answer for him if he couldn't. Well, yeah, he said. Is it . . . what you want? I could feel my mouth tightening, the grinding machinery of my own jaw.

You know, sometimes you don't seem that enthusiastic, I said.

He laughed, which wasn't really the sympathetic response I expected. He looked down, his face was a little flushed. Do I not? he said.

I felt hurt then, and said: I mean, I talk a lot about how much I want you and how much fun I'm having and it's never really reciprocal. I feel like I don't fulfil you a lot of the time.

He lifted his hand and started rubbing the back of his neck. Oh, he said. Okay. Well, I'm sorry.

I am trying, you know. If there are things I'm doing wrong I want you to tell me.

In a slightly pained voice he said: you're not doing anything wrong. It's me, you know, I'm just awkward.

That was all he said. I didn't really know what to add, and anyway it seemed clear that no matter how unsubtly I fished for his reassurance he wasn't going to provide it. We went on kissing and I tried not to think about it. He asked if I wanted to get on my hands and knees this time and I said sure. We undressed without watching each other. I put my face in the mattress and felt him touch my hair. He put his arm around my body and said: come here for a second. I knelt upright, I could feel his chest against my back, and when I turned my head his mouth touched the rim of my ear. Frances, I want you so badly, he said. I closed my eyes. The words seemed to go past my mind, like they went straight into my body and stayed there. When I spoke, my voice sounded low and sultry. Will you die if you can't have me? I said. And he said: yes.

When he was inside me, I felt as though I had forgotten how to breathe. He had his hands around my waist. I kept asking him to do it harder, although it hurt a little when he did. He said things like, are you sure that doesn't hurt? I told him I wanted it to hurt, but I don't know whether I really did. And all Nick said was, okay. After a while it felt so good that I couldn't see clearly any more, and I wasn't sure if I could pronounce whole sentences. I kept saying, please, please, though I didn't know what I was asking him for. He held a finger to my lips as if to tell me to be quiet and I took it into my mouth, until he touched the back of my throat. I heard him say oh, no, don't. But it was already too late, he came. He was sweating, and he kept saying: fuck, I'm so sorry. Fuck. I was shivering badly. I felt that I had no understanding of what was happening between us.

By then it had started getting light outside and I had to leave. Nick sat up watching me put my dress back on. I didn't know what to say to him. We looked at one another with agonised expressions and then looked away. Downstairs in my room I couldn't sleep. I sat on my bed, holding my knees against my chest and watching the light move through the chink in the shutters. Eventually I opened up the window and looked out at the sea. It was dawn, and the sky was silvery blue and exquisite. In the room above I could hear Nick walking around. If I closed my eyes I felt that I was very close to him, close enough to hear him breathing. I sat at the window that way until I heard doors opening upstairs, and the dog barking, and the coffee machine switched on for breakfast.

CHAPTER
FIFTEEN

The following night, Evelyn wanted to play a game where we split into teams and entered names of famous people into a large bowl. You drew a name out of the bowl and your teammates had to ask yes or no questions about the name until they figured out who it was. It was dark and we were sitting in the living room with the lights on and the shutters open. Occasionally a moth would fly in through the window and Nick would catch it in his hands and throw it back out again, while Derek encouraged him to kill it. Bobbi told Derek to stop and he said, don't tell me animal rights extend to moths now, do they? Bobbi's lips were stained dark with wine, she was drunk.

No, Bobbi said. Just kill it yourself if you want it to die.

Melissa and Derek and I were on one team together, and Nick and Bobbi and Evelyn were on the other. Melissa brought out another bottle of wine while we were writing down the names and putting them into the bowl, though we'd already had a lot of wine at dinner. Nick put his hand over his empty water glass when Melissa offered. They seemed to share a look of some kind before she went away to refill her own.

First it was the other team's turn, and Nick was drawing out the names. He read the first one and frowned and then went oh, okay. Bobbi asked if it was a man and he said no. Is it a woman? she said. Yes, yeah. Evelyn asked if she was a politician or an actress or a sportsperson, she wasn't any of those. Bobbi said, a musician? And Nick said, not that I know of, no.

Is this person famous? Bobbi said.

Well, define famous, he said.

Do we all know who this person is? said Evelyn.

You both definitely do, Nick said.

Oh, said Bobbi. Okay, so, is this someone we know in real life?

He said it was. Melissa and Derek and I were sitting wordlessly watching this. I became very conscious of the wine glass in my hand, holding the stem too hard against my thumb.

Is it someone you like? Bobbi said. Or don't like?

Me personally? Yeah, I like her.

And does she like you? said Bobbi.

Is that really going to help you figure out who it is? he said.

It might, said Bobbi.

I don't know, he said.

So you like her, but you don't know if she likes you, said Bobbi. Do you not know her very well? Or is she mysterious?

He shook his head and laughed to himself, like he found this line of questioning extremely stupid. I sensed that Melissa and Derek and I had all become quite still. No one was talking or drinking any more.

I guess it's a little of both, he said.

You don't know her very well and she's mysterious? said Evelyn.

Is she smarter than you? Bobbi said.

Yeah, though a lot of people are. These questions don't seem very strategic.

Okay, okay, said Bobbi. Is this person more emotional, or more rational?

Oh, rational, I guess.

Like, unemotional, said Bobbi. Emotionally unintelligent.

What? No. That's not what I said.

A dull heat rose into my face and I looked into my glass. I thought Nick seemed faintly agitated, or at least not cool and relaxed like he usually pretended to be, and then I wondered when I'd decided he was pretending.

Extrovert or introvert? said Evelyn.

Introvert I would think, Nick said.

Young or old? said Evelyn.

Young, definitely young.

This person is a child? said Bobbi.

No, no, an adult. Jesus.

An adult woman, okay, said Bobbi. And do you think you'd find her attractive in a swimsuit?

Nick looked at Bobbi for an excruciatingly long second, and then put the piece of paper down.

Bobbi already knows who it is, said Nick.

We all know who it is, Melissa said quietly.

I don't, said Evelyn. Who is it? Is it you, Bobbi?

Bobbi grinned a little mischievous grin and said, it was Frances. I watched her, but I couldn't figure out who this performance had been aimed at. Bobbi herself was the only person who found it amusing, but that didn't seem to bother her; she looked like it had played out just as she intended. I realised, stupidly late, that she had almost certainly put my name into the bowl in the first place. I was reminded of her wildness, her tendency to get inside things and break them open, and I felt fearful of her, not for the first time. She wanted to expose something private about how I felt, to turn it from a secret into something else, a joke or a game.

The atmosphere in the room changed after that round ended. At first I was afraid that the others knew about us, that people had heard us at night, that even Melissa knew, but then I realised it was a different quality of tension. Derek and Evelyn seemed instead to feel awkward on Nick's behalf, like they thought he had been trying to conceal his feelings from me; and toward me they expressed a kind of unspoken concern, maybe that I would be offended or upset. Evelyn kept glancing at me with a sympathetic expression. After Melissa correctly guessed the name Bill Clinton, I excused myself to go to the bathroom, which was across the hall. I ran cold water over my hands and dabbed it under my eyes, then dried my face with a clean towel.

Outside in the hallway, Melissa was waiting to use the bathroom. Before I could step past her she said: are you all right?

I'm fine, I said. Why?

She drew her lips together. She was wearing a blue dress that day, with a low scooped neckline and a pleated skirt. I had a pair of rolled-up jeans and a crinkled white shirt on.

He hasn't done anything, has he? she said. I mean, he's not bothering you.

I realised she was talking about Nick, and I felt faint. Who? I said.

She gave me an unwelcome look then, a look that suggested she was disappointed in me.

It's okay, she said. Forget about it.

I felt guilty, knowing that she was making an effort to care for me, an effort that was probably painful to her. Quietly I said: no, look, of course he hasn't. I don't know . . . I think it's nothing. I'm sorry. I think it's just Bobbi.

Well, it's a crush or something, she said. I'm sure it's probably harmless, I just want you to know you can tell me if anything happens to make you uncomfortable.

I appreciate that, it's very kind of you. But really, it doesn't . . . it doesn't bother me.

She smiled at me then, like she was relieved that I was all right, and that her husband had not been doing something untoward. I smiled back gratefully and she wiped her hands on the skirt of her dress.

It's not like him, she said. But I guess you're his type.

I looked down at our feet, I felt dizzy.

Or am I flattering myself? she said.

I met her eye then, and I realised she was trying to make me laugh. I did laugh, out of gratitude for her kindness and her apparent trust.

I think I'm the one who should be flattered, I said.

Not by him, he's completely useless. Great taste in women, though.

She pointed at the bathroom. I moved out of the way and she went inside. I wiped my face with my wrist and felt it was damp. I wondered what she had meant by calling Nick "useless". I couldn't tell whether she was being affectionate or vitriolic; she had a way of making them seem like the same thing.

We didn't play for very much longer after that. I didn't talk to Bobbi at all before she went to bed. I sat on the sofa until everyone else had gone too, and after a few minutes Nick came back. He closed the shutters and then leaned against the windowsill. I yawned and touched my hair. He said hey, that was weird, wasn't it? With Bobbi. I agreed it was weird. Nick seemed cautious on the subject of Bobbi, as if he wasn't sure how I felt about her.

Have you given up drinking? I said.

It just makes me tired. And I prefer being sober for all this anyway.

He sat on the arm of the sofa, as if he expected we would be getting up again shortly. I said: what do you mean all this? And he said, oh, all this stimulating late-night conversation we have.

You don't like having sex when you're drunk? I said.

I think it's probably better for everyone if I'm not.

What, it's like a performance issue? I don't have any complaints.

No, you're very easy to please, he said.

138

I didn't like him saying that, though it was true and he probably did think so. He touched the inside of my wrist with his hand and I felt myself shudder.

Not really, I said. I just know you like it when I lie there telling you how great you are.

He grimaced and said: that's harsh. I laughed and said, oh no, am I ruining the fantasy for you? I'll go back to sighing over how strong and masculine you are if you prefer. He didn't say anything then.

I should go to bed anyway, I said. I'm exhausted.

He touched his hand against my back, which felt like an uncharacteristically tender gesture. I didn't move at all.

Why haven't you had any affairs before? I said.

Oh. I guess because I didn't really meet anyone.

What does that mean?

For a second I really thought he would say: I never met anyone I desired, the way I desire you. Instead he said: yeah, I don't know. We were pretty happy together for a long time, so I never really thought about it then. You know, you're in love, you don't really think about these things.

When did you stop being in love?

He lifted his hand away then, so no parts of our bodies were touching any more.

I don't think I did stop as such, he said.

So you're saying you still love her.

Well, yeah.

I stared at the light fixture on the ceiling. It was switched off. We had put the table lamp on instead,

139

before the game started, and it cast elongated shadows toward the window.

I'm sorry if that hurts you, he said.

No, of course not. But so, is this like a game you're playing with her? Like you're trying to get her to notice you by having an affair with a college student.

Wow. Okay. To get her to notice me?

Well? It's not like she hasn't seen you looking at me. She asked me earlier if you were making me uncomfortable.

Jesus, he said. Okay. Am I?

I didn't feel in the mood to tell him no, so I rolled my eyes instead and got off the sofa, smoothing down my shirt.

You're going to bed then, he said.

I said yes. I put my phone into my handbag to bring it downstairs and didn't look up at him.

You know, that was hurtful, he said. What you said just now.

I picked up my cardigan from the floor and draped it over my bag. My sandals were lined up beside the fireplace.

You think I would do this just for attention, he said. What makes you feel that way about me?

Maybe the fact that you're still in love with your wife even though she's not interested in you any more.

He laughed but I didn't look at him. I glanced in the mirror over the fireplace, and my face looked awful, so bad it shocked me. My cheeks were blotched like someone had slapped me, and my lips were dry and almost white.

You're not jealous, Frances, are you? he said.

Do you think I have feelings for you? Don't be embarrassing.

I went downstairs then. When I got into my own bed I felt terrible, not so much from sadness as from shock and a strange kind of exhaustion. I felt like someone had gripped my shoulders and shaken me firmly back and forth, even while I pleaded with them to stop. I knew it was my own fault: I had gone out of my way to provoke Nick into fighting with me. Now, lying on my own in the silent house, I felt I'd lost control of everything. All I could decide was whether or not to have sex with Nick; I couldn't decide how to feel about it, or what it meant. And although I could decide to fight with him, and what we would fight about, I couldn't decide what he would say, or how much it would hurt me. Curled up in bed with my arms folded I thought bitterly: he has all the power and I have none. This wasn't exactly true, but that night it was clear to me for the first time how badly I'd underestimated my vulnerability. I'd lied to everyone, to Melissa, even to Bobbi, just so I could be with Nick. I had left myself no one to confide in, no one who would feel any sympathy for what I'd done. And after all that, he was in love with someone else. I screwed my eyes shut and pressed my head down hard into the pillow. I thought of the night before, when he told me that he wanted me, how it felt then. Just admit it, I thought. He doesn't love you. That's what hurts.

CHAPTER
SIXTEEN

The next morning at breakfast, the day before Bobbi and I flew home, Melissa told us that Valerie was coming to visit. There was some discussion of which room should be made up, while I watched a metallic-looking red ladybird cross the table valiantly toward the sugar cubes. The insect looked like a miniature robot with robotic legs.

And we'll have to get dinner things, Melissa was saying. A few of you can go to the supermarket, can't you? I'll make a list.

I don't mind going, Evelyn said.

Melissa was slathering salted butter on a splayed-open croissant and then waving her knife around vaguely while she spoke.

Nick can take you in the car, she said. We'll need to get a dessert, one of the nice fresh ones. And flowers. Take someone else in the car to help you. Take Frances. You won't mind, will you?

The ladybird made it to the sugar bowl and started to ascend the glazed white rim. I looked up with what I hoped was a polite expression and said: of course not.

And Derek, you can set up the bigger dining table in the garden for us, Melissa said. And Bobbi and I will tidy the house.

Having arranged the itinerary, we finished breakfast and brought our plates inside. Nick went to find the car keys and Evelyn sat on the front steps with her elbows on her knees, looking adolescent behind her spectacles. Melissa was leaning on the kitchen windowsill writing the list, while Nick lifted up couch cushions and said: has anyone else seen them? I stood in the hallway with my back pressed flat against the wall, trying not to be in the way. They're on the hook, I said, but so quietly that he didn't hear me. Maybe I left them in a pocket or something, said Nick. Melissa was opening cupboards to see if they had some ingredient or other. Did you see them? he said, but she ignored him.

Eventually I lifted the keys off the hook silently and put them into Nick's hand as he went past. Oh, aha, he said. Well, thank you. He was avoiding my eye, but not in a personal way. He seemed to be avoiding everyone's eyes. Did you get them? Melissa said from the kitchen. Did you look on the hook?

Evelyn and Nick and I went down to the car then. It was a foggy morning but Melissa had said it would clear up later. Bobbi appeared in her bedroom window just as I turned around to look for her. She was opening up the shutters. That's right, she said. Abandon me. Go have fun with your new friends in the supermarket.

Maybe I'll never come back, I said.

Don't, said Bobbi.

I got into the back of the car and put my seat belt on. Evelyn and Nick got in and closed the doors behind them, sealing us into a shared privacy where I felt I didn't belong. Evelyn gave an expressively weary sigh and Nick started the engine.

Did you ever get that thing with the car sorted? Nick said to Evelyn.

No, Derek won't let me call the dealership, she said. He's "taking care of it".

We pulled out of the driveway onto the road down toward the beach. Evelyn was rubbing her eyes behind her glasses and shaking her head. The mist was grey like a veil. I fantasised about punching myself in the stomach.

Oh, taking care of it, okay, said Nick.

You know what he's like.

Nick made a suggestive noise like: hm. We were driving along by the harbour, where the ships implied themselves as concepts behind the fog. I touched my nose to the car window.

She's been behaving herself quite well, Evelyn said. I thought. Until today.

Well, that's the Valerie production, he said.

But until all that started, said Evelyn. She's been relatively relaxed, hasn't she?

No, you're right. She has.

Nick hit the indicator to turn left and I said nothing. It was clear they were talking about Melissa. Evelyn had taken her glasses off and was cleaning the lenses on the soft cotton of her skirt. Then she put them back on and

144

looked at herself in the mirror. She noticed my reflection and made a kind of wry face.

Never get married, Frances, she said.

Nick laughed and said: Frances would never lower herself to such a bourgeois institution. He was working the steering wheel around to take the car through a corner, and he didn't look up from the road. Evelyn smiled and gazed out the window at the boats.

I didn't realise Valerie was coming, I said.

Did I not tell you? said Nick. I meant to say last night. She's only coming for dinner, she may not even stay. But she always gets the royal baby treatment.

Melissa has this little hang-up about her, Evelyn said.

Nick glanced over his shoulder out the back window, but he didn't look at me. I liked that he was busy driving because it meant we could talk without the intensity of having to acknowledge each other. Of course, he hadn't mentioned Valerie the night before because instead, he'd been telling me that he still loved his wife and that I meant nothing to him. The exchange about Valerie which he had been planning to have instead implied a kind of personal intimacy which I now felt we had lost forever.

I'm sure it'll all be fine, said Evelyn.

Nick said nothing, and neither did I. His silence was significant and mine was not because his opinion on whether things would be fine, unlike mine, was important.

It won't be totally insufferable at least, she said. Frances and Bobbi will be there to defuse the tension.

Is that what they do? he said. I've been wondering.

Evelyn gave me another little smile in the mirror and said: well, they're also very decorative.

Now that I object to, he said. Strenuously.

The supermarket was a large, glassy building outside town, with a lot of air conditioning. Nick took a trolley and we walked behind him, through the little one-way entry gates, into the section with the paperback books and men's watches displayed inside security-tagged plastic cases. Nick said the only things that really needed to be carried by hand were the dessert and the flowers, everything else could go in the trolley. He and Evelyn discussed what kind of dessert would be least likely to cause an argument and decided on something expensive with a lot of glazed strawberries. She went off to the dessert aisle and Nick and I walked along on our own.

I'll come and get the flowers with you on our way out, he said.

You don't have to.

Well, if we end up getting the wrong ones, I'd rather say it was my fault.

We were standing in the coffee aisle and Nick had stopped to examine various kinds of ground coffee, in different-sized packages.

You needn't be so chivalrous, I said.

No, I just think you and Melissa fighting might be more than I could handle today.

I put my hands down into the pockets of my skirt while he loaded various black-wrapped packages of coffee into the trolley.

At least we know whose side you'd be on, I said.

146

He looked up, with a bag of Ethiopian coffee in his left hand and a faintly humorous expression.

Who? he said. The one who isn't interested in me any more, or the one who's just using me for sex?

I felt my whole face wash over in a forceful blush. Nick put the bag of coffee down, but before he could say anything I had already walked away. I walked all the way to the deli counter and the tank of live crustaceans at the back of the supermarket. The crustaceans looked ancient, like mythological ruins. They batted their claws uselessly against the glass sides of the tank and stared at me with accusatory eyes. I held the cold side of my hand against my face and glared back at them malevolently.

Evelyn came back along the deli, holding a large box of thin bluish plastic with a strawberry tart inside.

Don't tell me lobsters are on the list, she said.

Not that I know of, no.

She looked at me and gave me another encouraging smile. Encouragement seemed to be Evelyn's primary mode of relating to me for some reason.

Everyone's just a little highly strung today, she said.

We saw Nick exiting another aisle with the trolley, but he turned without seeing us. He had Melissa's handwritten list in his right hand and he was directing the trolley with his left.

There was a bit of an incident last year, she said. With Valerie.

Oh.

We walked after Nick's trolley together while I waited for her to elaborate, but she didn't. The supermarket had an in-house florist near the tills, with fresh potted plants and buckets of cut carnations and chrysanthemums. Nick chose two bouquets of pink roses and one mixed bouquet. The roses had huge, sensuous petals and tight, unrevealing centres, like some kind of sexual nightmare. I didn't look at him as he handed me the bouquets. I carried them to the checkout in silence.

We left the supermarket together, not saying a great deal. Rain beaded our skin and hair and parked cars looked like dead insects. Evelyn started to tell a story about a time she and Derek had brought their car on the ferry and punctured a tyre on the way over to Étables and Nick had had to come in his car to change the tyre for them. I gathered that the story was intended, obliquely and perhaps not even consciously, to cheer Nick up by recalling nice things he had done in the past. I've never been so happy to see you in my life, Evelyn said. You could have changed that tyre yourself, said Nick. If you weren't married to an autocrat.

When we parked up back at the house, Bobbi ran outside with the dog at her ankles. It was still foggy, though nearly noon by then. Bobbi was wearing linen shorts, and her legs looked long and tanned. The dog yelped twice. Let me help with the things, Bobbi said. Nick handed her a bag of groceries obligingly and she looked at him as if trying to communicate something.

Everything all right while we were gone? he said.

Tensions have been running high, said Bobbi.

Oh God, Nick said.

He handed her another bag, which she carried up against her stomach. He took the remaining groceries in his arms while Evelyn and I walked inside carefully, carrying the flowers and dessert like two sombre Edwardian servant women.

Melissa was in the kitchen, which looked empty without the chairs and table. Bobbi went upstairs to finish sweeping Valerie's bedroom. Nick put the shopping bags on the windowsill wordlessly and started to put away the groceries, while Evelyn placed the dessert box on top of the fridge. I wasn't sure what to do with the flowers, so I just kept holding them. They smelled fresh and suspicious. Melissa wiped her lips with the back of her hand and said: oh, you've decided to come back after all.

We weren't gone that long, were we? Nick said.

Apparently it's going to rain, said Melissa, so we've had to move the table and chairs into the front dining room. It looks terrible, the chairs don't even match.

They're Valerie's chairs, he said. I'm sure she knows whether they match or not.

It didn't seem to me that Nick was making the best possible effort at assuaging Melissa's temper. I stood there gripping the flowers and waiting to say something like: did you want me to leave these somewhere? But the words didn't arrive. Evelyn was now helping Nick to unpack the groceries, while Melissa was inspecting the fruit we had purchased.

And you remembered lemons, didn't you? said Melissa.

No, Nick said. Were they on the list?

Melissa dropped her hand from the nectarines and then lifted it to her forehead, as if she were about to faint.

I don't believe this, she said. I told you as you were going out the door, I specifically said don't forget lemons.

Well, I didn't hear you, he said.

There was a pause. I realised that the soft pad of skin at the base of my thumb was held against a thorn and beginning to turn purple. I tried to rearrange the flowers so that they weren't injuring me but without calling attention to my continued presence in the room.

I'll go get some in the corner shop, Nick said eventually. It's not the end of the world.

I don't believe this, said Melissa again.

Should I leave these somewhere? I said. I mean, can I put them in a vase, or?

Everyone in the room turned to look at me. Melissa took one bouquet out of my arms and looked into it. These stems need to be cut, she said.

I'll do that, I said.

Fine, said Melissa. Nick will show you where we keep the vases. I'll go and help Derek fix the dining room up. Thank you all very much for your hard work this morning.

She left the room and shut the door hard behind her. I thought: this woman? This is the woman you love? Nick took the flowers out of my arms and left them on the countertop. The vases were in a cupboard under the sink. Evelyn was watching Nick anxiously.

I'm sorry, Evelyn said.

150

Don't you apologise, said Nick.

Maybe I should go and help.

Sure, you may as well.

Nick was cutting the bouquets out of their plastic with a scissors when Evelyn left. I can do all this, I said. You go get the lemons. He didn't look at me. She likes the stems cut diagonally, he said. You know what I mean, diagonally? Like this. And he clipped one of the ends off at a slant. I didn't hear her say anything about lemons either, I said. He smiled then, and Bobbi came into the room behind us. You're going to take my side now, are you? he said.

I knew you were making friends without me, said Bobbi.

I thought you were tidying the bedroom, Nick said.

It's one room, said Bobbi. It can only get so tidy. Are you trying to get rid of me?

What happened while we were gone? he said.

Bobbi hopped up on the windowsill and swung her legs to and fro while I clipped the flowers stem by stem, letting the cut ends fall into the sink.

I think your wife is a little on edge today, said Bobbi. She was not impressed with my linen-folding technique earlier. Also, she told me she didn't want me "making any snide remarks about rich people" when Valerie gets here. Quote.

Nick laughed a lot at that. Bobbi always amused and delighted him, whereas I could see I had on balance probably caused him more distress than joy.

For the rest of the afternoon Melissa sent us around to do various menial tasks. She didn't think the glasses were quite clean, so I rewashed them in the sink. Derek brought one vase of flowers up to Valerie's room, along with a bottle of sparkling water and a clean glass for her bedside table. Bobbi and Evelyn ironed some pillowcases together in the living room. Nick went out for lemons and went out again later for sugar cubes. Early in the evening, while Melissa was cooking and Derek was polishing silverware, Nick and Evelyn and Bobbi and I sat in Nick's room looking around vacantly and not saying much. Like bold children, Evelyn said.

Let's open a bottle of wine, said Nick.

Do you have a death wish? Bobbi said.

No, let's, said Evelyn.

Nick went down to the garage and brought up some plastic cups and a bottle of Sancerre. Bobbi was lying face up on his bed, just the way I usually lay there after he made me come. Evelyn and I were sitting side by side on the floor. Nick poured the wine into cups and we listened to Derek and Melissa talking in the kitchen.

What's Valerie like, actually? Bobbi said.

Evelyn coughed and then said nothing.

Oh, said Bobbi.

After we had all finished our first cup of wine, we heard Melissa calling Nick from the kitchen. He got up and handed me the bottle. Evelyn said: I'll come with you. They went out together and shut the door. Bobbi and I sat in the room silently. Valerie had said she would be in town by seven. It was now half past six. I refilled Bobbi's cup and my own, then sat down again with my back against the bed.

You know Nick has a thing for you, don't you? Bobbi said. Everyone else has noticed. He's always looking at you to check if you're laughing at his jokes.

I chewed on the edge of my plastic cup until I could hear it crack. When I looked down, a vertical white line had formed from the rim. I thought of Bobbi's performance in the game the night before.

We get along, I said eventually.

It could totally happen. He's a failed actor and his marriage is dead, those are the perfect ingredients.

Isn't he more like a moderately successful actor?

Well, apparently he was expected to get famous and then he didn't, and now he's too old or something. Having an affair with a younger woman would probably be good for his self-esteem.

He's only thirty-two, I said.

I think his agent dropped him though. Anyway he seems like he's embarrassed to be alive.

I felt a growing sense of dread, a thin and physical dread that began in my shoulders, as I listened. At first I couldn't figure out what it was. It felt like dizziness, or the strange blurry sensation that precedes being violently ill. I tried to think of what might be causing it, things I had eaten, or the car journey earlier. It was only when I remembered the night before that I knew what it was. I felt guilty.

I'm pretty sure he's still in love with Melissa, I said.

People can be in love and have affairs.

It would depress me to sleep with someone who loved someone else.

Bobbi sat up then, I could hear her. She swung her legs down off the bed, and I knew she was looking down at me, onto my scalp.

I get the sense you've given this some consideration, she said. Did he make a pass at you or something?

Not as such. I just don't think I would enjoy being someone's second choice.

Not as such?

I mean, he's probably just trying to make her jealous, I said.

She slipped down off the bed, holding the wine bottle, which she passed to me. We were sitting on the floor together then, our upper arms pressed together. I splashed a little wine into the cracked plastic cup.

You can love more than one person, she said.

That's arguable.

Why is it any different from having more than one friend? You're friends with me and you also have other friends, does that mean you don't really value me?

I don't have other friends, I said.

She shrugged and took back the bottle of wine. I turned the cup around so nothing would spill from the crack and swallowed two warm mouthfuls.

Did he come on to you? she said.

No. I'm just saying I wouldn't be interested if he did.

You know, I kissed Melissa once. I never told you about that, did I?

I turned around and stared at her, craning my neck to see her face. She laughed. She was wearing a funny, dreamy expression, which made her look even more attractive than usual.

154

What? I said. When?

I know, I know. It was at her birthday party, out in the garden. We were both drunk, you were in bed. It was stupid.

She was staring into the bottle of wine. I looked at her face in profile, the strange half-shape of it. She had one tiny cut beside her ear, maybe she'd scratched it, and it was the bright red colour of a flower.

What? she said. Are you judging me?

No, no.

I heard Valerie's car pull into the driveway outside, and we stashed the bottle of wine under Nick's pillow. Bobbi linked her arm under mine and gave my cheek a little kiss, which surprised me. Her skin was very soft and her hair smelled of vanilla. I was wrong about Melissa, she said. I swallowed and said: well. We've all been wrong about things.

CHAPTER
SEVENTEEN

We had duck for dinner, with roast baby potatoes and salad. The meat tasted sweet like cider and fell off the bone in dark, buttery shreds. I tried to eat slowly to be polite, but I was hungry and exhausted. The dining room was large, wood-panelled and had a window out onto the rainy street. Valerie spoke with a moneyed British accent, too rich to be comical. She and Derek talked about publishing, and the rest of us were quiet. Valerie thought a lot of people in publishing were charlatans and hacks, but she seemed to find it funny rather than depressing. At one point she removed a smudge from her wine glass with a corner of her napkin and we all watched Melissa's face, which contracted and fell like a piece of wire spring.

Though Melissa had taken care to introduce us all at the beginning of dinner, Valerie asked which one of us was Bobbi during dessert. When Bobbi identified herself, Valerie replied: oh yes, of course. But a face like that won't last, I'm afraid. I can tell you that because I'm an old woman now.

Fortunately Bobbi is blessed with more than just good looks, said Evelyn.

Well, marry young, that's my advice, Valerie said. Men are very fickle.

Cool, said Bobbi. But actually I'm gay.

Melissa flushed and stared into her glass. I pressed my lips together wordlessly. Valerie raised an eyebrow and pointed her fork between Bobbi and myself.

I see, Valerie said. And are you two . . . ?

Oh no, said Bobbi. Once, but no.

No, I suppose not, Valerie said.

Bobbi and I glanced at one another and looked away so as not to laugh or scream.

Frances is a writer, Evelyn said.

Well, kind of, I said.

Don't say kind of, said Melissa. She's a poet.

Is she any good? Valerie said.

She had not looked up at me during this exchange.

She is good, said Melissa.

Oh well, Valerie said. I've always thought poetry rather lacks a future.

As an amateur without a real opinion on the future of poetry, and because Valerie hadn't appeared to notice my presence anyway, I said nothing. Bobbi stepped on my toe under the table and coughed. After dessert, Nick went to the kitchen to make coffee, and as soon as he left, Valerie put down her fork and peered at the closed door.

He doesn't look very well, does he? she said. How has his health been?

I stared at her. She had not addressed a single comment or question to me directly, and I knew she would pretend not to notice I was looking.

Up and down, said Melissa. He was great for a while but I think he had a bit of an episode last month. Over in Edinburgh.

Well, he had pneumonia, Evelyn said.

It wasn't just pneumonia, said Melissa.

It's a shame, Valerie said. But he's very passive really. He lets himself get overwhelmed by these things. You remember last year.

We don't need to drag the girls through all this, do we? Evelyn said.

There's no need to be secretive, said Valerie. We're all friends here. Nick suffers from depression, I'm afraid.

Yes, I said. I know.

Melissa looked up at me and I ignored her. Valerie looked at the floral arrangement and distractedly moved one blossom slightly to the left.

You're a friend of his, are you, Frances? Valerie said.

I thought we were all friends here, I said.

Finally she looked at me. She was wearing some artistic brown resin jewellery and had handsome rings on her fingers.

Well, I know he wouldn't mind me asking after his health, said Valerie.

Then maybe you can ask after it when he's actually in the room, I said.

Frances, Melissa said. Valerie is a very old friend of ours.

Valerie laughed and said: please, Melissa, I'm not that old, am I? My jaw was trembling. I pushed my seat back from the table and excused myself from the room. Evelyn and Bobbi watched me go, like little nodding dogs in the back window of a disappearing car. Nick was in the hallway bringing in two cups of coffee. Hello, he said. Oh, what's happened? I shook my head and shrugged, silly gestures that meant nothing. I walked past him, down the back staircase and into the garden. I didn't hear him follow me, I supposed he had gone into the dining room with the others.

I walked down to the bottom of the garden and opened the gate onto the back lane. It was raining and I was wearing a short-sleeved blouse but I didn't feel the cold. I slammed the gate shut and went on walking away from the house, toward the beach. My feet were getting wet and I rubbed my face hard with the back of my hand. The headlights of cars passed by in blazes of white but there were no other pedestrians. The path to the beach wasn't lit by streetlights and I did begin to feel cold then. I couldn't go back to the house. I stood there shivering with my arms crossed, feeling the rain soak through my blouse, the cotton sticking to my skin.

It seemed unlikely that Nick would be distressed by what Valerie had said. He'd probably just shrug it off, even if he did find out. My anguish on his behalf seemed to be unrelated to anything he might personally feel, a phenomenon I had experienced before. In our final year of school Bobbi had run for president of the student council, and one of the boys had beaten her by thirty-four votes to twelve. Bobbi had been disappointed, I could see that, but not upset. She'd smiled and congratulated the winner and then the bell had gone and we'd collected our books. Instead of going to class I had locked myself in a cubicle in the upstairs bathrooms and cried until I heard the lunchtime bell, cried until my lungs hurt and my face was rubbed raw. I couldn't explain what made me feel that furious, consuming misery, but sometimes even still when I thought about that election my eyes filled up stupidly with tears.

Eventually I heard the back gate open again and the clap of sandals, and Bobbi's voice saying: you complete goose. What are you like? Come inside and have coffee. I couldn't see her in the darkness at first and then I felt her arm slip under mine, the crackle of her raincoat. That was a nice little performance, she said. I haven't seen you lose your temper like that in some time.

Fuck this, I said.

Don't be upset.

She nestled her small warm head into my neck. I thought of her taking all her clothes off at the lake.

I hate that woman, I said.

I could feel Bobbi's breath on my face, the bitter aftertaste of unsweetened coffee, and then she kissed my lips. I gripped her wrist when she pulled away, trying to stare at her, but it was too dark. She slipped out of my grasp like a thought.

We shouldn't, she said. Obviously. But you are very lovable when you're self-righteous.

I dropped my arm uselessly by my side and she started walking back to the house. Illuminated by passing headlights I saw she had her hands down in the pockets of her raincoat and was splashing along through the puddles. I followed, with nothing at all to say.

160

Inside the house, the party had broken up into the living room and kitchen, and there was music playing. I was dripping wet and in the mirror my face was a livid, unnatural pink. I went through with Bobbi to the kitchen, where Evelyn and Derek and Nick were standing around drinking their coffees. Oh, Frances, Evelyn said. You're drenched. Nick was standing against the sink and he filled a coffee cup from the pot and handed it to me. Our eyes seemed to be having a conversation of their own. Sorry, I said. Evelyn touched my arm. I swallowed the coffee and Bobbi said: I'll get her a towel, shall I? You people, really. She shut the door behind her.

I'm sorry, I said again. I just lost my temper.

Yeah, I'm sorry I missed it, said Nick. I didn't know you had a temper to lose.

We kept looking at one another. Bobbi came back in the room and handed me a towel. I thought of her mouth, the strange familiar taste of it, and shivered. I seemed to have no power any longer over what was happening, or what was going to happen. It felt as if a long fever had broken and I simply had to lie there and wait for the illness to pass.

Once my hair was dry we rejoined Melissa and Valerie in the other room. Valerie acted exaggeratedly pleased to see me and expressed interest in reading my work. I gave a sickly smile and cast around for something to say or do. Sure, I said. I'll send you some of my stuff, sure. Nick brought out some brandy, and when he poured a measure for Valerie she clasped his wrist maternally and said, ah Nick, if only my sons were as handsome as you are. He handed her the glass and said: is anyone?

After Valerie went to bed we fell into a kind of tense, resentful silence. Evelyn and Bobbi tried to talk about a film they had both seen, but it transpired they were thinking of two different films, which put a halt to the discussion. Melissa got up to bring the empty glasses to the kitchen and said: Frances, maybe you could give me a hand. I stood up. I could feel Nick watching me, like a schoolchild watching his mother step into the principal's office.

We picked up the rest of the glasses and went to the kitchen, which was dark. Melissa didn't switch the light on. She deposited the glasses in the sink and then stood there, holding her hands over her face. I left what I was carrying down on a countertop and asked if she was all right. She paused for so long that I thought she was about to scream or throw something. Then in one quick motion she switched the tap on and began to fill the basin.

You know I don't like her either, said Melissa.

I just watched her. In the almost-darkness her skin looked silver and ghostly.

I don't want you to think that I like her, Melissa said, or that I appreciate the way she talks about Nick, or that I think her behaviour is appropriate. I don't feel that way. I'm sorry you were upset at dinner.

No, I'm sorry, I said. I'm sorry I made a scene like that. I don't know why I did it.

Don't apologise. It's what I would have done if I had a spine.

162

I swallowed. Melissa turned off the tap and started to rinse the glasses in the basin, sloppily, with no particular care for whether they were smudged any more.

I don't think I could have this next book published without her, Melissa said. It's kind of mortifying to tell you that.

No, it shouldn't be.

And I'm sorry for being so unreasonable this afternoon. I know what you must think of me. I just felt so anxious after everything that happened last year. But I want to tell you, I don't usually speak to Nick that way. Obviously things aren't perfect between us, but I do love him, you know. I really do.

Of course, I said.

She kept rinsing the glasses. I stood there by the fridge not knowing what to say. She lifted one wet hand and dabbed at something under her eye and then went back to the basin.

You're not sleeping with him, are you, Frances? she said.

Oh Jesus, I said. No.

Okay. I'm sorry. I shouldn't have asked that.

He's your husband.

Yes, I'm aware.

I kept standing there by the fridge. I had broken out in a sweat. I could feel it trickling from the back of my neck between my shoulders. I said nothing, I bit on my tongue.

You can go back and sit with the others if you'd like, she said.

I don't know what to say, Melissa.

Go on, it's all right.

I went back into the living room. They all turned their faces up to look at me. I think I'll get some sleep, I said. Everyone agreed it was a good idea.

That night when I knocked on Nick's door he had his bedroom light off. I heard him say come in, and as I closed the door behind me, I whispered: it's Frances. Well, I should hope it is, he said. He sat up and put the lamp on, and I stood beside his bed. I told him what Melissa had asked me and he said she had asked him the same thing, but earlier, while I was outside being rained on.

I said no, Nick said. Did you say no?

Of course I said no.

The bottle of Sancerre was on his bedside cabinet. I lifted it up and worked the cork out. Nick watched me while I drank and then accepted the bottle when I offered it. He drained what was left of it and then placed it back on the cabinet top. He looked at his fingernails, and then at the ceiling.

I'm not very good at these conversations, he said.

We don't have to talk, I said.

Okay.

I got into bed, and he lifted my nightdress off. I put my arms around his neck and held him very closely against me. He kissed the firm upturned bowl of my stomach, he kissed the inside of my thigh. When he went down on me I bit on my hand to keep quiet. His mouth felt hard. My teeth started to draw blood from my thumb and my face was wet. When he looked up, he said, is it okay? I nodded and felt the headboard nudge the wall. He knelt upright and I let my mouth form a kind of long, murmured syllable, like an animal would make. Nick touched me and I snapped my legs shut and said no, I'm too close now. Oh, that's good, he said.

He took the box out of the bedside drawer and I closed my eyes. I felt his body then, his heat and complex weight. I held his hand tightly between my finger and thumb, like I was trying to press it down into some absorbable size. Yes, I said. I tried not to make it end too quickly. He was so deep inside me it felt like I might die. I wrapped my legs around his back, and he said, God, I love that, I love it when you do that. We whispered one another's names over and over. Then it was finished.

Afterwards I lay with my head on his chest and listened to his heart beat.

Melissa seems like a good person, I said. You know, I mean, deep down.

Yeah, I believe she is.

Does that make us bad people?

I hope not, he said. Not you anyway. Me, maybe.

His heart continued to beat like an excited or miserable clock. I thought about Bobbi's dry and ideological reading of non-monogamous love, and I felt like bringing it up with Nick, as a joke maybe, not being completely serious but just floating the possibility to see what he thought.

Have you considered telling her about us? I said.

165

He sighed, the kind of audible sigh that's like a word. I sat up and he looked at me with sad eyes, as if the subject weighed on him.

I know I should tell her, he said. I feel bad making you lie to people for my sake. And I'm not even good at lying. Melissa asked me the other day if I had feelings for you and I said yes.

The palm of my hand was resting on his sternum and I could still feel his blood pumping below the surface of his skin. Oh, I said.

But what happens if I do tell her? he said. I mean, what would you want to happen? I don't get the impression that you want me to move in with you.

I laughed and so did he. Although we were laughing about the impossibility of our relationship, it still felt nice.

No, I said. But she's had affairs and she never moved out of your house.

Yeah, but you know, circumstances were very different. Look, obviously the ideal thing is that I tell her and she says, well go ahead and live your life, what do I care. I'm not even saying that won't happen, I'm just saying it might not.

I ran my finger along his collarbone and said: I can't remember if I thought about this at the beginning. How it was doomed to end unhappily.

He nodded, looking at me. I did, he said. I just thought it would be worth it.

For a few seconds we were silent. What do you think now? I said. I guess it depends how unhappy it gets.

166

No, said Nick. In a weird way I don't think it does. But look, I will tell her, all right? We'll work it out.

Before I could say anything, we heard footsteps coming up the back staircase. We both went quiet, while the footsteps came to the door. There was a knock, and Bobbi's voice said: Nick? He switched the light off and said: yeah, one second. He got out of bed and pulled on a pair of sweatpants. I lay on the mattress watching him. Then he answered the door. I couldn't see Bobbi through the crease of light, I could only see the silhouette of Nick's back and his arm leaning against the frame.

Frances isn't in her room, Bobbi said. I don't know where she is.

Oh.

I checked in the bathroom and outside in the garden. Do you think I should go and look for her? Should we wake up the others?

No, don't, Nick said. She's, um. Oh, Jesus Christ. She's in here with me.

There was a long silence then. I couldn't see Bobbi's face, or his. I thought of her kissing my lips earlier and calling me self-righteous. It was terrible that Nick had told her like this. I could see how terrible it was.

I didn't realise, said Bobbi. I'm sorry.

No, of course.

Well, sorry. Goodnight then.

He wished her goodnight and closed the door. We listened to her footsteps descending the back staircase to the basement rooms. Oh fuck, Nick said. Fuck. Expressionlessly I said: she won't tell anyone. Nick made an irritable sighing noise and said: well yeah, I hope not. He seemed distracted, as if he no longer noticed I was in the room. I put my nightdress back on and said I would sleep downstairs. Sure, okay, he said.

Nick was still in bed when Bobbi and I left the next morning. Melissa walked us down to the station with our luggage and watched us, quietly, as we boarded the bus.

PART TWO

CHAPTER
EIGHTEEN

It was late August. In the airport Bobbi asked me: how long has that been going on for, between the two of you? And I told her. She shrugged like, okay. On the bus back from Dublin airport, we heard a news report about a woman who had died in hospital. It was a case I had been following some time ago and forgotten about. We were too tired to talk about it then anyway. It was raining against the bus windows as we pulled up outside college. I helped Bobbi lift her suitcase out of the luggage compartment and she rolled down the sleeves of her raincoat. Lashing, she said. Typical. I was getting the train back to Ballina to stay with my mother for a few nights, and I told Bobbi I would call her. She flagged a taxi and I walked toward the bus stop to get the 145 to Heuston.

When I arrived in Ballina that night, my mother put on a bolognese and I sat at the kitchen table teasing the knots out of my hair. Outside the kitchen window the leaves dripped rain like squares of watered silk. She said I was tanned. I let a few split hairs fall from my fingers to the kitchen floor and said: oh, am I? I knew I was.

Did you hear from your father at all while you were over there? she said.

He called me once. He didn't know where I was, he sounded drunk.

She took a plastic packet of garlic bread from the fridge. My throat hurt and I couldn't think of what to say.

He wasn't always this bad, right? I said. It's gotten worse.

He's your father, Frances. You tell me.

I don't exactly hang out with him on the day-to-day.

The kettle came to the boil, releasing a cloud of steam over the hob and toaster. I shivered. I couldn't believe I had woken up in France that morning.

I mean, was he like this when you married him? I said.

She didn't reply. I looked out at the garden, at the bird-feeder hanging off the birch tree. My mother favoured some species of birds over others; the feeder was for the benefit of small and appealingly vulnerable ones. Crows were completely out of favour. She chased them away when she spotted them. They're all just birds, I pointed out. She said yes, but some birds can fend for themselves.

I could feel a headache coming on while I set the table, though I didn't want to mention it. Whenever I told my mother I had headaches she always said it was because I didn't eat enough and I had low blood sugar, although I had never looked up the science behind that claim. By the time the food was ready I could feel a

172

pain in my back too, like a kind of nerve or muscular pain that made sitting straight uncomfortable.

After we ate, I helped load up the dishwasher and my mother said she was going to watch TV. I carried my suitcase to my room, though as I went up the stairs I was finding it physically difficult to walk upright. My vision seemed brighter and sharper than usual. I was scared of moving too vigorously, like I was afraid it would shake the pain out and make it worse. Slowly I walked to the bathroom, closed the door and steadied my hands against the sink.

I was bleeding again. This time the blood had soaked through my clothes, and I wasn't feeling strong enough to take them all off right away. In various stages, using the sink to brace myself, I managed to get undressed. My clothes peeled off wet like skin from a wound. I wrapped myself in a bathrobe that was left hanging on the back of the door, then sat on the rim of the bath with my hands pressed hard into my abdomen, bloody clothes discarded on the floor. At first I felt better, then worse. I wanted to shower, but I was worried I was too weak and I'd fall over or faint.

I noticed that along with the blood were thick grey clots of what looked like skin tissue. I had never seen anything like this before and it scared me so badly that the only comforting idea I could think of was: maybe it's not happening. I kept returning to this thought every time I felt myself starting to panic, as if going insane and hallucinating an alternate reality was less frightening than what was really going on. Maybe it's not happening. I let my hands tremble and waited to start feeling normal again, until I realised that it wasn't just a feeling, something I could dismiss to myself. It was an outside reality that I couldn't change. The pain was like nothing I had ever felt before.

I crouched down to get my phone and then dialled the house number. When my mother answered I said: can you come up here for a second? I'm not feeling very well. I could hear her come up the stairs saying: Frances? Sweetheart? Once she came in I told her what had happened. I was in too much pain to feel embarrassed or squeamish.

Was your period late? she asked.

I tried to think about this. My periods had never really been regular, and I estimated it had been about five weeks since the last one, though it might have been closer to six.

I don't know, maybe, I said. Why?

I suppose there's no chance at all you were pregnant?

I swallowed. I said nothing.

Frances? she said.

It's extremely unlikely.

It's not impossible?

I mean, practically nothing is impossible, I said.

Well, I don't know what to tell you. We'll have to go up to the hospital if you're in that kind of pain.

I held the rim of the bath with my left hand, until the knuckles went white. Then I turned my head and vomited into the bathtub. After a few seconds, when I knew I wouldn't be sick again, I wiped my mouth with the back of my hand and said: maybe we should go to hospital, yeah.

174

* ★ * ★ * ★ *

After a lot of waiting around they gave me a bed in the Accident & Emergency ward. My mother said she would go home and get some sleep for a couple of hours, and that I was to ring her if there was any news. The pain had thinned out a little, but it wasn't gone. I held onto her hand when she said goodbye, the big warm plane of it, like something that could grow from the earth.

Once I got into bed, a nurse hooked me up to a drip, but she didn't tell me what the drip was doing. I tried to look calmly up at the ceiling and count down from ten in my head. The patients I could see from my bed were mostly elderly, but there was one young guy on the ward who seemed to be drunk or high. I couldn't see him, but I could hear him crying, and apologising to all the nurses who went past. And the nurses said things like, okay Kevin, you're all right, good man.

The doctor who came to take my blood sample didn't look much older than I was. He seemed to need a lot of blood, and a urine sample also, and he asked questions about my sexual history. I told him I had never had unprotected sex, and he moved his lower lip disbelievingly and said: never, okay. I coughed and said: well, not fully. Then he looked at me over his clipboard. It was clear from his expression that he thought I was an idiot.

Not fully unprotected? he said. I don't follow you.

I could feel my face get hot, but I replied in as dry and unconcerned a voice as possible.

No, I mean, not full sex, I said.

175

Right.

Then I looked at him and said: I mean he didn't come inside me, am I not being clear? He looked back down at his clipboard then. We hated each other energetically, I could see that. Before he went away, he said they would test the urine for pregnancy. Typically the hCG levels would remain elevated for up to ten days, that's what he said before he left.

I knew that they were testing for pregnancy because they thought I was having a miscarriage. I wondered if the clots of tissue were making them think that. A searing anxiety developed inside me at this thought, in the same form it always took no matter what external stimulus triggered it: first the realisation that I would die, then that everyone else would die, and then that the universe itself would eventually experience heat death, a kind of thought sequence that expanded outward endlessly in forms too huge to be contained inside my body. I trembled, my hands were clammy, and I felt sure I would be sick again. I punched my leg meaninglessly as if that would prevent the death of the universe. Then I found my phone under my pillow and dialled Nick's number.

He answered after several rings. I couldn't hear my own voice when I spoke, but I think I said something about wanting to talk to him. My teeth were chattering and I might have been talking gibberish. When he spoke it was in a whisper.

Are you drunk? he said. What are you doing calling me like this?

I said I didn't know. My lungs were burning and my forehead felt wet.

It's only 2a.m. here, you know, he said. Everyone's still awake, they're in the other room. Are you trying to get me in trouble?

I said again that I didn't know and he told me again that I sounded drunk. His voice contained both secrecy and anger in a special combination: the secrecy enriching the anger, the anger related to the secrecy.

Anyone could have seen you trying to call me, he said. Jesus Christ, Frances. How am I supposed to explain if someone asks?

I began to feel upset then, which was a better feeling than panic. Okay, I said. Goodbye. And I hung up the phone. He didn't call back, but he did send a text message consisting of a string of question marks. I'm in hospital, I typed. Then I held down the delete key until this message disappeared, character after evenly timed character. Afterwards I tucked my phone back underneath my pillow.

I tried to make myself think about things logically. Anxiety was just a chemical phenomenon producing bad feelings. Feelings were just feelings, they had no material reality. If I ever had been pregnant, then I was probably miscarrying anyway. So what? The pregnancy was already over, and I didn't need to consider things like Irish constitutional law, the right to travel, my current bank balance, and so on. Still, it would mean that at some time I had been unknowingly carrying Nick's child, or rather a child that consisted of a mysterious half-and-half mixture of myself and Nick, inside my own body. This seemed like something I should have to adjust to, though I didn't know how or what "adjusting" meant or whether I was being strictly logical about it any more. I was exhausted at this point and my eyes were shut. I found myself thinking about whether it had been a boy.

The doctor came back several hours later and confirmed that I had not been pregnant, that it was not a miscarriage, and that there was no sign of infection or any other irregularities in my blood work. He could see while he spoke to me that I was shivering, my face was damp, I probably looked like a spooked dog, but he didn't ask me if I was all right. So what, I thought, I am all right. He told me the gynaecologist would see me when her rotation started at eight. Then he went away, leaving the curtain open behind him. It was beginning to get light outside and I hadn't slept. The non-existent baby entered a new category of non-existence, that is, things which had not stopped existing but in fact had never existed. I felt foolish, and the idea that I had ever been pregnant now seemed wistfully naive.

The gynaecologist arrived at eight. She asked me some questions about my menstrual cycle and then drew the curtains closed to give me a pelvic exam. I didn't really know what she was doing with her hands, but whatever it was, it was grievously painful. It felt like some extremely sensitive wound inside me was being twisted around. Afterwards I held my arms around my chest and nodded at what she was saying, though I wasn't sure I could really hear her. She had just reached inside my body and caused some of the worst pain I had ever experienced, and the fact that she continued to speak as if she expected me to remember what she was saying struck me as truly crazy.

I do remember that she told me I needed an ultrasound, and that it could have been a number of things. Then she wrote me a script for the contraceptive pill and told me that if I wanted to I could run two boxes of pills together and only have one period every six weeks. I said I would do that. She told me I would get a letter about the ultrasound in the next couple of days.

That's it, she said. You're free to go.

My mother picked me up from the front of the hospital. When I shut the passenger door, she said: you look like you've been through the wars all right. I told her that if childbirth was anything like that pelvic exam I was surprised the human race had survived this long. She laughed and touched my hair. Poor Frances, she said. What will we do with you?

When I got home I fell asleep on the sofa until the afternoon. My mother had left me a note saying she had gone into work and to let her know if I needed anything. I was feeling well enough by then to walk around without hunching over and to make myself some instant coffee and toast. I buttered the toast thickly and ate it in small, slow bites. Then I showered until I felt really clean and padded back to my room wrapped in towels. I sat on the bed, water running from my hair down onto my back, and cried. It was okay to cry because nobody could see me, and I would never tell anyone about it.

By the time I was finished, I was very cold. The tips of my fingers had started to turn a creepy whitish-grey colour. I towelled my skin off properly and blow-dried my hair until it crackled. Then I reached for the soft part on the inside of my left elbow and pinched it so tightly between my thumbnail and forefinger that I tore the skin open. That was it. It was over then. It was all going to be okay.

CHAPTER
NINETEEN

My mother came home early from work that afternoon and fixed some cold chicken while I sat at the table drinking tea. She seemed a little cool with me while preparing the food and didn't really speak until we both sat down to eat.

So you're not pregnant, she said.

No.

You didn't seem so sure about that last night.

Well, the test is pretty definitive, I said.

She gave a funny little smile and picked up the salt shaker. Carefully she applied a small amount of salt to her chicken and replaced the shaker beside the pepper grinder.

You didn't tell me you were seeing anyone, she said.

Who says I'm seeing someone?

It's not that friend of yours you went on holiday with. The handsome guy, the actor.

I swallowed some tea calmly, but I was no longer hungry for the food.

You know his wife was the one who invited us on the holiday, I said.

I don't hear much about him any more. You used to mention his name a lot.

And yet for some reason you don't seem to be able to remember it.

She laughed out loud then. She said, I remember it, it's Nick something. Nick Conway. Nice-looking guy. I actually saw him on TV one night, I think I put it on the Sky Plus for you.

That was very thoughtful of you, mother.

Well, I wouldn't like to think it has anything to do with him.

I said the food was nice, and that I appreciated her fixing it for me.

Do you hear me talking to you, Frances? she said.

I don't feel up to this, I really don't.

We finished the meal in silence. I went upstairs afterwards and looked at my arm in the mirror, where I'd pinched it. It was red and a little swollen and when I touched it, it stung.

I stayed at home for the next few days, lying around and reading. I had a lot of academic reading I could have been doing in advance of the college term, but instead what I started reading was the gospels. For some reason my mother had left a small leather-bound copy of the New Testament on the bookshelf in my room, sandwiched between *Emma* and an anthology of early American writing. I read online that you were supposed to start with Mark and then read the other gospels in this order: Matthew, then John, then Luke. I got through Mark pretty quickly. It was divided up into very small parts which made it easy to read, and I noted down interesting passages in a red notebook. Jesus didn't talk very much during Mark's gospel, which made me more interested in reading the others.

I'd hated religion as a child. My mother had taken me to Mass every Sunday until I was fourteen, but she didn't believe in God and treated Mass as a social ritual in advance of which she made me wash my hair. Still, I came at the Bible from the perspective that Jesus was probably philosophically sound. As it turned out I found a lot of what he said cryptic and even disagreeable. Whoever does not have, even what he has will be taken away from him, I didn't like that, though I also wasn't sure I fully understood it. In Matthew there was a passage where the Pharisees were asking Jesus about marriage, which I was reading at eight or nine in the evening, while my mother was looking at the papers. Jesus said that in marriage, man and wife are no longer two but one flesh. Therefore what God has joined together, let not man separate. I felt pretty low when I read that. I put away the Bible, but it didn't help.

The day after the hospital I'd received an email from Nick.

hey. sorry about how i acted on the phone last night. i was just afraid someone had seen your name come up on the screen and it would become a thing. anyway no one saw and i told them it was my mother calling (let's not get too psychological about that). i did notice you sounded weird though. is everything ok?

183

ps everyone tells me that i've been in a bad mood
since you left. also evelyn thinks i'm "pining" for you,
which is awkward.

I read it many times but didn't reply. The next
morning the letter from the hospital arrived, scheduling
the ultrasound for some time in November. I thought it
seemed like a long time to wait, but my mother said
that was public health care for you. But they don't
know what's wrong with me, I said. She told me that if
it was anything serious they never would have
discharged me. I didn't know about that. Anyway I
filled out my prescription for the pill and started taking
it.

I called my father a couple of times, but he didn't
pick up the phone or return my calls. My mother
suggested I could "drop by" his house, on the other
side of town. I said I was still feeling ill and that I didn't
want to walk over for nothing, since he wasn't
answering his phone. In response she just said: he's
your father. It was like some kind of mantric prayer
with her. I let the issue go. He wasn't in touch.

My mother hated the way I talked about my father,
like he was just another normal person rather than my
distinguished personal benefactor, or a minor celebrity.
This irritation was directed toward me, but it was also a
symptom of her disappointment that my father had
failed to earn the respect she wanted me to give him. I
knew she'd had to sleep with her purse tucked inside
her pillowcase when they were married. I'd found her
crying the time he fell asleep on the stairs in his

underwear. I saw him lying there, gigantic and pink, his head cradled in one of his arms. He was snoring like it was the best sleep of his life. She couldn't understand that I didn't love him. You must love him, she told me when I was sixteen. He's your father.

Who says I have to love him? I said.

Well, I want to believe you're the kind of person who loves her own parents.

Believe what you want.

I believe I raised you to be kind to others, she said. That's what I believe.

Was I kind to others? It was hard to nail down an answer. I worried that if I did turn out to have a personality, it would be one of the unkind ones. Did I only worry about this question because as a woman I felt required to put the needs of others before my own? Was "kindness" just another term for submission in the face of conflict? These were the kind of things I wrote about in my diary as a teenager: as a feminist I have the right not to love anyone.

I found a video of the documentary that Bobbi had mentioned in France, a 1992 TV production called *Kid Genius!* Nick wasn't the primary kid genius on the programme, there were six featured children, each with different areas of interest. I skipped until I found some footage of Nick looking at books, while a voiceover explained that at the age of only ten, "Nicholas" had read several significant works of ancient philosophy and written essays on metaphysics. As a child Nick was very thin like a stick insect. The first shot showed a gigantic family home in Dalkey, with two imposing cars parked outside. Later in the show Nick appeared with a blue backdrop behind him and a female interviewer asked him questions about Platonic idealism, which he answered competently, without seeming haughty. At one point the interviewer asked: What makes you love the ancient world so much? And Nick cast his eyes around nervously like he was looking for his parents. Well, I don't love it, he said. I just study it. You don't see yourself as a budding philosopher king? the interviewer said humorously. No, Nick said very seriously. He tugged on the sleeve of his blazer. He was still looking around like he expected someone to appear and help him. That would be my worst nightmare, he said. The interviewer laughed, and Nick relaxed visibly. Women laughing always relaxed him, I thought.

A few days after the hospital I called Bobbi to ask if we were still friends. I could feel my voice getting stupid when I asked her, though I was trying to make it sound like a joke. I thought you were going to call me the other night, she said. I was in hospital, I told her. My tongue felt huge and traitorous in my mouth.

What do you mean? she said.

I explained what had happened.

They thought you were miscarrying a pregnancy, she said. That's kind of intense, isn't it?

Is it? I don't know, I didn't know what to feel about it.

She sighed audibly into the receiver. I wanted to explain that I didn't know how much I was allowed to feel about it, or how much of what I felt at the time I was still allowed to feel in retrospect. I panicked, I

186

wanted to tell her. I started thinking about the heat death of the universe again. I called Nick and then hung up on him. But these were all things I did because I thought something was happening to me which turned out not to happen. The idea of the baby, with all its huge emotional gravity and its potential for lasting grief, had disappeared into nothing. I had never been pregnant. It was impossible, maybe even offensive, to grieve a pregnancy that had never happened, even though the emotions I'd felt had still been real at the time that I felt them. In the past Bobbi had been receptive to my analyses of my own misery, but this time I couldn't trust myself to deliver the argument without weeping into the phone.

I'm sorry that you feel like I lied to you about Nick, I said.

You're sorry that I feel that way, okay.

It was just complicated.

Yeah, Bobbi said. I guess extramarital relationships can be.

Are you still my friend?

Yes. So when are you getting this ultrasound thing?

I told her November. I also told her about the doctor asking about unprotected sex, which made her snort. I was sitting on my bed, with my feet under the coverlet. In the mirror on the other wall I could see my left hand, my free hand, moving nervously up and down the seam of a pillowcase. I dropped it and watched it lie dead on the quilt.

Still, I can't believe Nick would try to get away with not using a condom, Bobbi said. That's fucked up.

187

I mumbled something defensive like: oh, we didn't . . . you know, it wasn't really . . .

I'm not blaming you, she said. I'm surprised at him, that's all.

I tried to think of something to say. None of the idiotic things we did felt like they were Nick's fault because he always just followed along with what I suggested.

It was probably my idea, I said.

You sound brainwashed when you talk like that.

No, but he's actually very passive.

Right, but he could have said no, Bobbi said. Maybe he just likes to act passive so he doesn't have to take the blame for anything.

In the mirror I noticed that my hand had started doing the thing again. This wasn't the conversation I was trying to have.

You're making him sound very calculating, I said.

I didn't mean he was doing it consciously. Have you told him you were in hospital?

I said no. I felt my mouth opening again to explain about the phone call when he accused me of being drunk, then I decided against telling her, instead pronouncing the phrase: yeah, no.

But you're close with him, she said. You tell him things.

I don't know. I don't know really how close we are.

Well, you tell him more than you tell me.

No, I said. Less than you. He probably thinks I never tell him anything.

That night I decided to start reading over my old instant message conversations with Bobbi. I'd taken on a similar project once before, shortly after our break-up, and now I had whole additional years of messages to read. It comforted me to know that my friendship with Bobbi wasn't confined to memory alone, and that textual evidence of her past fondness for me would survive her actual fondness if necessary. This had been foremost in my mind at the time of the break-up also, for obvious reasons. It was important to me that Bobbi would never be able to deny that at one point she had liked me very much.

This time I downloaded our exchanges as one huge text file with time stamps. I told myself it was too large to read from start to finish, and it also didn't take a coherent narrative shape, so I decided to read it by searching for particular words or phrases and reading around them. The first one I tried was "love", which brought up the following exchange, from six months previously:

Bobbi: if you look at love as something other than an
    interpersonal phenomenon
Bobbi: and try to understand it as a social value
    system
Bobbi: it's both antithetical to capitalism, in that it
    challenges the axiom of selfishness
Bobbi: which dictates the whole logic of inequality
Bobbi: and yet also it's subservient and facilitatory
Bobbi: i.e. mothers selflessly raising children without
    any profit motive

Bobbi: which seems to contradict the demands of the
    market at one level
Bobbi: and yet actually just functions to provide work-
    ers for free
me: yes
me: capitalism harnesses "love" for profit
me: love is the discursive practice and unpaid labour is
    the effect
me: but I mean, I get that, I'm anti love as such
Bobbi: that's vapid frances
Bobbi: you have to do more than say you're anti
    things

I got out of bed after I read that exchange and
stripped my clothes off to look in the mirror.
Periodically I found myself doing this out of a kind of
compulsion, though nothing about me ever seemed to
change. My hip bones still jutted out unattractively on
either side of my pelvis, and my abdomen was still hard
and round to the touch. I looked like something that
had dropped off a spoon too quickly, before it had time
to set. My shoulders were freckled with broken,
violet-coloured capillaries. For a while I stood there just
looking at myself and feeling my repulsion get deeper
and deeper, as if I was experimenting to see how much
I could feel. Eventually I heard a ringing noise in my
bag and went to try and find it.

When I retrieved my phone it said I'd missed a call
from my father. I tried calling back but he didn't
answer. By then I was getting cold so I put all my
clothes back on and went downstairs to tell my mother

I was going to drop by my father's house. She was sitting at the table reading the paper; she didn't look up. Good woman, she said. Tell him I was asking after him.

I walked the same old route through town. I hadn't brought a jacket, and at his house I rang the doorbell and jogged from foot to foot to warm myself up. My breath fogged the glass. I rang again and nothing happened. When I opened the door, I could hear nothing inside the house. The hall smelt of damp and of something worse than damp too, something slightly sour. A refuse sack was tied up and abandoned under the hall table. I called my father's name: Dennis?

I could see the light was on inside the kitchen so I pushed open the door and reflexively lifted a hand against my face. The smell was so rancid that it felt physical, like heat or touch. Several half-eaten meals had accumulated around the table and countertops, in various states of decay, surrounded by dirty tissues and empty bottles. The fridge door was ajar, leaking a triangle of yellow light onto the floor. A bluebottle crawled along a knife which had been abandoned in a large jar of mayonnaise, and four others were batting themselves against the kitchen window. In the bin I could see a handful of white maggots, writhing blindly like boiling rice. I stepped backwards out of the room and closed the door.

In the hallway I tried calling Dennis's phone again. He didn't answer. Standing in his house was like watching someone familiar smile at me, but with missing teeth. I wanted to hurt myself again, in order to

191

feel returned to the safety of my own physical body. Instead I turned around and walked out. I pulled my sleeve over my hand to shut the door.

CHAPTER
TWENTY

My internship in the agency ended formally at the start of September. We each had one last meeting with Sunny, to talk about our plans for the future and what we'd learned from our experiences, though I didn't foresee having anything to say about any of that. I came into her office on my last day and she asked me to close the door and sit down.

Well, you don't want to work in a literary agency, she said.

I smiled like she was joking, while she looked at some papers and then put them aside. She put her elbows up on her desk, holding her chin in her hands contemplatively.

I wonder about you, she said. You don't seem to have a plan.

Yeah, that's something I definitely don't have.

You're just hoping to fall on your feet.

I looked out the window behind her onto the beautiful Georgian buildings and the buses passing. It was raining again.

Tell me about the holiday, she said. How is Melissa's piece coming on?

I told her about Étables, about Derek, whom Sunny knew, and about Valerie, whom she had heard of. Sunny called her a "formidable woman". I grimaced a little bit and we laughed. I realised that I didn't want to leave Sunny's office, that I felt as if I was letting go of something I wasn't finished with.

I don't know what I'm going to do, I said.

She nodded and then gave an expressive, accepting shrug.

Well, your reports were always very good, she said. If you ever want a reference you know where to find me. And I'm sure I'll see you again soon.

Thank you, I said. For everything.

She gave me one last sympathetic or despairing look and then went back to the papers on her desk. She told me I could call Philip in on my way out. I did.

That night in my apartment I was up late tinkering with commas in a long poem I was working on. I saw Nick was online and I sent him a message: hello. I was sitting at the kitchen table drinking peppermint tea because the milk in the fridge was sour. He replied, asking if I'd received his email five days ago and I said yes, and not to worry about the awkward phone call. I didn't want to tell him I had been in hospital, or why. It was a story with no conclusion, and anyway it was embarrassing. He told me they were all missing Bobbi and me over in France.

me: equally?
Nick: haha

Nick: well maybe i miss you like, slightly more
me: thanks
Nick: yeah i keep waking up at night when i hear
    people on the stairs
Nick: and then i remember you're gone
Nick: crushing disappointment

I laughed to myself although there was no one there to see me. I loved when he was available to me like this, when our relationship was like a Word document which we were writing and editing together, or a long private joke which nobody else could understand. I liked to feel that he was my collaborator. I liked to think of him waking up at night and thinking of me.

me: that's actually very cute
me: I miss your sweet handsome face
Nick: i wanted to send you a song earlier because it
    reminded me of you
Nick: but i anticipated your sarcastic reply and
    chickened out
me: hahaha
me: please send it!
me: I promise not to be sarcastic
Nick: would it be ok if i called you on the phone
Nick: ive been drinking and the effort of typing is kill-
    ing me
me: oh you're drunk, is that why you're being nice
Nick: i think john keats had a name for women like
    you
Nick: a french name

Nick: you see where i'm going with this
me: please call

He called me. He didn't really sound drunk on
the phone, he sounded sleepy in a nice way. We said
again that we missed one another. I held the cup of
peppermint tea in my fingers, feeling it get cool.
Nick apologised again about the phone call the
other night. I'm a bad person, he said. I told him not
to say that. No, I'm bad, he said. I'm a bad guy. He
told me about what they'd been up to in Étables,
about the weather, and some castle they went to
visit. I told him about my internship finishing up, and
he said I had never seemed invested in it anyway.
Maybe I was distracted by drama in my personal life,
I said.

Oh yeah, I meant to ask, he said. How are things
with you and Bobbi? That wasn't the best way for her
to find out about us I guess.

Yeah, it's been awkward. It's kind of bothering me.

This is the first relationship you've been in since you
two were together, isn't it?

I guess so, I said. Do you think that's why it's weird?

Well, you didn't really seem to separate that much
after you broke up. In the sense that you still spend all
your time together.

She was the one who broke up with me.

Nick paused, and when he spoke he sounded like he
was smiling curiously. Yes, I know that, he said. Is it
relevant?

I rolled my eyes, but I was enjoying him. I put down the cup of tea on the table. Oh I see, I said. I see why you're calling me, okay.

What?

You want us to have phone sex.

He started laughing. This was the intended effect and I basked in it. He laughed a lot. I know, he said. Classic me. I wanted to tell him about the hospital then, because he was in such a nice mood with me, and he might say consoling things, but I knew it would make the conversation serious. I didn't like cornering him into having serious conversations. By the way, he said, I saw a girl on the beach today who looked like you.

People are always saying someone looks like me, I said. And then when I see the person it's always someone plain-looking and I have to pretend not to mind.

Oh, not this woman. This woman was very attractive.

You're telling me about an attractive stranger you saw, how sweet.

She looked like you! he said. She was probably less hostile, though. Maybe I should have an affair with her instead.

I took a mouthful of tea and swallowed. I felt silly for not replying to his email for so long and grateful that he didn't dwell on it or act hurt. I asked what he had been doing that day and he told me he was avoiding his parents' calls and feeling guilty about it.

Is your dad as handsome as you are? I said.

Why, are you thinking about going there? He's very right-wing. I would point out he's also still married, but when has that stopped you before?

Oh, that's nice. Now who's hostile?

I'm sorry, he said. You're so right, you should seduce my dad.

Do you think I'm his type?

Oh yeah. In the sense that you greatly resemble my mother, anyway.

I started to laugh. It was a sincere laugh but I still wanted to make sure he would hear it.

That's a joke, said Nick. Are you laughing there, or weeping? You don't resemble my mother.

Is your dad actually right-wing or was that a joke too?

Oh no, he's a real wealth creator. Hates women. Absolutely detests the poor. So you can imagine he loves me, his camp actor son.

I was really laughing then. You're not camp, I said. You're aggressively heterosexual. You even have a twenty-one-year-old mistress.

That I think my father would actually approve of. Happily he'll never know.

I looked around the empty kitchen and said: I cleaned my room today in advance of you getting back from France.

Did you really? I love that. I think this actually counts as phone sex now.

Will you visit me?

After a pause he said: of course. I didn't feel I had lost him exactly, but I knew he was thinking about something else. Then he said: you sounded really out of it on the phone the other night, were you drunk?

Let's forget about it.

You're just not a big person for phone calls usually. You weren't upset or anything, were you?

I heard something in the background on Nick's end of the line, and then a little crackling noise. Hello? he called out. A door opened and then I heard Melissa's voice say: oh, you're on the phone. Nick said: yeah, give me one second. The door closed again. I said nothing.

I'll visit you, he said quietly. I have to go, all right?

Sure.

Sorry.

Go ahead, I said. Live your life.

He hung up.

The next day, our friend Marianne came back from Brooklyn and told us about all the celebrities she had met. She showed us photographs on her phone over coffee: Brooklyn Bridge, Coney Island, Marianne herself smiling with a blurry man who I privately did not believe was actually Bradley Cooper. Wow, Philip said. Cool, I agreed. Bobbi licked the back of her teaspoon and said nothing.

I was happy to see Marianne again, happy to listen to her problems as if my own life was going exactly how it always went. I asked about her boyfriend Andrew, how he liked his new job, whatever happened with his ex messaging him on Facebook. I boasted to her about Philip's internship in the agency, how he was going to become a predatory literary agent and make millions, and I could see I was pleasing him. It's better than the arms trade, he said. Bobbi snorted. Jesus, Philip, is that your gold standard? she said. At least I'm not selling arms?

At this point the conversation slipped away from me. Before I could direct another question toward Marianne, Philip started to ask us about Étables. Nick and Melissa were still over there, they weren't coming back for another two weeks. Bobbi told him we'd had "fun".

Any luck with Nick yet? he asked me.

I stared at him. To Marianne he added: Frances is having an affair with a married man.

No I'm not, I said.

Philip is joking, said Bobbi.

Famous Nick? Marianne said. I want to hear about him.

We're friends, I said.

But he definitely has a crush, said Philip.

Frances, you temptress, said Marianne. Isn't he married?

Blissfully, I said.

To change the subject, Bobbi mentioned something about wanting to move out and find an apartment closer to town. Marianne said there was an accommodation crisis, she said she'd heard about it on the news.

And they won't take students, Marianne said. I'm serious, look at the listings.

You're moving out? said Philip.

It shouldn't be legal to say No Students, Marianne said. It's discrimination.

Where are you looking? I asked. You know we'll be letting the second bedroom in my place.

Bobbi looked at me and then let out a little laugh.

We could be flatmates, she said. How much?

I'll talk to my dad, I said.

I hadn't spoken to my father since I'd visited his house. When I called him after coffee that evening, he answered, sounding relatively sober. I tried to repress the image of the mayonnaise jar, the noise of bluebottles hammering themselves against glass. I wanted to be speaking to someone who lived in a clean house, or someone who was only a voice, whose life I didn't have to know about. On the phone we talked about the apartment's second bedroom. He told me his brother had some viewings arranged and I explained that Bobbi was looking for a place.

Who's this? he said. Who's Bobbi?

You know Bobbi. We were in school together.

Your friend, is it? Which friend now?

Well, I really only had one friend, I said.

I thought you'd want another girl living with you.

Bobbi is a girl.

Oh, the Lynch girl, is it? he said.

Bobbi's surname was actually Connolly, but her mother's name was Lynch, so I let that one go. He said his brother could give her the room for six fifty a month, a price Bobbi's father was willing to pay. He wants me to have somewhere quiet to study, she said. Little does he know.

The next day her father drove her over in his jeep with all her belongings. She had brought some bedlinen and a yellow anglepoise, and also three boxes of books. When we unloaded the car, her father drove off again and I helped Bobbi to dress the bed. She started sticking some postcards and photographs onto the wall while I put the pillows into cases. She put up a photograph of the two of us in our school uniforms, sitting on the basketball court. We had long tartan skirts on and ugly, dimpled shoes, but we were laughing. We looked at it together, our two little faces peering back at us like ancestors, or perhaps our own children.

Term didn't start up for another week, and in the meantime Bobbi bought a red ukulele and took to lying on the couch playing "Boots of Spanish Leather" while I cooked dinner. She made herself at home by moving items of furniture around while I was out for the day and sticking magazine cut-outs on the mirrors. She took a great interest in getting to know the neighbourhood. We stopped into the butcher's one day for mince and Bobbi asked the guy behind the counter how his hand was. I had no idea what she was talking about, I didn't even know she'd been in the place before, but I did notice the guy was wearing a blue cast on his wrist. Stop, he said. Needs surgery now and everything. He was shovelling red meat into a plastic bag. Oh no, said Bobbi. When will that be? He told her Christmas. Fucked if I'm getting a day off either, the guy said. You'd have to be across in Massey's before you get a day off in this place. He handed her the bag of meat and added: in your coffin.

The profile was published just before classes started up again. I went to Easons the morning it came out and flicked through the magazine looking for my name. I stopped at a full-page photograph of Bobbi and me, taken in the garden in Étables. I had no recollection of Melissa taking such a photograph. It depicted us sitting at the breakfast table together, me leaning over as if to whisper something in Bobbi's ear, and Bobbi was laughing. It was an arresting image, the light was beautiful, and it conveyed spontaneity and warmth in a way the earlier posed photographs hadn't. I wondered what Bobbi would say about it. The article that followed was a short, admiring account of our spoken word performances and of the spoken word scene in Dublin generally. Our friends read it and said the photograph was flattering, and Sunny sent me a nice email about it. For a while, Philip liked to carry a copy of the magazine around and read from it in a phony accent, but that joke exhausted itself eventually. Pieces like this were published in small magazines all the time, and anyway Bobbi and I hadn't performed together in months.

Once term started, I had academic work to keep me busy again. Philip and I walked to seminars together having minor disagreements about various nineteenth-century novelists, which always ended with him saying things like: look, you're probably right. One evening Bobbi and I called Melissa to thank her for the article. We put her on speakerphone so we could sit at the table to talk. Melissa told us all about what we'd missed in Étables, the thunderstorms, and the day they went to visit the castle, things I had already heard about. We told her we had moved in together and she sounded pleased. Bobbi said: we must have you over some time. And Melissa said that would be lovely. She told us they were coming home the next day. I pulled my sleeve over my hand and rubbed absent-mindedly at a little stain on the tabletop.

I continued to read through my log of conversations with Bobbi, entering search terms which seemed wilfully calculated to annoy me. Searching for the word "feelings" unearthed this conversation, from our second year of college:

> Bobbi: well you don't really talk about your feelings
> me: you're committed to this view of me
> me: as having some kind of undisclosed emotional life
> me: I'm just not very emotional
> me: I don't talk about it because there's nothing to
>   talk about
> Bobbi: i don't think "unemotional" is a quality
>   someone can have
> Bobbi: that's like claiming not to have thoughts
> me: you live an emotionally intense life so you think
>   everyone else does
> me: and if they're not talking about it then they're
>   hiding something
> Bobbi: well, ok
> Bobbi: we differ on that

Not all the exchanges were like this. The "feelings" search also brought up the following conversation, from January:

me: I mean I always had negative feelings about authority figures
me: but really only when I met you did I formulate the feelings into beliefs
me: you know what I mean
Bobbi: you would have gotten there on your own though
Bobbi: you have a communist intuition
me: well no, I probably only hated authority because I resent being told what to do
me: if not for you I could have become a cult leader
me: or an ayn rand fan
Bobbi: hey, i resent being told what to do!!
me: yes but out of spiritual purity
me: not a will to power
Bobbi: you are in many ways, the very worst psychologist

I remembered having this conversation; I remembered how effortful it felt, the sense that Bobbi was misunderstanding me, or even intentionally averting her gaze from what I was trying to say. I'd been sitting in the upstairs bedroom in my mother's house, under the quilt, and my hands were cold. Having spent Christmas in Ballina away from Bobbi, I wanted to tell her that I missed her. That was what I had started to say, or thought about saying.

Nick came over to the apartment a few days after they got back, an afternoon when Bobbi was busy with lectures. When I let him in we looked at one another for a couple of seconds and it felt like drinking cold water. He was tanned, his hair was fairer than before. Oh, fuck, you look so good, I said. That made him laugh. His teeth were gorgeously white. He glanced around at the hall and said: yeah, nice apartment. It's pretty central, what's the rent like? I said my dad's brother owned it and he looked at me and said: oh, you little trust fund baby. You didn't tell me your family had property in the Liberties. The whole building or just the apartment? I punched his arm lightly and said: just the apartment. He touched my hand and then we were kissing again, and under my breath I was saying: yes, yes.

CHAPTER
TWENTY-ONE

The following week, Bobbi and I went to the launch of a book in which one of Melissa's essays appeared. The event was in Temple Bar, and I knew that Melissa and Nick would be there together. I selected a blouse that Nick particularly liked, and left it partly unbuttoned so my collarbone was visible. I spent several minutes carefully disguising the small blemishes on my face with make-up and powder. When Bobbi was ready to go she knocked on the bathroom door and said: come on. She didn't comment on my appearance. She was wearing a grey turtleneck and looked much better than I did anyway.

Nick and I had seen each other a couple of times during the week, always while Bobbi was at lectures. He brought me little gifts when he visited. One day he brought ice cream, and on Wednesday a box of doughnuts from the booth on O'Connell Street. The doughnuts were still hot when he arrived and we ate them with coffee and talked. He asked me if I had been in touch with my father lately, and I wiped a crust of sugar from my lips and said: I don't think he's doing too well. I told Nick about the house. Jesus, he said.

That sounds traumatic. I swallowed a mouthful of coffee. Yeah, I said. It was upsetting.

After this conversation I asked myself why it was that I could talk to Nick about my father, even though I'd never been able to broach the subject with Bobbi. It was true that Nick was an intelligent listener, and I often felt better after we spoke, but those things were true of Bobbi too. It was more that Nick's sympathy seemed unconditional, like he rooted for me regardless of how I acted, whereas Bobbi had strong principles that she applied to everyone, me included. I didn't fear Nick's bad judgement like I did Bobbi's. He was happy to listen to me even when my thoughts were inconclusive, even when I told stories about my own behaviour that showed me in an unflattering light.

Nick wore nice clothes when he visited the apartment, like he always did, clothes I suspected were expensive. Instead of leaving them on the floor when he undressed, he folded them over the back of my bedroom chair. He liked to wear pale-coloured shirts, sometimes linen ones that looked vaguely rumpled, sometimes Oxford shirts with button-downs, always worn with the sleeves rolled back over his forearms. He had a canvas golf jacket he seemed to like a lot, but on cold days he wore a grey cashmere coat with blue silk lining. I loved this coat, I loved how it smelled. It had only a shallow lip of collar and a single row of buttons.

On Wednesday I tried the coat on while Nick was in the bathroom. I got out of bed and slipped my naked arms through the sleeves, feeling the cool silk run over my skin. The pockets were heavy with personal items:

his phone and wallet, his keys. I weighed them in my hands like they were mine. I gazed at myself in the mirror. Inside Nick's coat my body looked very slim and pale, a white wax candle. He came back into the room and laughed at me in a good-natured way. He always dressed to go to the bathroom in case Bobbi came home unexpectedly. Our eyes met in the mirror.

You're not keeping it, he said.

I like it.

Unfortunately, I like it too.

Was it expensive? I said.

We were still looking at each other in the mirror. He stood behind me and lifted the coat open with his fingers. I watched him looking at me.

It was, uh . . . he said. I don't remember how much it was.

A thousand euro?

What? No. Two or three hundred maybe.

I wish I had money, I said.

He slipped his hand inside the coat then and touched my breast. The sexual way you talk about money is kind of interesting, he said. Though also disturbing, obviously. You don't want me to give you money, do you?

In a way I do, I said. But I wouldn't necessarily trust that impulse.

Yeah, it's weird. I have money that I don't urgently need, and I would rather you had it. But the transaction of giving it to you would bother me.

You don't like to feel too powerful. Or you don't like to be reminded how powerful you like to feel.

He shrugged. He was still touching me underneath the coat. It was nice.

I think I struggle enough with the ethics of our relationship already, he said. So giving you money would probably push it too far for me. Although, I don't know. You'd probably be happier with the cash.

I looked at him, seeing my own face in my peripheral vision, my chin raised slightly. Blurred out on the periphery I thought I looked quite formidable. I slipped out of the coat and left him holding it. I got back onto the bed and ran my tongue between my lips.

Are you conflicted about our relationship? I said.

He stood there holding the coat kind of limply in his hands. I could tell he was enjoying himself and too distracted to think about hanging it up.

No, he said. Well, yes, but only in the abstract.

You're not going to leave me?

He smiled, a shy smile. Would you miss me if I did? he said.

I lay back on the bed, laughing at nothing. He hung the coat up. I lifted one of my legs in the air and crossed it over the other one slowly.

I would miss dominating you in conversation, I said.

He lay down beside me and flattened his hand against my stomach. Go on, he said.

I think you would miss it too.

Being dominated? Of course I would. That's like foreplay for us. You say cryptic things I don't understand, I give inadequate responses, you laugh at me, and then we have sex.

I laughed. He sat up a little to watch me laughing.

210

It's nice, he said. It gives me an opportunity to enjoy being so inadequate.

I propped myself up on one elbow and kissed his mouth. He leaned into it, like he really wanted to be kissed, and I felt a rush of my own power over him.

Do I make you feel bad about yourself? I said.

You can be a little hard on me from time to time. Not that I blame you really. But no, I think we're getting along well at the moment.

I looked down at my own hands. Carefully, like I was daring myself, I said: if I lash out at you it's just because you don't seem very vulnerable to it.

He looked at me then. He didn't even laugh, it was just a kind of frowning look, like he thought I was mocking him. Okay, he said. Well. I don't think anyone likes being lashed out at.

But I mean you don't have a vulnerable personality. Like, I find it hard to imagine you trying on clothes. You don't seem to have that relationship with yourself where you look at your reflection wondering if you look good in something. You seem like someone who would find that embarrassing.

Right, he said. I mean, I'm a human being, I try clothes on before I buy them. But I think I understand what you're saying. People do tend to find me kind of cold and like, not very fun.

I was excited that we shared an experience I found so personal, and quickly I said: people find me cold and lacking in fun.

Really? he said. You always seemed charming to me.

211

I was gripped by a sudden and overwhelming urge to say: I love you, Nick. It wasn't a bad feeling, specifically; it was slightly amusing and crazy, like when you stand up from your chair and suddenly realise how drunk you are. But it was true. I was in love with him.

I want that coat, I said.

Oh, yeah. You can't have it.

When we arrived at the launch the following night, Nick and Melissa were there already. They were standing together talking to some other people we knew: Derek, and a few others. Nick saw us coming in, but he didn't hold my gaze when I tried to look at him. He noticed me and looked away, that was all. Bobbi and I flicked through the book and didn't buy it. We said hello to the other people we knew, Bobbi texted Philip to ask where he was, and I pretended to read the author bios. Then the readings started.

Throughout Melissa's reading, Nick watched her face very attentively and laughed in the right places. My discovery that I was in love with Nick, not just infatuated but deeply personally attached to him in a way that would have lasting consequences for my happiness, had prompted me to feel a new kind of jealousy toward Melissa. I couldn't believe that he went home to her every evening, or that they ate dinner together and sometimes watched films on their TV. What did they talk about? Did they amuse each other? Did they discuss their emotional lives, did they confide in one another? Did he respect Melissa more than me? Did he like her more? If we were both going to die in a burning building and he could only save one of us, wouldn't he certainly save Melissa and not me? It seemed practically evil to have so much sex with someone who you would later allow to burn to death.

After her reading, Melissa beamed while we all applauded. When she sat back down Nick said something in her ear and her smile changed, a real smile now, with her teeth and the sides of her eyes. He was always calling her "my wife" in front of me. At the beginning I thought it was playful, maybe kind of sarcastic, like she wasn't his real wife at all. Now I saw it differently. He didn't mind me knowing that he loved someone else, he wanted me to know, but he was horrified by the idea that Melissa would find out about our relationship. It was something he was ashamed of, something he wanted to protect her from. I was sealed up in a certain part of his life that he didn't like to look at or think about when he was with other people.

Once all the readings were finished, I went to get a glass of wine. Evelyn and Melissa were standing nearby holding glasses of sparkling water, and Evelyn waved me over. I congratulated Melissa on her reading. Behind her shoulder I saw Nick coming toward us, and then he spotted me and hesitated. Evelyn was talking about the editor of the book. Nick arrived at her shoulder and they embraced, so warmly that it knocked Evelyn's glasses sideways and she had to fix them. Nick and I nodded at each other politely. This time he held my eyes for a second longer than he had to, like he was sorry we were meeting this way.

You're looking so well, Evelyn said to him. You really are.

He's been practically living in the gym, said Melissa.

I took a huge mouthful of white wine and washed it around my teeth. Is that what he tells you, I thought.

Well, it's working, said Evelyn. You have a look of radiant good health about you.

Thanks, he said. I'm feeling well.

Melissa was watching Nick with a kind of pride, like she had nursed him back to health after a long illness. I wondered what he meant by "I'm feeling well", or what he meant for me to hear in it.

And how about you, Frances? said Evelyn. How are you keeping?

Fine, thanks, I said.

You're looking a little glum tonight, said Melissa.

Cheerfully Evelyn said: I'd be glum if I were you, spending all your time around ancient people like us. Where's Bobbi?

Oh, she's here, I said. I gestured toward the cash register, though I didn't actually know where she was.

Are you getting tired of ancient people? said Melissa.

No, not at all, I said. If anything I could go more ancient.

Nick stared into his glass.

We'll have to find you a nice older girlfriend, Melissa said. Someone with a lot of money.

I didn't have the nerve to look at Nick. Around the stem of my wine glass I sank my thumbnail into the side of my finger to feel it sting.

I'm not sure what my role would be in that relationship, I said.

You could write her love sonnets, said Evelyn.

214

Melissa grinned. Don't underestimate the effect of youth and beauty, she said.

That sounds like a recipe for disastrous unhappiness, I said.

You're twenty-one, said Melissa. You should be disastrously unhappy.

I'm working on it, I said.

Someone else joined the conversation then to talk to Melissa, and I took the opportunity to go and find Bobbi. She was talking to the cashier near the front door. Bobbi had never had a job and she loved to talk to people about what they did at work. Even mundane details interested her, though she often forgot them quickly. The cashier was a lanky young man with acne, who was telling Bobbi enthusiastically about his band. The bookshop manager came over then and started to talk about the book, which none of us had read or bought. I stood beside them, watching Melissa from across the room as she put her arm absently on Nick's back.

When I saw Nick look over at us, I turned to Bobbi, smiling, and moved her hair aside to whisper something in her ear. She looked at Nick and then suddenly grabbed my wrist, hard, harder than she had ever touched me in my life before. It hurt me, it drew a little gasp from my throat, and then she dropped my arm again. I cradled it against my ribs. In a deathly calm voice, staring directly into my face, Bobbi said: don't fucking use me. She held my eyes for a second, with a terrifying seriousness, and then she turned back to the cashier.

I went to get my jacket. I knew that no one was watching me, that no one cared what I thought or did, and I seemed to feel myself almost vibrating with the power of this perverse new freedom. I could scream or take my clothes off if I wanted, I could walk in front of a bus on my way home, who would know? Bobbi wouldn't follow me. Nick wouldn't even be seen speaking to me in public.

I walked home on my own without telling anyone I was leaving. My feet were throbbing by the time I unlocked the front door. That night in bed I sat up and downloaded a dating app on my phone. I even put up a picture of myself, one of Melissa's pictures, where my lips were parted and my eyes looked big and spooky. I heard Bobbi come home, I heard her drop her bag in the hall instead of hanging it up. She was singing "Green Rocky Road" to herself, loudly enough that I knew she was drunk. I sat in the dark scrolling through a series of strangers in my area. I tried to think about them, to think about letting them kiss me, but instead I kept thinking of Nick, his face looking up at me from my pillow, reaching to touch my breast like he owned it.

I didn't tell my mother that I'd brought the little leather copy of the New Testament back to Dublin with me. I knew she wouldn't notice it was gone, and if I tried to explain, she wouldn't understand why it interested me. My favourite part of the gospels was in Matthew, when Jesus said: love your enemies, bless those who curse you, do good to those who hate you, and pray for those who spitefully use you and persecute you. I shared in this desire for moral superiority over my enemies. Jesus always wanted to be the better person, and so did I. I underlined this passage in red pencil several times, to illustrate that I understood the Christian way of life.

The Bible made a lot more sense to me, almost perfect sense, if I pictured Bobbi as the Jesus character. She didn't deliver his lines entirely straight; often she pronounced them sarcastically, or with a weird, distant expression. The bit about husbands and wives was satirical, whereas the passage about loving your enemies she played sincerely. It made sense to me that she would befriend adulteresses, and also that she would have a pack of disciples spreading her message.

The day after the book launch, a Friday, I wrote Bobbi a long email apologising for what had happened between us in the bookshop. I tried to explain that I had felt vulnerable, but I did so without using the word "vulnerable" or any synonyms. I did say sorry, I said that several times. She replied within a few minutes:

it's okay, i forgive you. but lately i sometimes feel like i'm watching you disappear.

I stood up from my desk after reading this email and remembered I was in the college library, but without really seeing the library environment around me. I found my way to the bathrooms and locked myself in a stall. A mouthful of sour fluid washed up from my stomach and I leaned over the toilet basin to be sick. My body was gone then, vanished somewhere no one would ever see it again. Who would miss it? I wiped my mouth with a single square of tissue paper, flushed the toilet and went back upstairs. My MacBook screen had gone black and radiated a perfect rectangular glow from the reflected ceiling light. I sat back down, logged out of my email, and continued reading a James Baldwin essay.

I didn't exactly start praying that weekend after the book launch, but I did look up online how to meditate. It mainly involved closing my eyes and breathing, while also calmly letting go of passing thoughts. I focused on my breathing, you were allowed to do that. You could even count the breaths. And then at the end you could just think about anything, anything you wanted, but after five minutes of counting my breath, I didn't want to think. My mind felt empty, like the inside of a glass jar. I was appropriating my fear of total disappearance as a spiritual practice. I was inhabiting disappearance as something that could reveal and inform, rather than totalise and annihilate. A lot of the time my meditation was unsuccessful.

My father called me on Monday night at about eleven to say he had put my allowance in the bank that day. His voice rolled around on the line uncertainly and I felt a drenching sense of guilt. Oh, thanks, I said.

I put in a few extra quid for you, he said. You never know when you'll need it.

You shouldn't have. I have enough money.

Well, treat yourself to something nice.

After this phone call I felt restless and too warm, as if I had just run up a staircase. I tried lying down, but it didn't help. Nick had sent me an email that day containing a link to a Joanna Newsom song. I sent back a link to the Billie Holiday recording of "I'm a Fool to Want You", but he didn't reply.

I went into the living room, where Bobbi was watching a documentary about Algeria. She patted the couch cushion beside her and I sat down.

Do you ever feel like you don't know what you're doing with your life? I said.

I'm actually watching this, said Bobbi.

I looked at the screen, where old wartime footage was overlaid with a voice-over explaining the role of the French military. I said: sometimes I just feel. And Bobbi placed a finger over her lips and said: Frances. I'm watching.

On Wednesday night I matched with somebody called Rossa on the dating thing and he sent me a couple of messages. He asked me if I wanted to meet up and I said: sure. We went for a drink together in a bar on Westmoreland Street. He was in college too, studying medicine. I didn't tell him about the problems I'd had with my uterus. Actually I bragged about how healthy I was. He talked about how hard he had worked in school, which he seemed to consider a formative experience, and I said I was happy for him.

I've never worked hard at anything, I said.

That must be why you study English.

Then he said that he was just joking, and actually he had won his school's gold medal for composition. I love poetry, he said. I love Yeats.

Yeah, I said. If there's one thing you can say for fascism, it had some good poets.

He didn't have anything else to say about poetry after that. Afterwards he invited me back to his apartment and I let him unbutton my blouse. I thought: this is normal. This is a normal thing to do. He had a small, soft upper body, not at all like Nick, and he did none of the usual things that Nick did to me before we had sex, like touching me for a long time and talking in a low voice. It started right away, with no introduction really. Physically I felt almost nothing, just a mild discomfort. I let myself become rigid and silent, waiting for Rossa to notice my rigidity and stop what he was doing, but he didn't. I considered asking him to stop, but the idea that he might ignore me felt more serious than the situation needed to be. Don't get yourself into a big legal thing, I thought. I lay there and let him continue. He asked me if I liked it rough and I told him I didn't think so, but he pulled my hair anyway. I wanted to laugh, and after that I hated myself for feeling superior.

When I got home, I went to my room and took a single plastic-wrapped bandage from the drawer. I am normal, I thought. I have a body like anyone else. Then I scratched my arm open until it bled, just a faint spot of blood, widening into a droplet. I counted to three and afterwards opened the bandage, placed it carefully over my arm, and disposed of the plastic wrap.

CHAPTER
TWENTY-TWO

The next day I started to write a story. It was a Thursday, I didn't have class until three, and I was sitting up in bed with a cup of black coffee on my bedside cabinet. I didn't plan to write a story, I just noticed after some time that I wasn't hitting the return key and that the lines were forming full sentences and attaching to each other like prose. When I stopped, I had written over three thousand words. It was past three o'clock and I hadn't eaten. I lifted my hands from the keyboard and in the light from the window they looked emaciated. When I did get out of bed, a wave of dizziness came over me, breaking everything into a shower of visual noise. I made myself four slices of toast and ate them without butter. I saved the file as "b". It was the first story I ever wrote.

Bobbi and Philip and I went for milkshakes after the cinema that night. During the film I had checked my phone six times to see if Nick had replied to a message I sent him. He hadn't. Bobbi was wearing a denim jacket and a lipstick that was such a dark purple it was nearly black. I folded our milkshake receipt up into a complex geometrical pattern, while Philip tried to convince us to start performing together again. We were being evasive about it, though I didn't know why exactly.

I have college work, Bobbi said. And Frances has a secret boyfriend.

I looked up at her with an expression of total horror. I could feel it in my teeth, a hard banging of shock in the nerve endings. She frowned.

What? Bobbi said. He already knows, he was talking about it the other day.

Talking about what? said Philip.

About Frances and Nick, Bobbi said.

Philip stared at her, and then at me. Bobbi lifted her hand to her mouth, slowly, the hand flat and horizontal, and gave one tiny shake of her head. It was enough to signal to me that she was really freaked out and not playing a game.

I thought you knew, said Bobbi. I thought you said it the other day.

You're joking, Philip said. You're not really having some kind of affair with him, are you?

I tried to work my mouth into a sort of casual expression. Melissa was going away to visit her sister for the weekend, and I had messaged Nick asking if he wanted to come and stay with me while she was gone. Bobbi won't mind, I wrote. He had seen the message and not replied.

He's fucking married, said Philip.

Don't be a moralist, Bobbi said. That's all we need.

I just continued folding my mouth up smaller and smaller and didn't look at anyone.

222

Is he going to leave his wife? said Philip.

Bobbi scrubbed at her eye with a fist. Quietly and with a tiny mouth I said: no.

After a long and uninterrupted silence at our table, Philip looked at me and said: I didn't think you would let someone take advantage of you like that. He had a choked, embarrassed expression on his face while he pronounced these words, and I felt sorry for all of us, like we were just little children pretending to be adults. He left then and Bobbi slid his half-finished milkshake across the table toward me.

I'm sorry, she said. I honestly thought he knew.

I decided to drink as much milkshake as I could without taking a breath. When my mouth started hurting I didn't stop. I didn't stop when my head started hurting either. I didn't stop until Bobbi said: Frances, are you planning to drown there? Then I looked up like everything was normal and said: what?

Nick invited me to come out and stay in his house that weekend. He was cooking when I arrived on Friday evening and I was so relieved to see him that I wanted to make some kind of silly romantic gesture, like throwing myself into his arms. I didn't. I sat at the table chewing my fingernails. He told me I was being quiet and I tore a piece off my thumbnail with my teeth and looked at the nail critically.

So maybe I should tell you, I said, I slept with this guy I met on Tinder the other day.

Oh, really?

Nick was cutting vegetables into small pieces in the neat methodical way he always did. He liked to cook, he told me it relaxed him.

You're not angry or anything, are you? I said.

Why would I be angry? You can sleep with other people if you want to.

I know. I just feel foolish. I think it was a stupid thing to do.

Oh really? he said. What was he like?

Nick hadn't looked up from the chopping board. He moved the diced onion pieces to one side of the board with the flat part of his knife and started to slice a red pepper.

He was awful, I said. He told me he loved Yeats, can you believe that? I practically had to stop him reciting "The Lake Isle of Innisfree" in the bar.

Wow, I feel terrible for you.

And the sex was bad.

No one who likes Yeats is capable of human intimacy.

We ate dinner without touching one another. The dog woke up and wanted to be let out, and I helped clear the plates into the dishwasher. Nick went outside for a cigarette and left the door open so we could talk. I felt like he wanted me to leave and he was too polite to say so. He asked how Bobbi was. Okay, I said. How's Melissa? He shrugged. Finally he put the cigarette out and we went upstairs. I got onto his bed and started to undress.

And you're sure this is what you want? Nick said.

He was always saying this kind of thing, so I just said yes or nodded and unbuckled the belt I was wearing.

Behind me I heard him say abruptly: because I just feel, I don't know. I turned around and he was standing there, rubbing his left shoulder with his hand.

You seem kind of distant, he said. If you'd rather be . . . If there's somewhere else you'd rather be, I don't want you to feel like you're trapped here.

No. I'm sorry. I didn't mean to seem distant.

No, I'm not . . . I feel like I'm having trouble talking to you. Maybe it's my fault, I don't know. I feel kind of . . .

He never usually trailed off his sentences this way. I started to feel agitated. I said again that I didn't mean to be distant with him. I didn't understand what he was trying to say and I was afraid of what it might have been.

If you're doing this for any reason other than just wanting to, he said, then don't do it. I really don't, you know, I don't have any interest in that.

I murmured something like sure, of course, but in fact it was unclear to me what he was talking about now. It sounded like he was worried that I'd developed feelings for him and he was trying to say that he wasn't interested in anything other than sex. Anyway I agreed with him whatever he meant.

In bed he went on top and we didn't make eye contact very much. Impulsively I lifted one of his hands and pressed it against my throat. He held it still for a few seconds and then said: what do you want me to do? I shrugged. I want you to kill me, I thought. He stroked the hard muscle of my throat with his fingers and then lifted his hand away.

After it was over, he asked me about the bandage on my arm. Did you hurt it? he said. I looked at it but didn't say anything. I could hear Nick breathing, hard, like he was tired. I felt a lot of things I didn't want to feel. I felt that I was a damaged person who deserved nothing.

Would you ever hit me? I said. I mean if I asked you to.

Nick didn't look over at me, his eyes were closed. He said: uh, I don't know. Why? Do you want me to? I closed my eyes too, and breathed out very slowly until there was no air in my lungs and my stomach was small and flat.

Yeah, I said. I want you to do it now.

What?

I want you to hit me.

I don't think I want to do that, he said.

I knew that he was sitting up now, looking down at me, though I kept my eyes closed.

Some people like it, I said.

You mean during sex? I didn't realise you were interested in that kind of thing.

I opened my eyes then. He was frowning.

Wait, are you okay? he said. Why are you crying?

I'm not crying.

Incidentally it turned out that I was crying. It was just something my eyes were doing while we were talking. He touched the side of my face where it was wet.

I'm not crying, I said.

Do you think I want to hurt you?

I could feel tears coming out of my eyes, but they didn't feel hot like real tears. They felt cool like little streams from a lake.

I don't know, I said. I'm just telling you that you can.

But is it something you want me to do?

You can do whatever you want with me.

Yeah, he said. I'm sorry. I don't really know what to say to that.

I dried my face with my wrist. Never mind, I said. Forget about it. Let's try and get some sleep. Nick didn't say anything at first, he just lay there. I didn't look over, but I sensed the tension of his body on the mattress, like he was preparing to sit up suddenly. Finally he said: you know we've talked about this, you can't just lash out at me whenever you feel bad.

I'm not lashing out, I said.

How would you feel if I was sleeping with other women and then coming to your house to brag about it?

I froze. I had actually forgotten by then about the date with Rossa. Nick's reaction when I'd told him had been so blank that the incident immediately felt insignificant, and I hadn't thought of it again. I hadn't even considered that it might have prompted Nick's strange mood. Privately I had to admit that if he'd done the same thing to me — sought out another woman, had meaningless sex with her, and then flippantly told me about it while I prepared his dinner — I would never have wanted to see him again. But that was different.

You're fucking married, I said.

Yeah, thanks. That's very helpful. I guess because I'm married that means you can just treat me however you want.

I can't believe you're trying to play the victim.

I'm not, he said. But I think if you're honest with yourself, you're actually glad I'm married, because it means you can act out and I have to take the blame for everything.

I wasn't used to being attacked like this and it was frightening. I thought of myself as an independent person, so independent that the opinions of others were irrelevant to me. Now I was afraid that Nick was right: I isolated myself from criticism so I could behave badly without losing my sense of righteousness.

You promised me you were going to tell Melissa about us, I said. How do you think I feel about lying to everyone all the time?

I don't think it bothers you that much. To be honest, I think you only want me to tell her because you'd like to see us fighting.

If that's what you think of me, why are we even doing this?

I don't know, he said.

I got out of bed then and started to put my clothes on. He thought I was a cruel and petty person intent on destroying his marriage. He didn't know why he was still seeing me; he didn't know. I buttoned my blouse, feeling a humiliation so deep it was difficult to breathe comfortably.

What are you doing? he said.

I think I should go.

He said okay. I pulled on my cardigan and stood up from the bed. I knew what I was going to tell him, the most desperate thing I could possibly tell him, as if even in the depths of my indignity I craved something worse.

The problem isn't that you're married, I said. The problem is that I love you and you obviously don't love me.

He took a deep breath in and said: you're being unbelievably dramatic, Frances.

Fuck you, I said.

I slammed his bedroom door hard on my way out. He shouted something at me on my way down the stairs but I didn't hear what it was. I walked to the bus stop, knowing that my humiliation was now complete. Even though I had known Nick didn't love me, I had continued to let him have sex with me whenever he wanted, out of desperation and a naive hope that he didn't understand what he was inflicting on me. Now even that hope was gone. He knew that I loved him, that he was exploiting my tender feelings for him, and he didn't care. There was nothing to be done. On the bus home I chewed the inside of my cheek and stared out the black window until I tasted blood.

CHAPTER
TWENTY-THREE

When I tried to withdraw some cash for food on Monday morning, the ATM said I had insufficient funds. I was standing in the rain on Thomas Street with a canvas bag under my arm, feeling a pain behind my eyes. I tried the card again, though a small queue had formed and I could hear someone quietly call me a "fucking tourist". The machine wheeled my card back out with a clicking noise.

I walked to the bank holding the canvas bag over my hair. Inside I stood in a line with people in business suits while a cool female voice announced things like: counter four, please. When I got to one of the windows, the boy behind the glass asked me to insert my card. His name badge read "Darren" and he looked like he had not quite entered adolescence. After looking at the computer screen quickly, Darren said I was thirty-six euro in overdraft.

Sorry? I said. Excuse me, sorry, what?

He turned the screen around and showed me the most recent figures from the account: twenty-euro notes I had taken out of ATMs, coffees I had paid for by card. No money had come in for over a month. I felt the blood drain out of my face, and I distinctly remember thinking: this child who works in the bank thinks I'm stupid now.

Sorry, I said.

Were you expecting a payment into the account?

Yeah. Sorry.

It could take three to five working days for the payment to come through, Darren said kindly. Depending on how it was lodged.

I saw my own reflected outline in the glass window, pale and unpleasant.

Thanks, I said. I see what's happened there. Thank you.

When I walked out of the bank, I stood outside the doors and dialled my father's number. He didn't pick up. I called my mother, still standing there in the street, and she answered. I told her what had happened.

Dad told me he paid my allowance, I said.

He must have just forgotten, love.

But he called me and told me that he did it.

Have you tried calling him? she said.

He won't answer.

Well, I can help you out, she said. I'll put fifty in your account this afternoon while you're waiting to hear back from him. All right?

I was about to explain that once the overdraft was paid, that would only make up fourteen euro, but I didn't.

Thanks, I said.

Don't you worry.

We hung up.

When I got home I had an email from Valerie. She reminded me that she was interested in reading my work and said Melissa had passed on my email address. That I had managed to leave any lasting impact on Valerie filled me with a sense of spiteful triumph. Although she had ignored me at dinner, I was now the interesting thing she wanted to unravel. In this triumphantly recriminatory mood, I sent her the new story, without even looking it over again for typos. The world was like a crumpled ball of newspaper to me, something to kick around.

That evening the sickness started to happen again. I'd finished my second sheet of pills two days before, and when I sat down to eat dinner the food felt gluey and wrong in my mouth. I scraped my plate into the bin but the smell turned my stomach and I started to sweat. My back hurt and I could feel my mouth watering. When I pressed the back of my hand against my forehead it felt damp and scalding. It was happening again, I knew that, but I could do nothing.

At about 4a.m. I went to the bathroom to get sick. Once my stomach was empty I lay on the bathroom floor shivering, while the pain moved up my spine like an animal. I thought: maybe I'll die, who cares? I was conscious that I was bleeding copiously. When I felt well enough to crawl, I crawled to bed. I saw that Nick had sent me a text in the middle of the night saying: i tried calling you, can we talk? I knew that he didn't want to see me any more. He was a patient person and I had exhausted the patience. I hated the terrible things I had said to him, I hated what they revealed about me.

I wanted him to be cruel now, because I deserved it. I wanted him to say the most vicious things he could think of, or shake me until I couldn't breathe.

The pain was still there in the morning but I decided to go to class anyway. I took a minor overdose of paracetamol and wrapped up in a coat before leaving the house. It rained all the way into college. I sat at the back of the classroom shivering and set up a stopwatch on my laptop to tell me when I could take my next dose. Several fellow students asked if I was okay, and after class even the lecturer asked me. He seemed nice, so I told him I had missed a lot of classes for medical reasons and now I wasn't allowed to miss any more. He looked at me and said: oh. I smiled winningly despite the shivering and then my alarm went off to tell me I could have more paracetamol.

I went to the library after that to start an essay that was due in two weeks' time. My clothes were still damp from the rain and I could hear a thin ringing noise in my right ear, but I mostly ignored that. My real concern was for the acuity of my critical faculties. I wasn't sure if I remembered exactly what the word "epistemic" meant, or if I was still able to read. For a few minutes I laid my head down on the library table and listened to the ringing noise get louder and louder, until it felt almost like a friend who was talking to me. You could die, I thought, and it was a nice relaxing thought at the time. I imagined death like a switch, switching off all the pain and noise, cancelling everything.

When I left the library it was still raining and it felt unbelievably cold. My teeth were chattering and I couldn't remember any words in English. Rain moved across the footpath in shallow waves like a special effect. I had no umbrella and I perceived that my face and hair were becoming wet, too wet to feel normal. I saw Bobbi sheltering outside the arts building and I started to walk toward her, trying to remember what people usually said to each other as a greeting. This felt effortful in an unfamiliar way. I raised my hand to wave at her and she came toward me, very quickly I thought, saying something I didn't understand.

Then I blacked out. When I woke up again I was lying under the shelter with some people standing around me, and I was saying the word: what? Everyone seemed relieved I was talking. A security guard was saying something into a walkie-talkie, but I couldn't hear him. The pain in my abdomen felt tight like a fist and I tried to sit up and see if Bobbi was there. I saw her on the phone, holding her free ear shut with a hand as if struggling to hear the other person. The rain was loud like an untuned radio.

Oh, she's awake, Bobbi said into the phone. One second.

Bobbi looked at me then. Are you okay? she said. She looked clean and dry like a model from a catalogue. My hair was leaking water onto my face. I'm fine, I said. She went back to talking on the phone, I couldn't hear what she was saying. I tried to wipe my face with my sleeve but my sleeves were even wetter than my face was. Outside the shelter the rain fell white like milk.

Bobbi put her phone away and helped me to sit up straight.

I'm sorry, I said. I'm so sorry.

Is it the thing you had before? said Bobbi.

I nodded my head. Bobbi pulled her sleeve over her hand and wiped my face. Her sweater was dry and very soft. Thanks, I said. People started to disperse, the security guard went to look around the corner.

Do you need to go back to hospital? she said.

I think they'll just tell me to wait for this scan.

Let's go home then. Okay?

She linked her arm under mine and we walked out onto Nassau Street, where there was a taxi passing right outside. The driver pulled up and let us get in the back even though the cars behind were beeping. Bobbi gave our address and I let my head loll back and gazed out the window while they talked. The streetlights bathed people's figures in angelic light. I saw shopfronts, and faces in bus windows. Then my eyes closed.

When we reached our street, Bobbi insisted on paying. Outside the building I gripped the iron railings and waited for her to unlock the door. Inside she asked me if I'd like a bath. I nodded, yes. I braced myself against the corridor wall. She went to run the bath and I slowly took off my coat. A terrific pain was beating inside my body. Bobbi reappeared in front of me and took my coat to hang it up.

Are you going to need help getting out of your clothes? she said.

I thought of the story I had sent to Valerie that morning, a story which I now remembered was explicitly about Bobbi, a story which characterised Bobbi as a mystery so total I couldn't endure her, a force I couldn't subjugate with my will, and the love of my life. I paled at this memory. Somehow I hadn't been conscious of it, or had forced myself not to be conscious, and now I remembered.

Don't get upset, she said. I've seen you undressed hundreds of times.

I tried to smile, although my breath moved in and out of my lips in a way that probably contorted the smile.

Don't remind me, I said.

Oh, come on. It wasn't all bad. We had some fun.

You sound like you're flirting.

She laughed. In the story I had described a house party after the Leaving Cert, when I drank a shoulder of vodka and then spent the night throwing up. Whenever anyone tried to look after me I would push them away and say: I want Bobbi. Bobbi wasn't even at the party.

I'll undress you in a very unsexy way, she said. Don't worry.

The bath was still running. We went inside the bathroom and I sat on the closed toilet seat while she rolled her sleeves up to test the temperature. She told me it was hot. I was wearing a white blouse that day, and I tried to undo the buttons but my hands were trembling. Bobbi shut the tap off and crouched down to finish unbuttoning for me. Her fingers were wet and left little dark prints around the buttonholes. She scooped my arms out of the sleeves easily, like she was peeling a potato.

And there's going to be blood everywhere, I said.

Lucky it's me here and not your boyfriend.

No, don't. I'm fighting with him. It's, uh. Things aren't very good.

She stood up and went to the bath again. She seemed distracted suddenly. In the white bathroom light her hair and fingernails gleamed.

Does he know you're sick? she said.

I shook my head. She said something about getting me a towel and then left the room. Gradually I stood up, finished undressing myself and managed to climb into the bath.

In the story I had included an anecdote in which I did not appear. Bobbi had gone to study in Berlin for six weeks when we were sixteen, staying with a family who had a daughter our age called Liese. One night, without saying anything, Bobbi and Liese went to bed together. They were quiet, not wanting Liese's parents to hear, and they never talked about it afterwards. Bobbi did not dwell on the sensory aspects of the incident, on whether she had nursed a desire for Liese before it happened, whether she knew of Liese's feelings, or even what it was like. If anyone else in school had told me the same thing, I wouldn't have believed them, but because it was Bobbi I knew immediately that it was true. I wanted Bobbi, and, like Liese, I would have done anything to be with her. She told me this story by way of explaining to me that she wasn't a virgin. She pronounced Liese's name without any particular love or hatred, just a girl she had known, and for months afterwards, maybe forever afterwards, I was afraid that someday she would say my name that way too.

The water was soapy and a little too hot. It left a rim of pink on my leg where it touched me. I forced myself to get all the way down into the tub, where the water licked me obscenely. I tried to visualise the pain draining out of my body, draining out into the water and dissolving. Bobbi knocked on the door and came in holding a big pink towel, one of the new ones she had brought with her from her parents' house. She started to hang it on the towel rack while I closed my eyes. I heard her leave the bathroom again, a tap running in the other room, her bedroom door opening and closing. I could hear her voice, she must have been on the phone.

After a few minutes, she came back into the bathroom holding her phone outstretched toward me.

It's Nick, she said.

What?

Nick's on the phone for you.

My hands were wet. I lifted one of them out of the water and reached to dry it clumsily on a bathtowel before accepting the phone from her hand. She left the room again.

Hey, are you okay? said Nick's voice.

I closed my eyes. He had a gentle tone in his voice and I wanted to climb into it, like it was something hollow I could be suspended inside.

I'm feeling all right now, I said. Thank you.

Bobbi told me what happened. It must have been really frightening.

For a few seconds neither of us said anything, and then we both started speaking.

You first, I said.

He told me he would like to come and see me. I said he was welcome to. He asked if I needed anything and I said no.

Okay, he said. I'll get in the car. What were you going to say?

I'll tell you when I see you.

I hung up and carefully placed the phone on the dry part of the bathmat. Then I closed my eyes again and let the warmth of the water into my body, the synthetic fruit scent of shampoo, the hard plastic of the tub, the fog of steam that wet my face. I was meditating. I was counting my breaths.

After what seemed like a long time, fifteen minutes or half an hour, Bobbi came back in. I opened my eyes and the room was very bright, radiantly bright, and strangely beautiful. All okay? Bobbi said. I told her Nick was coming over and she said: good. She sat on the side of the bath and I watched her take a packet of cigarettes and a lighter from her cardigan.

What she said to me after she lit the cigarette was: are you going to write a book? I realised then that she hadn't answered Philip's questions about our performances because on some level she knew that something had changed, that I was working on something new. The fact that she had noticed this gave me a kind of confidence but also served to demonstrate that nothing about me was impenetrable to Bobbi. When it came to sordid or mundane things, she might be slow to notice, but real changes that occurred inside me were never hidden from her.

I don't know, I said. Are you?

She screwed one eye shut like it was bothering her and then opened it again.

Why would I write a book? she said. I'm not a writer.

What are you going to do? After we graduate.

I don't know. Work in a university if I can.

This phrase, "if I can", made it clear that Bobbi was trying to tell me something serious, something that couldn't be communicated in words but instead through a shift in the way we related to each other. Not only was it nonsense for Bobbi to say "if I can" at the end of her sentence, because she came from a wealthy family, read diligently and had good grades, but it didn't make sense in the context of our relationship either. Bobbi didn't relate to me in the "if I can" sense. She related to me as a person, maybe the only person, who understood her ferocious and frightening power over circumstances and people. What she wanted, she could have, I knew that.

What do you mean "if"? I said.

This was too obvious, and for a while Bobbi said nothing and picked a loose hair off the sleeve of her cardigan instead.

I thought you were planning to bring down global capitalism, I said.

Well, not on my own. Someone has to do the small jobs.

240

I just don't see you as a small-jobs person.

That's what I am, she said.

I didn't really know what I'd meant by a "small-jobs person". I believed in small jobs, like raising children, picking fruit, cleaning. They were the jobs I considered the most valuable, the jobs that struck me as deserving the most respect of all. It confused me that suddenly I was telling Bobbi that a job in a university wasn't good enough for her, but it also confused me to imagine Bobbi doing something so sedate and ordinary. My skin was the same temperature as the water, and I moved one knee outside, into the cold air, before dipping it back down again.

Well, you'll be a world-famous professor, I said. You'll lecture at the Sorbonne.

No.

She seemed irritable, almost about to express something, but then her eyes became calm and remote.

You think everyone you like is special, she said.

I tried to sit up and the bathtub was hard on my bones.

I'm just a normal person, she said. When you get to like someone, you make them feel like they're different from everyone else. You're doing it with Nick, you did it with me once.

No.

She looked up at me, without any cruelty or anger at all, and said: I'm not trying to upset you.

But you are upsetting me, I said.

Well, I'm sorry.

I gave a little grimace. Down on the bathmat her phone started buzzing. She picked it up and said: hello? Yeah, give me one second. Then she hung up again. It was Nick, she was going out to the hall to buzz him in.

I lay there in the bath not thinking, not doing anything. After a few seconds, I heard her open the front door, and then her voice saying: she's had a really rough day, so just be nice to her. And Nick said: I know, I will. I loved them both so much in this moment that I wanted to appear in front of them like a benevolent ghost and sprinkle blessings into their lives. Thank you, I wanted to say. Thank you both. You are my family now.

Nick came into the bathroom and shut the door behind him. There's that beautiful coat, I said. He was wearing it. He smiled, he rubbed at one of his eyes. I was worried about you, he said. I'm glad you're feeling well enough to fetishise commodities as usual. Are you in pain? I shrugged. Not so much any more, I said. He kept looking at me. Then he started looking down at his shoes. He swallowed. Are you okay? I said. He nodded, he wiped at his nose with his sleeve. I'm happy to see you, he said. His voice sounded thick. Don't worry, I said. I'm fine. He looked up at the ceiling, like he was laughing at himself, and his eyes were wet. It's good to hear that, he said.

I told him I wanted to get out of the bath and he took the towel off the rack for me. When I stood up out of the water he looked at me in a way that was not at all vulgar, the kind of look you can give someone's body when you've seen it many times and it has a particular relationship to you. I didn't look away from him then or even feel embarrassed. I tried to imagine how I must have looked: dripping wet, flushed with steam heat, my hair leaking rivulets of water down my shoulders. I watched him standing there, not blinking, his expression calm and fathomless like an ocean. We didn't have to speak then. He wrapped the cloth around me and I got out of the bath.

CHAPTER
TWENTY-FOUR

In my room Nick sat on the bed while I dressed in clean pyjamas and towelled my hair. We could hear Bobbi strumming her ukulele in the other room. Peace seemed to radiate outwards from the inside of my body. I was tired and very weak, but these were also peaceful feelings in their own way. Eventually I came to sit beside Nick and he put his arm around me. I could smell cigarette smoke on the collar of his shirt. He asked about my health, and I told him I'd been to hospital in August and that I was waiting for an ultrasound. He touched my hair and said he was very sorry I hadn't told him about it before. I said I didn't want him to pity me and for a while he was quiet.

I'm really sorry about the other night, he said. I felt like you were trying to hurt my feelings and I overreacted, I'm sorry.

For some reason all I could say was: it's all right, don't worry. Those were the only words that would come, so I said them as soothingly as I could.

All right, he said. Well, can I tell you something?

I nodded.

I spoke to Melissa, he said. I told her we've been seeing each other. Is that okay?

I closed my eyes. What happened? I said quietly.

We talked for a while. I think she's all right. I told her that I wanted to keep seeing you and she understands that, so.

You didn't have to do that.

I should have done it at the beginning, he said. There was no need to put you through any of this, I was just being cowardly.

We were silent for a few seconds. I felt blissfully tired, like each cell in my body was winding down into a deep private sleep of its own.

I know I'm not a great guy, he said. But I do love you, you know. Of course I do. I'm sorry I didn't tell you before, but I didn't know if you wanted to hear it. I'm sorry.

I was smiling. My eyes were closed still. It felt good to be wrong about everything. Since when have you loved me? I said.

Since I met you, I would think. If I wanted to be very philosophical about it, I'd say I loved you before then.

Oh, you're making me very happy.

Am I? he said. That's good. I want to make you very happy.

I love you too.

He kissed my forehead. When he spoke, his words were light but in his voice I heard a concealed emotion, which moved me. All right, he said. Well, you've suffered enough. Let's just be very happy from now on.

The next day, I received an email from Melissa. I was sitting in the library, typing up a page of notes, when her email arrived. I decided that before reading it I would take a walk around the library desks. Slowly I arose from my seat and began my walk. Inside, everything was very brown. Out of the windows I could see a rattle of wind making its way through the trees. On the cricket green a woman in shorts was running with her elbows working up and down like small pistons. I cast a glance back at my own library desk to ensure my laptop was still there. It sat glowing ominously into the nothingness. I walked halfway around the room before looping back to my own seat, as if this circuit around the library desks was actually a physical endurance test of some kind. Then I opened the email.

> Hi Frances. I'm not angry at you, I want you to know that. I'm just getting in touch with you because I think it's important that we're on the same page with this. Nick doesn't want to leave me & I don't want to leave him. We are going to keep living together & being married. I'm putting this in an email because I don't trust Nick to be straight with you about it. He has a weak personality & compulsively tells people what they want to hear. In short if you're sleeping with my husband because you secretly believe that one day he will be your husband, then you're making a serious mistake. He's not going to divorce me & if he did he would never marry you. Equally if you're sleeping with him because you believe his affection proves you to be a good person, or even a smart or attractive person, you should know that Nick is not primarily attracted to

good-looking or morally worthy people. He likes partners who take complete responsibility for all his decisions, that's all. You will not be able to draw a sustainable sense of self-respect from this relationship you're in. I'm sure you find his total acquiescence charming now, but over the course of a marriage it actually becomes exhausting. Fighting with him is impossible because he's pathologically submissive, & you can't scream at him without hating yourself. I know because today I screamed at him for a long time. Because I myself have "made mistakes" in the past, it's hard to feel truly cathartically wronged by the fact that he's been having sex with a 21-year-old behind my back, & I hate that. I feel like any other person would feel in this situation. I've cried copiously, not only in fits & starts but also for sustained periods of over an hour each. But just because I once slept with another woman at a literary festival & then several years later while Nick was in psychiatric hospital began an affair with his best friend which continued even after I knew Nick had found out about it, my feelings don't count. I know I'm a monster & he probably tells you bad things about me. Sometimes I find myself thinking: if I'm so awful, why doesn't he leave me? And I know what kind of person has those thoughts about their own spouse. The kind of person who later murders their spouse, probably. I wouldn't murder Nick but it's important for you to know that if I tried, he would absolutely go with it. Even if he figured out that I was planning his murder he wouldn't bring it up in case it upset me. I've become so used to seeing him as pathetic & even contemptible that I forgot anybody else could love him. Other women have always lost interest once they got to know him. But not you. You love him, don't you? He tells me your father is an alcoholic, so was mine. I wonder if we gravitate toward Nick because he gives us a sense of control that was lacking in childhood. I actually believed him when he told me nothing had happened between you & it was just a crush. I felt relieved, isn't that terrible? I thought oh well, he only met you during the summer, he still wasn't really himself then, he's been so much better since. And now I realise that you're actually a function of the betterness, or it's a function of you. Are you making my husband better, Frances? What gives you the right to do that? He's awake during the day now, I've noticed. He's started replying to emails & answering the phone again. When I'm at work he sometimes sends me interesting articles about leftists in Greece. Does he send you the same ones or are they personalised? I admit I'm threatened by your extreme youth. It's very shocking thinking about your own husband being into younger women. I never noticed it before with him. 21 is young, right? But what if you were 19, would he still have done it then? Is he the kind of morbid guy in his 30s who secretly finds 15-year-old girls attractive? Has he ever used the search term "teen"? These are things I didn't have to think about before you came into our lives. Now I wonder if he hates me. I didn't hate him when it was me seeing someone else; in fact I think I liked him more, but if he tried to tell me that I'd want to spit at him. I think most of all I'm shocked that he doesn't want to do the easy thing & leave you. That's how I know I've been replaced. He says he still loves me, but if he doesn't do what I say any more, then how can I believe him? Of course he never overreacted like this in my case, & I always thought I was so lucky that he didn't. Now I wonder if he ever loved me at all. It's hard to imagine marrying someone you don't love, but actually it's just the kind of thing Nick would do, out of loyalty & a craving for punishment. Do you know him that way too, or am I the only one? Part of me wishes I could be friends with you. I used to find you very cold & unkind, and at first I thought it was because of Bobbi, which I resented. Now that I know it was just jealousy & fear, I feel differently about you. But you don't need to be jealous, Frances. For Nick you're probably indistinguishable from happiness. I don't doubt that he considers you the great love of his adult life. He & I never had a tempestuous affair behind anyone's back. I know I can't ask him to stop seeing you, although I want to. I could ask you to stop seeing him, but why should I? Things are better now, even I can see that. I used to come home in the evening & he'd be in bed already. Or else sitting in front of the TV having not changed the channel since he woke up. Once I came home & saw him watching some kind of softcore pornographic film where two cheerleaders were kissing each other, & when he saw me he shrugged & said "I'm not watching this, I just didn't know where the remote was." At the time I actually pretended not to believe him, because I thought it would be less upsetting if he were really watching the cheerleader film rather than just sitting there reluctantly allowing the film to keep playing because he was too depressed to find the remote. Now I keep thinking about all the evenings I've come home this month & he's been cooking & listening to something on the radio. And he's always clean-shaven & asking me how my day was & his gym clothes are always in the washing machine. I see him looking in the mirror sometimes with quite an appraising expression. Of course, how could I not have known? But I always said I wanted him to be happy, & now I know it was true all along. I do want that. Even when it looks like this I still want it. So. Anyway. Maybe we could all have dinner together some time. (I'll invite Bobbi too.)

I read the email several times. It seemed like an affectation on Melissa's part not to include paragraph breaks, as if she was saying: look at the tide of emotion that has swept over me. I also believed she had edited the email carefully for effect, the effect being: always remember who is the writer, Frances. It is me, and not you. These were the thoughts I sprang to, unkind thoughts. She didn't call me a bad person, she didn't say any of the horrible things about me that the situation would excuse. Maybe a tide of emotion really did sweep over her. The part of the email about my youth affected me, and I realised it didn't matter whether it was calculated or not. I was young and she was older. That was enough to make me feel bad, like I had put extra coins into the vending machine. On the second reading I let my eyes skip over that section.

The only part of the email I really wanted to know about was the information relating to Nick. He had been in psychiatric hospital, which was news to me. I wasn't repelled as such; I had read books, I was familiar with the idea that capitalism was the really crazy thing. But I had thought people who were hospitalised for psychiatric problems were different from the people I knew. I could see I had entered a new social setting now, where severe mental illness no longer had unfashionable connotations. I was going through a second upbringing: learning a new set of assumptions, and feigning a greater level of understanding than I really possessed. By this logic Nick and Melissa were like my parents bringing me into the world, probably hating and loving me even more than my original parents did. This also meant I was Bobbi's evil twin, which didn't seem at the time like taking the metaphor too far.

I followed this pattern of thought superficially, like letting my eyes follow the trajectory of a passing car. My body was twisted up in the library chair like a coiled spring and my legs were crossed twice over, the arch of my left foot pressed tightly into the base of the chair. I felt guilty that Nick had been so ill, and that I knew about it now even though he had chosen not to tell me. I didn't know how to handle the information. In the email Melissa had been callous about it, like Nick's illness was a dark comic backdrop to her affair, and I wondered if she felt that way or if that was a way of disguising what she really felt. I thought of Evelyn in the bookshop telling him again and again how well he looked.

After an hour, the email I wrote in response was as follows:

Lots to think about. Dinner sounds good.

CHAPTER
TWENTY-FIVE

It was the middle of October by then. I put some cash together from whatever I could find in my room, as well as some birthday and Christmas money I'd forgotten to lodge in the bank. Altogether this came to forty-three euro, four fifty of which I spent in a German supermarket buying bread, pasta and tinned tomatoes. In the mornings I asked Bobbi for the use of her milk and she waved me away like: use whatever you want. Jerry gave her an allowance every week, and I also noticed she had started wearing a new black wool coat with tortoiseshell buttons. I didn't want to tell her what had happened with my account, so I just described myself as "broke" in a tone of voice I calculated to be flippant. Every morning and evening I called my father, and every morning and evening he didn't pick up.

We did go to Melissa and Nick's house to have dinner. We went more than once. Increasingly I noticed that Bobbi had started to enjoy Nick's company, even to enjoy it more than the company of Melissa or myself. When the four of us spent time together, she and Nick often engaged in pretend arguments or other competitive activities from which Melissa and I were excluded. They played video games after dinner, or magnetic travel chess, while Melissa and I talked about impressionism. Once when they were drunk they even raced each other around the back garden. Nick won but he was tired afterwards, and Bobbi called him "elderly" and threw dead leaves on him. She asked Melissa: who's prettier, Nick or me? Melissa looked at me and in an arch tone she replied: I love all my children equally. Bobbi's relationship with Nick affected me in a curious way. Seeing them together, each giving the other all of their attention, gave me a weird aesthetic thrill. Physically they were perfect, like twins. At times I caught myself wishing they would move closer or even touch one another, as if I was trying to complete something which in my mind remained unfinished.

We often had political discussions, in which we all shared similar positions but expressed ourselves differently. Bobbi, for example, was an insurrectionist, while Melissa, from a grim pessimism, tended to favour the rule of law. Nick and I fell somewhere between the two of them, more comfortable with critique than endorsement. We talked one night about the endemic racism of criminal justice in the US, the videos of police brutality that we had all seen without ever seeking them out, and what it meant for us as white people to say they were "difficult to watch", which we all agreed they were although we couldn't fix on one exact meaning for this difficulty. There was one particular video of a black teenage girl in a bathing suit crying for her mother while a white police officer knelt on her back, which Nick said made him feel so physically ill he couldn't finish watching it.

I realise that's indulgent, he said. But I also thought, what good even comes of me finishing it? Which is depressing in itself.

We also discussed whether these videos in some way contributed to a sense of European superiority, as if police forces in Europe were not endemically racist.

Which they are, Bobbi said.

Yeah, I don't think the expression is "American cops are bastards," said Nick.

Melissa said she didn't doubt that we were all a part of the problem, but it was difficult to see how exactly, and seemingly impossible to do anything about it without first comprehending that. I said I sometimes felt drawn to disclaiming my ethnicity, as if, though I was obviously white, I wasn't "really" white, like other white people.

No offence, Bobbi said, but that's honestly very unhelpful.

I'm not offended, I said. I agree.

Certain elements of my relationship with Nick had changed since he told Melissa we were together. I sent him sentimental texts during daytime hours and he called me when he was drunk to tell me nice things about my personality. The sex itself was similar, but afterwards was different. Instead of feeling tranquil, I felt oddly defenceless, like an animal playing dead. It was as though Nick could reach through the soft cloud of my skin and take whatever was inside me, like my lungs or other internal organs, and I wouldn't try to stop him. When I described this to him he said he felt the same, but he was sleepy and he might not really have been listening.

Piles of dead leaves had formed all over campus, and I spent my time attending lectures and trying to find books in the Ussher Library. On dry days, Bobbi and I walked along underused paths kicking leaves and talking about things like the idea of landscape painting. Bobbi thought the fetishisation of "untouched nature" was intrinsically patriarchal and nationalistic. I like houses better than fields, I observed. They're more poetic, because they have people in them. Then we sat in the Buttery watching rain come down the windows. Something had changed between us, but I didn't know what it was. We still intuited each other's moods easily, we shared the same conspiratorial looks, and our conversations still felt lengthy and intelligent. The time she ran me that bath had changed something, had placed Bobbi in a new relation to me even as we both remained ourselves.

One afternoon toward the end of the month, when my supply of money was down to about six euro, I got an email from a man called Lewis, who was the editor of a literary journal in Dublin. The email said that Valerie had sent the story on with a view to having it published, and that if I was willing to give my permission, he would very much like to print it in an upcoming issue. He said he was "very excited" by the prospect and that he had some thoughts on possible revisions if I was interested.

I opened the file I had sent to Valerie and read it all in one go, without stopping to think about what I was doing. The figure in the story was recognisably Bobbi, her parents recognisable as her parents, myself identifiably myself. No one who knew us could fail to see Bobbi in the story. It wasn't an unflattering portrait, exactly. It emphasised the domineering aspects of Bobbi's personality and of my own, because the story was about personal domination. But, I thought, things always have to be selected and emphasised, that's writing. Bobbi would understand that more than anyone.

Lewis also mentioned I would be paid for the story, and included a scale of fees for first-time contributors. If published at its current length, my story would be worth over eight hundred euro. I sent Lewis a reply thanking him for his interest and telling him I would be delighted to work with him on whatever revisions he thought appropriate.

That evening Nick picked me up from the apartment to take me out to Monkstown. Melissa was staying with her family in Kildare for a few days. In the car I explained about the story, and about the conversation I'd had with Bobbi in the bath and what she'd said about not being special. Slow down, Nick said. You've sold this story for how much did you say? I didn't even know you wrote prose. I laughed, I liked when he acted proud of me. I told him it was my first one and he called me intimidating. We talked about Bobbi appearing in the story, and he said he appeared in Melissa's work all the time.

But only passingly, I said. Like "my husband was there." Bobbi is the main character in this one.

Yeah, I forgot you've read Melissa's book. You're right, she doesn't dwell on me that much. Anyway I'm sure Bobbi won't mind.

I'm contemplating never telling her. It's not like she reads the magazine.

Well, I think that's a bad idea, he said. It would involve a lot of other people also not telling her. That guy Philip who you hang around with, people like that. My wife. But you're the boss, obviously.

I made a "hm" noise, because I thought he was right but I didn't want to think so. I liked when he called me the boss. He tapped his hands on the steering wheel cheerfully. What is it with me and writers? he said.

You just like women who can wreck you intellectually, I said. I bet you had crushes on your teachers at school.

I was actually notorious for that kind of thing. I slept with one of my college lecturers, have I told you about that?

I asked him to, and he told me. The woman was not just a teaching assistant, she was a real professor. I asked what age she was and Nick smiled coyly and said: like forty-five? Maybe fifty. Anyway she could have lost her job, it was insane.

I see it from her perspective, I said. Didn't I kiss you at your wife's birthday party?

He said he struggled to understand why he made people feel that way, that it had happened rarely in his life but always with a violent intensity and no real sense of agency on his part. A friend of his elder brother had developed a similar thing for him when he was fifteen.

258

And this girl was nearly twenty, Nick said. Obsessed with me. That's how I lost my virginity.

Were you obsessed with her? I said.

No, I was just frightened of saying no to her. I didn't want to hurt her feelings.

I told him that sounded bleak and it made me sad. Quickly he said: oh, I wasn't going for sympathy points. I did say yes to her, it wasn't . . . Well, it probably was illegal, but I consented to it.

Because you were too frightened to say no, I said. Would you call it consent if it happened to me?

Well, no. But it wasn't like I felt physically threatened. I mean, it was weird behaviour from her, but we were both teenagers. I don't think she was an evil person.

We were still in town, sitting in traffic on the north quays. It was early evening, but dark already. I looked out the window at passers-by and at the veil of rain that moved around under the streetlights. I told him I thought he was such an appealing love object partly because he was so curiously passive. I knew I would have to be the one to kiss you, I said. And that you would never kiss me, which made me feel vulnerable. But I also felt this terrible power, like, you're going to let me kiss you, what else will you let me do? It was sort of intoxicating. I couldn't decide if I had complete control over you or no control at all.

And now what do you feel? he said.

More like complete control. Is that bad?

He said he didn't mind. He thought it was healthy for us to try and correct the power disparity, though he added that he didn't think we would ever be able to do it completely. I told him that Melissa thought he was "pathologically submissive" and he said it would be a mistake to assume that meant he was powerless in relationships with women. He told me he thought helplessness was often a way of exercising power. I told him he sounded like Bobbi and he laughed. The highest compliment a man can ever get from you, Frances, he said.

That night in bed we talked about his sister's baby, how much he loved her, how sometimes when he was depressed he would go over to Laura's house just to be closer to the baby and see her face. I didn't know if he and Melissa planned to have children, or why they didn't have them already if he loved children so much. I didn't want to ask, because I was afraid of finding out that they did plan to, so instead I affected an ironic tone and said: maybe you and I could have children together. We could raise them in a polyamorous commune and let them choose their own first names. Nick told me he already had sinister ambitions to that effect.

Would you still find me attractive if I was pregnant? I said.

Sure, yeah.

In a fetishistic way?

Well, I don't know, he said. I do feel like I'm more aware of pregnant women than I was ten years ago. I tend to imagine myself doing nice things for them.

That sounds fetishistic.

Everything is a fetish with you. I meant more like cooking them meals. But would I still want to fuck you if you were pregnant, yes. Rest assured.

I turned around then and put my mouth up next to his ear. My eyes were closed so I felt like I was just playing a game and not being completely real. Hey, I said, I really want you. And I could feel Nick nodding his head, this sweet eager nod. Thanks, he said. He said that. We kissed. I pressed my back against the mattress and he touched me cautiously like a deer touches things with its face. Nick, you're such a gift, I said. I left my wallet in my coat, he replied. One second. And I said: just do it like this, I'm on the pill anyway. He had his hand laid flat on the pillow beside my head, and for a second he did nothing and his breath felt very hot. Yeah, do you want to? he said. I told him that I did and he kept breathing and then said: you make me feel so good about myself.

I put my arms around his neck and he slipped his hand between my legs so he could get inside me. We had always used condoms before and this felt different to me, or maybe he was being different about it. His skin was damp and he was sighing very hard. I felt my body opening up and then closing like a stop-motion video of a flower with its petals blooming open and closed, and it was so real it was like hallucinating. Nick said the word fuck and then said: Frances, I didn't know it would feel so good, I'm sorry. His mouth was extremely soft and close. I asked if he needed to come already and he inhaled for a second and then said: sorry, I'm sorry. I thought of his sinister desire to get

261

me pregnant, how full and huge I would feel, how he would touch me so lovingly and with such pride, and then I heard that I was saying: no it's good, I want it. It felt very weird and nice then, and he was telling me that he loved me, I remember that. He was murmuring it in my ear: I love you.

I had several essay deadlines approaching at the time, so I drew up a rough personal timetable. In the mornings, before the library opened, I sat in bed and worked on the revisions Lewis sent me. I could see the story I had written gaining shape, unfolding itself, becoming longer and more solid. Then I showered and dressed in oversized sweaters to go and work in college all day. I often managed without eating until late in the evening, and when I got home I cooked two handfuls of pasta and ate it with olive oil and vinegar before falling asleep, sometimes without getting undressed.

Nick had started rehearsing for a production of *Hamlet* and after work on Tuesdays and Fridays he came to stay in the apartment. He complained that there was never any food in the kitchen, but after I said I was broke in a sarcastic voice, he said: oh really? I'm sorry, I didn't know that. Then he started to bring food with him when he visited. He brought fresh bread from the Temple Bar bakery, jars of raspberry jam, tubs of hummus and full-fat cream cheese. When he watched the way I ate this food, he asked me how broke I was. I shrugged. After that he started to bring over chicken breasts and plastic things of minced beef to put in my fridge. This makes me feel like a kept woman, I said. He said things like: well look, you can freeze them if you don't want them tomorrow. I felt I had to act amused and glib about the food, because I thought Nick would be uncomfortable if he knew I really had no money and I was living on the bread and jam he brought me.

Bobbi seemed to enjoy Nick's presence in our apartment, partly because he made himself so useful. He showed us how to fix the leaky tap in our kitchen. Man of the house, she said sarcastically. Once while he was cooking dinner for us, I heard him on the phone to Melissa, talking about some editorial dispute of hers and reassuring her that the other party was being "totally unreasonable". For most of the call he was just nodding and moving saucepans around on the hob while saying: mm, I know. This was the role that seemed to appeal to him more than anything, listening to things and asking intelligent questions that showed he had been listening. It made him feel needed. He was excellent on the phone that time. I had no doubt that Melissa was the one who'd made the call.

We stayed up late talking those nights, sometimes until we could see it getting bright behind the blinds. One night I told him I was on a financial assistance scheme to cover my college fees. He expressed surprise and then immediately said: sorry for sounding surprised, that's ignorant of me. I shouldn't presume everyone's parents can pay for that stuff.

Well, we're not poor, I said. I'm not saying that defensively. I just don't want you to get the impression that I grew up very poor or anything.

Of course.

You know, but I do feel different from you and Bobbi. Maybe it's a small difference. I feel self-conscious about the nice things I have. Like my laptop, that's second-hand, it was my cousin's. But I feel self-conscious with it, still.

You're allowed to have nice things, he said.

I pinched the duvet cover between my thumb and finger. It was hard, scratchy cloth, not like the Egyptian cotton Nick had in his house.

My dad's been kind of unreliable about paying my allowance, I said.

Oh, really?

Yeah. Like at the moment I basically have no money.

Are you serious? said Nick. What are you living on?

I rolled the duvet cover between my fingers, feeling the grain of it. Well, Bobbi lets me share her things, I said. And you're always bringing food.

Frances, that's insane, he said. Why didn't you tell me? I can give you money.

No, no. You said yourself it would be weird. You said there were ethical concerns.

I would be more concerned about you starving yourself. Look, you can pay me back if you want, we can call it a loan.

I stared down at the duvet, its ugly printed pattern of flowers. I have money coming in from that story, I said. I'll pay you back then. The next morning, he went out to an ATM while Bobbi and I ate breakfast. When he came back, I could see he was too shy to give me the money while she was there, and I was glad. I didn't want her to know I needed it. I went into the hallway with him when he was leaving and he took out his wallet and counted out four fifty-euro notes. I found it unsettling to watch him handle money like that. That's too much, I said. He gave me a pained expression and said: then give it back another time, don't worry about it. I opened my mouth and he interrupted: Frances, it's nothing. For him it probably was nothing. He kissed my forehead before he left.

On the last day of October, I handed in one of my essays and Bobbi and I went out afterwards to meet friends for coffee. I was happy with my life then, happier than I could ever remember. Lewis was pleased with my revisions and ready to go ahead with printing the story in the January issue of the magazine. With Nick's loan, and the money I would have left over from the magazine even after I repaid him, I felt invincibly wealthy. It was like I'd finally escaped my childhood and my dependence on other people. There was no way for my father to harm me any more, and from this vantage point I felt a new and sincere compassion toward him, the compassion of a good-natured observer.

We met Marianne that afternoon, as well as her boyfriend Andrew, who nobody really liked. Philip was there too, with Camille, a girl he had started seeing. Philip seemed awkward in my company, careful to catch my eye when he could and smile at my jokes but in a way that seemed to communicate sympathy, or even pity, rather than real friendship. I found his behaviour too silly to be offensive, though I remember hoping that Bobbi would notice it too so we could talk about it later.

We were sitting upstairs in a small cafe near College Green, and at some point the conversation turned to monogamy, a subject I didn't have anything to say about. At first Marianne was discussing whether non-monogamy was an orientation, like being gay, and some people were "naturally" non-monogamous, which led Bobbi to point out that no sexual orientation was "natural" as such. I sipped on the coffee Bobbi had bought me and said nothing, just wanting to hear her talk. She said that monogamy was based on a commitment model, which served the needs of men in patrilineal societies by allowing them to pass property to their genetic offspring, traditionally facilitated by sexual entitlement to a wife. Non-monogamy could be based on an alternative model completely, Bobbi said. Something more like spontaneous consent.

Listening to Bobbi theorise in this way was exciting. She spoke in clear, brilliant sentences, like she was making shapes in the air out of glass or water. She never hesitated or repeated herself. Every so often she would catch my eye and I would nod: yes, exactly. This agreement seemed to encourage her, like she was searching my eyes for approval, and she would look away again and continue: by which I mean . . .

She didn't seem to be paying attention to the other people at the table while she spoke, but I noticed that Philip and Camille were exchanging glances. At one point Philip looked at Andrew, the only other man seated with us, and Andrew raised both his eyebrows as if Bobbi had started talking gibberish or promoting anti-Semitism. I thought it was cowardly of Philip to look at Andrew, whom I knew he didn't even like, and it made me uncomfortable. Gradually I realised that no one else had spoken in some time and that Marianne had started staring at her lap awkwardly. Even though I loved to listen to Bobbi when she was like this, I started to wish she would stop.

I just don't think it's possible to love more than one person, Camille said. I mean, with all your heart, really love them.

Did your parents have a favourite child? said Bobbi. That must have been hard for you.

Camille laughed nervously, unable to tell whether Bobbi was joking and not knowing Bobbi well enough to know that this was normal.

It's not really the same with children, Camille said. Is it?

Well, it depends whether you believe in some kind of transhistorical concept of romantic love consistent across diverse cultures, said Bobbi. But I guess we all believe silly things, don't we?

Marianne glanced at me, just briefly, but I could tell that she felt the same way I did: that Bobbi was being more than usually aggressive now, that she was going to hurt Camille's feelings, and that Philip would be annoyed. I looked at Philip and saw it was too late. His nostrils were flared slightly, he was angry, and he was going to argue with Bobbi and lose.

Lots of anthropologists agree that humans are a naturally monogamous species, said Philip.

Is that really where you're at theoretically? Bobbi said.

Not everything goes back to cultural theory, said Philip.

Bobbi laughed, an aesthetically gorgeous laugh, a performance of total self-assurance which made Marianne wince.

Oh my God, and they're going to let you graduate? Bobbi said.

What about Jesus? I said. He loved everybody.

He was also celibate, said Philip.

A matter of historical dispute, Bobbi said.

Why don't you tell us about your Bartleby essay, Philip? I said. You handed that in today, didn't you?

Bobbi grinned at my awkward intervention and sat back in her chair. Philip wasn't looking at me, but at Camille, smiling like they were sharing a private joke. I bristled, since I had stepped in to save him from humiliation, and it was graceless of him not to acknowledge my effort. He turned away then and talked about his essay, as if he was humouring me, and I pretended not to listen. Bobbi began to search her bag for a packet of cigarettes, lifting her head once to say: you should have read Gilles Deleuze. Philip glanced at Camille again.

I did read him, said Philip.

You missed his point then, Bobbi said. Frances? Do you fancy coming out for a cigarette?

I followed her. It was still early evening, and the air was crisp and navy blue. She started to laugh and I laughed too, from the joy of being alone with her. She lit both our cigarettes and then exhaled, a white cloud, and coughed with laughter.

Human nature, I ask you, she said. You're such a pushover.

I think I only appear smart by staying quiet as often as possible.

That amused her. She fixed a strand of my hair behind my ear fondly.

Is that a hint? she said.

Oh no. If I could talk like you I would talk all the time.

We smiled at one another. It was cold. The tip of Bobbi's cigarette glowed a spectral orange colour and released tiny sparks into the air. She lifted her face toward the street like she was showing off the perfect line of her profile.

I feel like shit lately, she said. All this stuff at home, I don't know. You think you're the kind of person who can deal with something and then it happens and you realise you can't.

She balanced her cigarette on her lower lip, near the corner of her mouth, and started to gather her hair back in a knot with her hands. It was Halloween, the streets were busy, and little knots of people went by dressed in capes or fake spectacles or tiger costumes.

What do you mean? I said. What happened?

You know Jerry's kind of temperamental, right? It doesn't really matter. Family drama, what do you care?

I care about everything that happens to you.

She put her cigarette back between her fingers and wiped her nose with her sleeve. In her eyes the orange light reflected like fire.

He's not really on board with the divorce, Bobbi said.

I didn't realise that.

Yeah, he's being a real jerk about it. He has all these conspiracy theories about Eleanor, like she's out to get his money or whatever. And the worst thing is that he actually expects me to be on his side.

I thought of her saying to Camille: did your parents have a favourite child? I knew Bobbi had always been Jerry's favourite, that he thought her sister was spoilt, that he considered his wife hysterical. I knew he told Bobbi these things in order to win her confidence. I had always thought that being Jerry's favourite was a privilege for Bobbi, but now I saw it was also something cumbersome and dangerous.

I didn't know you were going through all that, I said.

Everyone's always going through something, aren't they? That's life, basically. It's just more and more things to go through. You have all this shit going on with your dad that you never talk about. It's not like things are so perfect for you.

I said nothing. She exhaled a thin stream of smoke from her lips and then shook her head.

Sorry, she said. I didn't mean that.

No, you're right.

For a moment we stood there like that, huddled together behind the smoking barrier. I became aware that our arms were touching, and then Bobbi kissed

270

me. I accepted the kiss, I even felt my hand reaching for hers. I could sense the soft pressure of her mouth, her lips parting, the sweet chemical scent of her moisturiser. I thought she was about to put her arm around my waist, but instead she drew away. Her face was flushed and extraordinarily pretty-looking. She stubbed her cigarette out.

Should we go back upstairs? she said.

The inside of my body hummed like a piece of machinery. I searched Bobbi's face for some acknowledgement of what had just happened but there was none. Was she just confirming that she felt nothing for me any more, that kissing me was like kissing a wall? Was it some kind of experiment? Upstairs we got our coats and then walked home together talking about college, about Melissa's new book, about things that didn't really concern us.

CHAPTER
TWENTY-SIX

The next evening, Nick and I went to see an Iranian film about a vampire. On the way to the cinema I told him about Bobbi kissing me and he thought about it for a few seconds and then said: Melissa kisses me sometimes. Not knowing what I felt, I started to make jokes. You kiss other women behind my back! We were nearly at the cinema anyway. I do want to make her happy, he said. Maybe you'd prefer not to talk about it. I stood at the door of the cinema with my hands in my coat pockets. Talk about what? I said. About you kissing your wife?

We're getting along better now, he said. Than we were before all this. But I mean, maybe you don't want to know about that.

I'm glad you're getting along.

I feel like I should thank you for making me a tolerable person to live with.

Our breath hung between us like fog. The door of the cinema swung open with a rush of warmth and the smell of popcorn grease.

We're going to be late for the film now, I said.

I'll stop talking.

Afterwards we went to get falafel on Dame Street. We sat in the booth, and I told him my mother was coming to Dublin the next day to visit her sister and that she was taking me home in the car after that for my ultrasound. Nick asked me what day the appointment was and I told him the afternoon of November third. He nodded, he wasn't forthcoming on these kinds of topics. I changed the subject by saying: my mother is suspicious of you, you know.

Is that bad? said Nick.

Then the woman brought us our food and I stopped talking to eat. Nick was saying something about his parents, something about not seeing them much "after everything last year".

Last year seems to come up a lot, I said.

Does it?

In fragments. I'm picking up that it was a bad time.

He shrugged. He went on eating. He probably didn't know that I knew he had been in hospital. I sipped on my glass of Coke and said nothing. Then he wiped his mouth on a napkin and started to talk. I hadn't really expected him to start, but he did. There was nobody in either of the booths near us, nobody listening in, and he talked in a sincere, self-effacing way, not trying either to make me laugh or to make me feel bad.

Nick told me that last summer he had been working in California. He said the schedule was gruelling and he was run-down and smoking too much, and then one of his lungs collapsed. He couldn't finish filming, he said he ended up in some awful hospital in the States with no one he knew anywhere nearby. At the time

Melissa was travelling around Europe for an essay about immigrant communities and they weren't in touch very much.

By the time they were both back in Dublin, he told me, he was exhausted. He didn't want to go out anywhere with Melissa, and if she had friends over he would mostly stay upstairs trying to sleep. They were bad-tempered with one another and argued frequently. Nick told me that when they first married they had both wanted to have children, but increasingly when he brought it up Melissa would refuse to talk about it. She was thirty-six by then. One night in October she told him she had decided she didn't want children after all. They fought. He told me that he'd said some unreasonable things. We both did, he said. But I regret what I said to her.

Eventually he moved into the spare room. He slept a lot during the day, he lost a lot of weight. At first, he said, Melissa was angry, she thought he was punishing her, or trying to force her into something she didn't want. But then she realised he was really sick. She tried to help, she made appointments with doctors and counsellors, but Nick never went. I can't really explain it now, he said. I look back on how I behaved and I don't understand it myself.

Finally in December he was admitted to a psychiatric unit. He stayed there for six weeks, and during that time Melissa started seeing someone else, a mutual friend of theirs. He realised it was going on because she sent him a text that was intended for the other person. It probably wasn't great for my self-esteem, he said. But

I don't want to exaggerate. I don't know if at that point I had any self-esteem left anyway. When he came out, Melissa said she wanted a divorce, and he said okay. He thanked her for everything she had done to try and help him and suddenly she started crying. She told him how scared she had been, how guilty she felt just for leaving the house in the morning. I thought you were going to die, she said. They talked for a long time, they apologised to one another. In the end they agreed to keep living together until they could find some other arrangement.

Nick started working again in the spring. He was exercising more, he took a small part in an Arthur Miller play one of his friends was directing. Melissa fell out with Chris, the man she was seeing, and Nick said their lives just sort of continued. They tried to negotiate what he described as a "quasi-marriage". They saw one another's friends, they ate together in the evenings. Nick renewed his gym membership, took the dog down to the beach in the afternoons, started reading novels again. He drank protein shakes, he put the weight back on. Life was okay.

At this point you have to understand, he said, I was used to everyone seeing me as a burden. Like my family and Melissa, they all wanted me to get better, but it's not as if they enjoyed my company. In as much as I was functioning again, I still felt like this very worthless, pathetic person, you know, like I was just a waste of everyone's time. So that's kind of where I was at when I met you.

I stared at him across the table.

And it was so hard to believe you had any interest in me, he said. You know, you were sending me these emails, and sometimes I'd find myself thinking, is this a thing? And as soon as I thought about it, I'd feel mortified that I would even let myself imagine that. Like, what's more depressing than some awful married man who convinces himself that a beautiful younger woman wants to sleep with him? You know.

I didn't know what to say. I shook my head or shrugged. I didn't know you were feeling like that, I said.

No, well, I didn't want you to know. I wanted to be like this cool person you thought I was. I know sometimes you felt like I wasn't expressive enough. It was hard for me. That probably sounds like I'm making excuses.

I tried to smile back, I shook my head again. No, I said. We let a little pause form between us.

I was so cruel sometimes, I said. I feel horrible about that now.

Oh no, don't be hard on yourself.

I stared at the tabletop. We were both quiet then. I finished my glass of Coke. He folded up his napkin and put it on his plate.

After a while, he told me that was the first time he had ever told the story of that year and what had happened. He said he had never actually heard the story from his own point of view before, because he was used to Melissa telling it, and of course their versions were different. It feels strange, he said, hearing myself talk about it like I was the main character. It almost feels like I'm lying, although I think everything I said was true. But Melissa would tell it differently.

I like the way you tell it, I said. Do you still want to have children?

Sure, but it's off the table now I think.

You don't know. You're young.

He coughed. He seemed on the point of saying something and then he didn't. He watched me sipping my Coke and I looked back up at him.

I think you'd be a great parent, I said. You have a kind nature. You're very loving.

He made a funny, surprised face, then exhaled through his mouth.

That's intense, he said. Thank you for saying that. I have to laugh now or I'm going to start crying.

We finished our food and left the restaurant. Once we crossed Dame Street and got down to the quays, Nick said: we should go away together. For a weekend or something, would you like that? I asked where and he said, what about Venice? I laughed. He put his hands in his pockets, he was laughing too, I think because he was pleased at the idea of us going away together, or just that he had made me smile.

That was when I heard my mother. I heard her say: well, hello, missus. And there she was on the street in front of us. She had a Bally black winter coat on, and a beanie hat with the Adidas logo. I remember Nick was wearing his beautiful grey overcoat. He and my mother looked like characters from different films, made by totally dissimilar directors.

I didn't realise you were coming up tonight, I said.

I've just this minute parked the car, she said. I'm meeting your auntie Bernie for dinner.

Oh, this is my friend Nick, I said. Nick, this is my mother.

I could only glance at him quickly, but I saw that he was smiling and he held out his hand.

The famous Nick, she said. I've heard all about you.

Well, likewise, he said.

She did mention you were handsome all right.

Mum, for God's sake, I said.

But I had you pictured older, said my mother. You're only a young fellow.

He laughed and said he was flattered. They shook hands again, she told me she would see me the next morning, and we parted. It was the first of November. Lights sparkled on the river and buses ran past like boxes of light, carrying faces in the windows.

I turned to look at Nick, who had his hands back in his pockets. That was nice, he said. And no pointed remarks about me being married, that's a bonus.

I smiled. She's a cool lady, I said.

When I got home that night, Bobbi was in the living room. She was sitting at the table, staring at a print-out which was stapled together in one corner. Nick had gone back to Monkstown and said he would email me later about Venice. Bobbi's teeth were chattering faintly. She didn't look at me when I came in, which gave me a weird sensation of disappearance, like I was already dead.

Bobbi? I said.

Melissa sent it to me.

She held up the print-out. I could see it was double-spaced, with long paragraphs like an essay.

Sent you what? I said.

For a second she laughed, or maybe exhaled a breath she had been holding very tightly, and then she threw the pages at me. I caught them awkwardly against my chest. Looking down I saw the words printed in a light sans-serif font. My words. It was my story.

Bobbi, I said.

Were you ever going to tell me?

I stood there. My eyes ran over the lines I could see at the top of the page, the page where I described myself getting sick at a house party without Bobbi when I was still a teenager.

I'm sorry, I said.

Sorry for what? said Bobbi. I'm so curious. Sorry for writing it? I doubt you are.

No. I don't know.

It's funny. I think I've learned more about your feelings in the last twenty minutes than in the last four years.

I felt light-headed, staring down at the manuscript until the words wriggled like insects. It was the first draft, the one I had sent to Valerie. She must have let Melissa read it. ·

It's fictionalised, I said.

Bobbi stood up from her chair and looked my body up and down critically. A strange energy wound itself up in my chest, as if we were going to fight.

I heard you're getting good money for it, she said.

Yeah.

Fuck you.

I actually need the money, I said. I realise that's an alien concept for you, Bobbi.

She grabbed the pages out of my hands then, and the back of the staple tugged against my index finger and broke the skin. She held the manuscript in front of me.

You know, she said. It's actually a good story.

Thanks.

Then she tore the pages in half, threw them in the trash and said: I don't want to live with you any more. She packed up her things that night. I sat in my room listening. I heard her wheel the suitcase out into the hall. I heard her close the door.

The next morning my mother picked me up outside the apartment building. I got into the car and strapped my seat belt on. She had the classical station on the radio, but she turned it off when I shut the door. It was eight in the morning and I complained about having to get up so early.

Oh, I'm sorry, she said. We could have given the hospital a ring and arranged for you to have a lie-in, would that have been better?

I thought the scan was tomorrow.

It's this afternoon.

Fuck, I said mildly.

She placed a little bottle of water on my lap and said: you can start that any time you like. I unscrewed the cap. No preparation was necessary for the scan except drinking a lot of water, but I still felt like the whole thing had been thrown at me unexpectedly. We didn't speak for a while, and then my mother glanced at me sideways.

It was funny meeting you like that yesterday, she said. You looked like a real young lady.

As opposed to what?

She didn't answer at first, we were going round a roundabout. I stared out the windscreen at the passing cars.

You looked very elegant together, she said. Like film stars.

Oh, that's Nick. He's just glamorous.

My mother reached suddenly and grabbed my hand. The car was stopped in traffic. Her grip was tighter than I expected, almost hard. Mum, I said. Then she let me go. She tidied her hair back with her fingers and then settled her hands on the steering wheel.

You're a wild woman, she said.

I learned from the best.

She laughed. Oh, I'm afraid I'm no match for you, Frances. You'll have to figure things out all on your own.

CHAPTER
TWENTY-SEVEN

In the hospital I was advised to drink even more water, so much that I was in active discomfort while sitting in the waiting room. The place was busy. My mother bought me a bar of chocolate from the vending machine and I sat there tapping my pen against the front cover of *Middlemarch*, which I had to read for a class on the English novel. The cover depicted a sad-eyed lady from Victorian times doing something with flowers. I doubted Victorian women actually touched flowers as often as art from the period suggested they did.

While I was waiting, a man came in with two little girls, one of them in a pushchair. The older girl climbed onto the seat next to me and leaned over her father's shoulder to say something, although he wasn't listening. The girl wriggled around to get his attention, so her light-up sneakers pushed against my handbag and then my arm. When her father finally turned around he said: Rebecca, look what you're doing! You're kicking that woman's arm! I tried to catch his eye and say: it's fine, it's no problem. But he didn't look at me. To him, my arm was not important. He was only concerned with making his child feel bad, making her feel ashamed. I thought about the way Nick handled his little dog whom he loved so much, and then I stopped thinking about it.

The registrar called me up and I went into a little room with an ultrasound machine and a medical couch covered in white filmy paper. The technician asked me to get onto the couch and she rolled some gel onto a plastic instrument while I lay there looking at the ceiling. The room was dim, evocatively dim, as if it contained a hidden pool of water somewhere. We chatted, I don't remember about what. I had the sense that my voice was coming from somewhere else, like a small radio I kept in my mouth.

The technician pressed the plastic thing down hard into my lower abdomen then, and I stared upward and tried not to make any noise. My eyes were watering. I felt like at any moment she was going to show me a grainy image of a foetus and say something about a heartbeat, and I would nod wisely. The idea of making images of a uterus that had nothing in it struck me as sad, like photographing an abandoned house.

After it was over I thanked her. I went to the bathroom and washed my hands a number of times under the hot hospital taps. I may have scalded them a little, since my skin came up very pink and the tips of my fingers looked slightly swollen. Then I went back to wait for the consultant to call me. Rebecca and her family were gone.

The consultant was a man in his sixties. He squinted up at me as if I'd disappointed him in some way and then told me to sit down. He was looking at a folder with some writing in it. I sat on a hard plastic chair and looked at my fingernails. My hands were definitely scalded. He asked me some questions about the time I had been admitted to the hospital in August, what my symptoms were, and what the gynaecologist had said, and then asked more general questions about my menstrual cycle and sexual activity. While he asked these questions he was flipping sort of non-committally through his folder. Eventually he looked up at me.

Well, your ultrasound is clear, he said. No fibroids, no cysts, nothing like that. So that's the good news.

What's the other news?

He smiled, but it was a weird smile, as if he was admiring me for being brave. I swallowed, and I knew that I had made a mistake.

The doctor told me that I had a problem with the lining of my uterus, which meant that cells from inside the uterus were growing elsewhere in my body. He said these cells were benign, meaning non-cancerous, but the condition itself was incurable and in some cases progressive. It had a long name which I had never heard before: endometriosis. He called it a "difficult" and "unpredictable" diagnosis, which could only be confirmed with exploratory keyhole surgery. But it fits with all your symptoms, he said. And as many as one in ten women suffer from it. I sort of chewed on my scalded thumb and said things like, hm. He said there were some surgical interventions possible but they were only recommended in particularly severe cases. I wondered if that meant I wasn't a severe case; or just that they didn't know yet.

284

He told me that the primary problem for sufferers was "pain management". He said that patients often experienced pain during ovulation, menstrual pain, and discomfort during sexual intercourse. I bit down into the side of my thumbnail and started to peel it away from my skin. The idea that sex could hurt me felt apocalyptically cruel. The doctor said "we" wanted to prevent the pain from becoming debilitating or "reaching the level of disability". My jaw started to hurt and I wiped at my nose mechanically.

The secondary problem he said was "the issue of fertility". I recall these words very clearly. I said, oh, really? Unfortunately, he said, the condition does leave many women infertile, that's one of our biggest concerns. But then he talked about IVF treatments and how rapidly they were advancing. I nodded with my thumb in my mouth. Then I blinked several times quickly, as if I could blink the thought out of my mind, or blink the entire hospital away.

After that the consultation was over. I went back out to the waiting room and saw my mother reading my copy of *Middlemarch*. She was only about ten pages in. I went to stand beside her and she looked up at me with an expectant face.

Oh, she said. There you are. What did the doctor say?

Something seemed to close up over my body, like a hand held hard over my mouth or my eyes. I couldn't begin to phrase the explanation of what the doctor had told me, because there were so many parts to it, and it would take so long, and involve so many individual words and sentences. The thought of saying so many words about it made me feel physically sick. Out loud I heard myself say: oh, he said the ultrasound was clear.

So they don't know what it is? my mother said.

Let's get in the car.

We went out to the car and I strapped my seat belt on. I'll explain more when we get home, I thought. I'll have more time to think about it when we're home. She started the engine and I ran my fingers through a knot in my hair, feeling it stretch and then give way, the little pieces of dark hair snapping off and falling away through my hand. My mother was asking questions again and I could feel my mouth formulating responses.

It's just bad period pain, I said. He says it'll get better now that I'm on the pill.

She said oh. Well. That's a relief then, isn't it? You must be feeling good about that. I wanted to be hard and frictionless. I produced some kind of facial expression by reflex and she indicated left out of the car park.

When we got back home I went up to my room to wait for the train while my mother stayed downstairs tidying up. I could hear her putting away pots and pans into kitchen drawers. I got into bed and looked at the internet for a while, where I found a number of health features on women's websites about this incurable disease I had. Usually these took the form of interviews with people whose lives had been destroyed by suffering. There were a lot of stock photographs of white women looking out windows with concerned expressions, sometimes with a hand on their abdomen to indicate pain. I also found some online communities where people shared gruesome after-surgery images with questions like "how long should it take for hydronephrosis to improve once a stent is in place?" I viewed this information as dispassionately as possible.

When I had read as much of this as I could, I closed my laptop and took the little bible out of my bag. I turned to the part of Mark where Jesus says: Daughter, thy faith hath made thee whole; go in peace, and be whole of thy plague. All sick people were good for in the Bible was to be healed by people who were well. But Jesus didn't really know anything, and neither did I. Even if I had any faith, it wasn't going to make me whole. There was no use thinking about it.

My phone started to ring then and I saw it was Nick calling. I picked up and we said hello. Then he said: hey, I should probably tell you something. I asked what, and there was a short but perceptible pause before he spoke again.

So, Melissa and I have started sleeping together again, he said. I feel weird telling you about it on the phone, but then I also feel weird keeping it from you. I don't know.

At this I lifted the phone away from my face, slowly, and looked at it. It was just an object, it didn't mean anything. I could hear Nick say: Frances? But I could only hear it faintly, and it was like any other sound. I put the phone down carefully onto my bedside table, though I didn't hang up. Nick's voice became a kind of buzzing noise, with no identifiable words in it. I sat on my bed breathing in and out very slowly, so slowly I almost wasn't breathing at all.

Then I picked the phone up and said: hello?

Hey, Nick said. Are you there? I think the signal did something weird just now.

No, I'm here. I heard you.

Oh. Are you all right? You sound upset.

I closed my eyes. When I spoke I could hear my voice thinning out and hardening like ice.

About you and Melissa? I said. Be real, Nick.

But you did want me to tell you, didn't you?

Sure.

I just don't want things to change between us, he said.

Relax about it.

I could hear him breathe in apprehensively. He wanted to reassure me, I could tell, but I wasn't going to let him. People were always wanting me to show some weakness so they could reassure me. It made them feel worthy, I knew all about that.

How are you otherwise? he said. That scan is happening tomorrow, right?

Only then I remembered that I had given him the wrong date. He hadn't forgotten, it was my mistake. He had probably set a reminder on his phone for the next day: ask Frances how the scan went.

Right, I said. I'll let you know about it. The other phone is ringing so I'm going to go, but I'll give you a call after the thing.

Yeah, do that. I hope it goes okay. You're not worried about it, are you? I guess you don't worry about things.

I held the back of my hand to my face silently. My body felt cold like an inanimate object.

No, that's your job, I said. Talk soon, okay?

Okay. Keep in touch.

I hung up the phone. After that I put some cold water on my face and dried it, the same face I had always had, the one I would have until I died.

On the way to the station that evening my mother kept glancing at me, as if something about my behaviour was off-putting, and she wanted to reprimand me for it but couldn't decide what it was. Eventually she told me to take my feet off the dashboard, which I did.

You must be relieved, she said.

Yeah, delighted.

How are you managing for money?

Oh, I said. I'm okay.

She glanced in the rear-view mirror.

The doctor didn't say anything else, did he? she said.

No, that was it.

I looked out the window at the station. I had the sense that something in my life had ended, my image of myself as a whole or normal person maybe. I realised my life would be full of mundane physical suffering, and that there was nothing special about it. Suffering wouldn't make me special, and pretending not to suffer wouldn't make me special. Talking about it, or even writing about it, would not transform the suffering into something useful. Nothing would. I thanked my mother for the lift to the station and got out of the car.

TWENTY-EIGHT

That week I went to class every day and spent every evening in the library writing CVs and printing them off on the library printers. I had to get a job so I could give Nick the money back. I had become obsessed with repaying the money, as if everything else depended on it. Whenever he called me I hit the reject button and sent him texts saying I was busy. I said the scan was clear and there was nothing to worry about. Okay, he texted back. Is that good news? I didn't reply. It would be really nice to see you, he wrote. Later he sent me an email saying: melissa mentioned bobbi moved out of your apartment, is everything all right? I didn't reply then either. By Wednesday he sent me another email.

> hey. i know you're angry at me and i feel really bad about it. i would like if we could talk about what's bothering you. at this point i'm presuming it has something to do with melissa but i guess i might be wrong about that too. i had the impression that you knew this kind of thing might happen and you just wanted me to tell you if it did. but maybe i was enormously naive about that and what you actually wanted was for it not to happen. i'd like to do what

you want but i can't if i don't know what it is. otherwise maybe you're not feeling well or something else has upset you. i find it hard not knowing if you're ok. it would be really good to hear from you.

I didn't write back.

Before class one day I bought myself a cheap grey notebook and used it to keep track of all my symptoms. I wrote them out very neatly with the date printed up at the top. It helped me to become more intimately acquainted with phenomena like fatigue and pelvic pain, which had previously seemed like vague discomforts with no particular beginning or end. Now I came to know them as personal nemeses which dogged me in various ways. The grey notebook even helped me to feel out the contours of words like "moderate" and "severe", which no longer felt ambiguous but definitive and categorical. I paid so much attention to myself that everything I experienced came to seem like a symptom. If I felt dizzy after getting out of bed, was that a symptom? Or what if I felt sad? I decided to be completist in my approach. For several days in the grey notebook, I noted down in tidy handwriting the phrase: mood swings (sadness).

Nick was having a birthday party that weekend in Monkstown, he was turning thirty-three. I didn't know whether to attend or not. I read his email again and again while I tried to decide. On one reading it might give an impression of devotion and acquiescence, and on another it appeared indecisive or ambivalent. I didn't know what I wanted from him. What I seemed to want, though I didn't like to believe this, was for him to renounce every other person and thing in his life and pledge himself to me exclusively. This was outlandish not only because I had also slept with someone else during our relationship but because even now I was often preoccupied by other people, particularly Bobbi and how much I missed her. I didn't believe that the time I spent thinking about Bobbi had anything to do with Nick, but the time he spent thinking about Melissa I felt as a personal affront.

On Friday I called him. I told him I was having a strange week and he said how nice it was to hear my voice. I rubbed my tongue against my teeth.

You kind of threw me with that phone call last week, I said. Sorry if I overreacted.

No, I don't think you did. Maybe I underreacted. Are you upset?

I hesitated and said: no.

Because if you are, we can talk about it, he said.

I'm not.

He was oddly quiet for a few seconds and I worried he had something else bad to tell me. Finally he said: I know you don't like to seem upset by things. But it's not a sign of weakness to have feelings. A kind of hard smile came over my face then, and I felt the radiant energy of spite fill my body.

Sure, I have feelings, I said.

Right.

I just don't have feelings concerning whether you fuck your wife or not. It's not an emotive topic for me.

Okay, he said.

You want me to have feelings about it. Because you were jealous when I slept with someone else and it makes you insecure that I'm not jealous.

He sighed into the phone, I could hear him. Maybe, he said. Yeah, maybe, that's something to think about. I was just trying to, uh . . . yeah. I'm glad you're not upset.

I was really smiling then. I knew he could hear my smile when I said: you don't sound glad. He sighed again, a weak sigh. I felt like he was lying on the floor and I was tearing his body apart with my smiling teeth. I'm sorry, he said. I'm just finding you kind of hostile.

You're interpreting your failure to hurt me as hostility on my part, I said. That's interesting. This party is tomorrow night, right?

He didn't say anything for so long then that I was afraid I had gone too far, that he would tell me I was not a nice person, that he had tried loving me and it wasn't possible. Instead he said: yeah, in the house. Do you think you'll come?

Sure, why wouldn't I? I said.

Great. It'll be nice to see you again, obviously. You can arrive whenever.

Thirty-three is so old.

Yeah, I guess it is, he said. I've been feeling it.

By the time I got to the party, the house was noisy and full of people I didn't know. I saw the dog hiding behind the TV set. Melissa kissed me on the face, she was obviously very drunk. She poured me a glass of red wine and told me I looked pretty. I thought about Nick shuddering into her body when he came. I hated them both, with the intensity of passionate love. I swallowed a huge mouthful of red wine and crossed my arms over my chest.

What's going on with you and Bobbi? said Melissa.

I looked at her. Her lips were stained with wine, also her teeth. Under her left eye was a small but visible shadow of mascara.

I don't know, I said. Is she here?

Not yet. You need to sort it out, you know. She's been sending me emails about it.

I stared at Melissa and a shiver of nausea ran over my skin. I hated that Bobbi had been emailing her. It made me want to step on her foot very hard and then look in her face and deny that I had done it. No, I would say. I don't know what you're talking about. And she would look at me and know that I was evil and insane. I said I would go and wish Nick a happy birthday and she pointed out the double doors to the conservatory.

You're in a bad mood with him, Melissa said. Aren't you?

I clenched my teeth. I thought of how hard I could step on her if I put my whole weight onto the foot.

I hope it's not my fault, she said.

No. I'm not in a bad mood with anyone. I should go say hello.

In the conservatory, the stereo was playing a Sam Cooke song and Nick was standing there in conversation with some strangers, nodding his head. The lights were dim and everything looked blue. I needed to leave. Nick saw me, our eyes met. I felt it like always, a key turning hard inside me, but this time I hated the key and hated being opened up to anything. He came toward me and I stood there holding my arms crossed, probably scowling, or maybe looking scared.

He was drunk too, so drunk his words sounded slurred and I didn't like his voice any more. He asked if I was okay and I shrugged. Maybe you should tell me what's wrong so I can apologise, he said.

Melissa seems to think we're fighting, I said.

Well, are we?

Is it any of her business if we are?

I don't know, he said. I don't know what you mean by that.

A rigidity had settled over my whole body so that my jaw felt painfully tight. He touched my arm and I pulled away from him like he had slapped me. He looked hurt, like any normal person would look hurt. There was something wrong with me, I knew that.

Two people I had never met came over to wish Nick happy birthday then: a tall guy and a dark-haired woman holding a little baby. Nick seemed very happy to see them. The woman kept saying: we're not staying, we're not staying, it's a flying visit. Nick introduced me to them, it was his sister Laura and her husband Jim and their baby, the baby Nick loved. I wasn't sure if Laura knew who I was. The infant had blonde hair and huge, celestial eyes. Laura said it was nice to meet me and I said: your baby is so gorgeous, wow. Nick laughed and said, isn't she? She's like a model baby. She could do ads for baby food. Laura asked me if I wanted to hold her and I looked at her and said: yes, can I?

Laura handed me the baby and said she was going to get herself a glass of soda water. Jim and Nick were talking about something, I don't remember what. The baby looked at me and opened and closed her mouth. Her mouth was very mobile, and for a while she put her entire hand into it. It was hard to believe that such a perfect creature was dependent on the whims of adults who drank soda water and handed her to strangers at parties. The baby looked up at me with her wet hand in her mouth and blinked. I held her tiny body against my chest and thought about how small she was. I wanted to talk to her, but the others would have heard me, and I didn't want anybody else to hear.

When I looked up I saw that Nick was watching me. We looked at one another for a few seconds and it felt so serious that I tried to smile at him. Yeah, I said. I love this baby. This is a great infant, ten out of ten. Jim replied: oh, Rachel is Nick's favourite member of the family. He likes her more than we do. Nick smiled at that, and he reached over and touched the baby's hand, which was waving around in the air like she was trying to balance herself. She held onto the joint of Nick's thumb then. Oh, I'm going to weep, I said. She's perfect.

Laura came back and said she would take the kid off my hands. She's heavy, isn't she? she said. I nodded dumbly and then said: she's so lovely. Without the baby my arms felt thin and empty. She's a little charmer, Laura said. Aren't you? And she touched the baby's nose lovingly. Wait until you have your own, she said. I just stared at her and blinked and said something like yeah or hm. They had to leave then, they went to say goodbye to Melissa.

When they were gone Nick touched my back and I told him how much I liked his niece. She's beautiful, I said. Beautiful is a stupid thing to say, but you know what I mean. Nick said he didn't think it was stupid. He was drunk, but I could tell he was trying to be nice to me. I said something like: actually I don't feel very well. He asked if I was okay and I didn't look at him. I said: you don't mind if I head off, do you? There are so many people here anyway, I don't want to monopolise you. He tried to look at me but I couldn't look back at him. He asked me what was wrong and I said: I'll talk to you tomorrow.

He didn't follow me out of the front door. I was shivering and my lower lip had started to tremble. I paid for a taxi back into town.

Late that night I got a call from my father. I woke up to the noise of the ringtone and knocked my wrist on the bedside cabinet trying to pick up the phone. Hello? I said. It was after three in the morning. I nursed my arm against my chest and squinted into the darkness, waiting for him to speak. The noise in the background of the call sounded like weather, like wind or rain.

Is that you, Frances? he said.

I've been trying to get in touch with you.

I know, I know. Listen.

He sighed then, into the phone. I didn't say anything, but neither did he. When he next spoke, he sounded immensely tired.

I'm sorry, love, he said.

Sorry for what?

You know, you know. You know yourself. I am sorry.

I don't know what you're talking about, I said.

Although I had spent weeks calling him about my allowance, I knew that I wouldn't mention it now and that I might even deny the money was missing if he brought it up.

Listen, he said. It's just been a bad year. It's gotten out of hand.

What has?

He sighed again. I said: Dad?

Sure, you'd be better off without me at this stage, he said. Wouldn't you?

Of course not. Don't say that. What are you talking about?

Ah. Nothing. Only nonsense.

I was shivering. I tried to think about things that made me feel safe and normal. Material possessions: the white blouse drying on a hanger in the bathroom, the alphabetised novels on my bookshelf, the set of green china cups.

Dad? I said.

You're a great woman, Frances. You've never given us a bit of bother.

Are you okay?

Your mother tells me you have a boyfriend up there now, he said. Nice-looking fellow, I've heard.

298

Dad, where are you? Are you outside somewhere?

He was quiet for a few seconds, and then he sighed again, almost like a groan this time, like he was suffering from some physical ailment he couldn't speak of or describe.

Listen, he said. I'm sorry, all right? I'm sorry.

Dad, wait.

He hung up. I closed my eyes and felt all the furniture in my room begin to disappear, like a backwards game of Tetris, lifting up toward the top of the screen and then vanishing, and the next thing that would vanish would be me. I dialled his number again and again, knowing he wouldn't answer. Eventually it stopped ringing, maybe his battery had run flat. I lay there in the dark until it was bright.

The next day Nick called me on the phone when I was still in bed. I'd fallen asleep at around ten in the morning and it was past noon by then. The window blinds were casting an ugly grey shadow on the ceiling. When I answered, he asked if he'd woken me up and I said: it's okay. I didn't sleep well. He asked if he could come over. I reached a hand to pull the blinds open and said all right, sure.

I waited in bed while he got in the car. I didn't even get up to shower. I put on a black T-shirt to buzz him into the building and he came through looking very freshly shaven and smelling like cigarettes. I gripped my throat when I saw him and said something like, oh, it didn't take you long to get into town. We went into my room together and he said yeah, the roads were pretty clear.

For a few seconds we stood there looking at each other and then he kissed me, on the mouth. He said: is this okay? I nodded and murmured something stupid. He said: sorry again about last night. I've been thinking about you a lot. I've missed you. It sounded like he'd prepared these statements in advance so that I couldn't later accuse him of not saying them. My throat hurt like I was going to cry. I felt him touch me underneath my T-shirt and then I did start crying, which was confusing. He said: oh no, what's wrong? Hey. And I shrugged and made weird meaningless hand gestures. I was crying very hard. He just stood there looking awkward. He was wearing a pale blue shirt that day, a button-down shirt, with white buttons.

Can we talk about it? he said.

I said there was nothing to talk about, and then we had sex. I was on my knees and he was behind me. He used a condom this time, we didn't discuss that. When he spoke to me I mostly pretended I couldn't hear him. I was crying pretty badly still. Certain things made me cry harder, like when he touched my breasts, and when he asked me if it felt okay. Then he said he wanted to stop, so we stopped. I pulled the bedsheets over my body and pressed my hand down on my eyes so I didn't have to look at him.

Was it not good? I said.

Can we talk?

You used to like it, didn't you?

300

Can I ask you something? he said. Do you want me to leave her?

I looked at him then. He looked tired, and I could see that he hated everything I was doing to him. My body felt completely disposable, like a placeholder for something more valuable. I fantasised about taking it apart and lining my limbs up side by side to compare them.

No, I said. I don't want that.

I don't know what to do. I've been feeling fucking awful about it. You seem so upset with me and I don't know how I can make you happy.

Well, maybe we shouldn't see each other any more.

Yeah, he said. Okay. I guess you're probably right.

I stopped crying then. I didn't look at him. I pulled my hair back from my face and took an elastic tie off my wrist to wrap around it. My hands were trembling and I was starting to see faint lights in my eyeline where there were no real lights. He said he was sorry, and that he loved me. He said something else also, like he didn't deserve me or something like that. I thought: if only I hadn't picked up the phone this morning, Nick would still be my boyfriend, and everything would be normal. I coughed to clear my throat.

After he left the apartment I took a small nail scissors and cut a hole on the inside of my left thigh. I felt that I had to do something dramatic to stop thinking about how bad I felt, but the cut didn't make me feel any better. Actually it bled a lot and I felt worse. I sat on the floor of my room bleeding into a rolled-up piece of tissue paper and thinking about my own death. I was like an empty cup, which Nick had emptied out, and now I had to look at what had spilled out of me: all my delusional beliefs about my own value and my pretensions to being a kind of person I wasn't. While I was full of these things I couldn't see them. Now that I was nothing, only an empty glass, I could see everything about myself.

I got cleaned up and found a plaster to put over the cut. Then I pulled the blinds and opened my copy of *Middlemarch*. Ultimately it didn't matter that Nick had taken the first opportunity to leave me as soon as Melissa wanted him again, or that my face and body were so ugly they made him sick, or that he hated having sex with me so much that he had to ask me to stop halfway through. That wasn't what my biographers would care about later. I thought about all the things I had never told Nick about myself, and I started to feel better then, as if my privacy extended all around me like a barrier protecting my body. I was a very autonomous and independent person with an inner life that nobody else had ever touched or perceived.

The cut kept on throbbing badly even after it stopped bleeding. By that time I was a little frightened that I had done something so stupid, although I knew I never had to tell anyone about it and it would never happen again. After Bobbi had broken up with me I hadn't cut any holes into my skin, although I did stand in the shower and let the hot water run out and then keep standing there until my fingers went blue. I privately termed these behaviours "acting out". Scratching my arm open was "acting out", and so was giving myself hypothermia by accident and having to explain it to a paramedic on the phone.

That evening I thought about my father's phone call from the night before, and how I had wanted to tell Nick about it, and for a moment I really thought: I will call Nick and he will come back. Things like this can be undone. But I knew that he would never come back again, not really. He wasn't only mine any more, that part was over. Melissa knew things that I didn't know. After everything that had happened between them they still desired one another. I thought about her email, and about how I was sick and probably infertile anyway, and how I could give Nick nothing that would mean anything to him.

For the next few days I stared at my phone for hours on end and accomplished nothing. The time moved past visibly on the illuminated onscreen clock and yet I still felt as though I didn't notice it passing. Nick didn't call me that evening, or that night. He didn't call me the next day, or the day after that. Nobody did. Gradually the waiting began to feel less like waiting and more like this was simply what life was: the distracting tasks undertaken while the thing you are waiting for continues not to happen. I applied for jobs and turned up for seminars. Things went on.

CHAPTER
TWENTY-NINE

I was offered a job working evenings and weekends serving coffee in a sandwich shop. On my first day a woman called Linda gave me a black apron and showed me how to make coffee. You pressed a little lever to fill the portafilter with grounds, once for a single shot and twice for a double shot. Then you screwed the filter tightly into the machine and hit the water switch. There was also a little steam nozzle and a jug for milk. Linda told me lots of things about coffee, the difference between a latte and a cappuccino, things like that. They served mochas, but Linda told me mochas were "complicated" so I could just let one of the others do it. People never order mochas, she said.

I never saw Bobbi in college, though I was convinced I would. I spent long periods lingering in the arts building, on the ramp where she usually smoked, or near the debating society rooms where they had free copies of the *New Yorker* and you could use their kitchen to make tea. She never appeared. Our timetables weren't similar anyway. I wanted to run into her at a time that suited me, a time when I would appear wearing my camel coat, maybe with my arms full of books, and I could smile at her with the tentative smile of someone who wants to forget an argument. My overriding fear was that she would come into the sandwich shop where I worked and see that I had a job. Whenever a slim woman with a dark fringe came through the door, I turned compulsively toward the coffee machine and pretended to steam milk. In the preceding months, I felt as if I'd glimpsed the possibility of an alternative life, the possibility of accumulating income just by writing and talking and taking an interest in things. By the time my story was accepted for publication, I even felt like I'd entered that world myself, like I'd folded my old life up behind me and put it away. I was ashamed at the idea that Bobbi might come into the sandwich shop and see for herself how deluded I had been.

I told my mother about the phone call from my father. In fact, we had a fight about it over the phone, after which I felt too tired to speak or move for an hour. I called her "an enabler". She said: oh it's my fault, is it? Everything is my fault. She said his brother had seen him in town the day before and that he was fine. I repeated the incident from my childhood where he had thrown a shoe at my face. I'm a bad mother, she said, that's what you're saying. If that's the conclusion you draw from the facts, that's your business, I said. She told me I had never loved my father anyway.

According to you the only way to love someone is to let them treat you like shit, I said.

She hung up on me. Afterwards I lay on my bed feeling like a light had been switched off.

305

One day toward the end of November, Evelyn posted a video link on Melissa's Facebook wall with the message: just came across this again and I'm DEAD. I could see from the thumbnail that the video had been filmed in the kitchen of Melissa's house. I clicked and waited for it to load. The lighting in the video was buttery yellow, there were fairy lights strung up in the background, and I could see Nick and Melissa standing side by side at the kitchen countertops. Then the sound came on. Someone behind the camera was saying: okay, okay, settle down. The camerawork was shaky, but I saw Melissa turn to Nick, they were both laughing. He was wearing a black sweater. He nodded along as if she was signalling something to him, and then he sang the words: I really can't stay. Melissa sang: but baby, it's cold outside. They were singing a duet, it was funny. Everyone in the room was laughing and applauding and I could hear Evelyn's voice saying, sh! sh! I had never heard Nick singing before, he had a sweet voice. So did Melissa. It was good the way they acted it out, Nick being reluctant and Melissa trying to make him stay. It suited them. They had obviously practised it for their friends. Anyone could see from the video how much they loved each other. If I had seen them like this before, I thought, maybe nothing would have happened. Maybe I would have known.

I only worked from 5 until 8p.m. on weekdays, but by the time I got home I felt so exhausted I couldn't eat. I fell behind on college work. With my hours in the sandwich shop, I had less time to finish my academic reading, but the real problem was my focus. I couldn't concentrate. Concepts refused to arrange themselves into patterns, and my vocabulary felt smaller and less precise. After my second pay cheque came in, I withdrew two hundred euro from my bank account and put it in an envelope. On a slip of notepaper I wrote: thank you for the loan. Then I mailed it to Nick's address in Monkstown. He never got back to me to say he received it, but by then I didn't expect him to.

It was almost December. I had three pills left in the cycle, then two, then one. As soon as I finished the packet the feeling came back, like before. It lasted days. I went to class as usual, gritting my teeth. The cramps came on in waves and left me weak and sweating when they receded. A teaching assistant called on me to say something about the character of Will Ladislaw and although I had actually finished *Middlemarch*, I just opened and closed my mouth like a fish. Eventually I managed to say: no. I'm sorry.

That evening I walked home down Thomas Street. My legs were trembling and I hadn't eaten a whole meal in days. My abdomen felt swollen, and for a few seconds I braced my body against a bicycle stand. My vision was beginning to disintegrate. My hand on the bicycle stand appeared translucent, like a photo negative held up in front of a light. The Thomas Street church was just a few steps ahead of me and I walked with a lopsided shuffle toward the door, holding my ribcage with one arm.

The church smelled of stale incense and dry air. Columns of stained glass rose up behind the altar like long piano-playing fingers and the ceiling was the white and mint-green colour of confectionery. I hadn't been in a church since I was a child. Two old women were sitting off to the side with rosary beads. I sat at the back and looked up at the stained glass, trying to fix it in my visual field, as if its permanence could prevent my disappearance. This stupid disease never killed anyone, I thought. My face was sweating, or else it had been damp outside and I hadn't noticed. I unbuttoned my coat and used the dry inside of my scarf to wipe my forehead.

I breathed in through my nose, feeling my lips part with the effort of filling my own lungs. I clasped my hands together in my lap. The pain kicked against my spine, radiating up into my skull and making my eyes water. I'm praying, I thought. I'm actually sitting here praying for God to help me. I was. Please help me, I thought. Please. I knew that there were rules about this, that you had to believe in a divine ordering principle before you could appeal to it for anything, and I didn't believe. But I make an effort, I thought. I love my fellow human beings. Or do I? Do I love Bobbi, after she tore up my story like that and left me alone? Do I love Nick, even if he doesn't want to fuck me any more? Do I love Melissa? Did I ever? Do I love my mother and father? Could I love everyone and even include bad people? I bowed my forehead into my clasped hands, feeling faint.

Instead of thinking gigantic thoughts, I tried to focus on something small, the smallest thing I could think of. Someone once made this pew I'm sitting on, I thought. Someone sanded the wood and varnished it. Someone carried it into the church. Someone laid the tiles on the floor, someone fitted the windows. Each brick was placed by human hands, each hinge fitted on each door, every road surface outside, every bulb in every streetlight. And even things built by machines were really built by human beings, who built the machines initially. And human beings themselves, made by other humans, struggling to create happy children and families. Me, all the clothing I wear, all the language I know. Who put me here in this church, thinking these thoughts? Other people, some I know very well and others I have never met. Am I myself, or am I them? Is this me, Frances? No, it is not me. It is the others. Do I sometimes hurt and harm myself, do I abuse the unearned cultural privilege of whiteness, do I take the labour of others for granted, have I sometimes exploited a reductive iteration of gender theory to avoid serious moral engagement, do I have a troubled relationship with my body, yes. Do I want to be free of pain and therefore demand that others also live free of pain, the pain which is mine and therefore also theirs, yes, yes.

When I opened my eyes I felt that I had understood something, and the cells of my body seemed to light up like millions of glowing points of contact, and I was aware of something profound. Then I stood up from my seat and collapsed.

Fainting had become normal for me. I assured the woman who helped me up that it had happened before and she seemed a little annoyed then, like: sort it out.

My mouth tasted bad, but I was strong enough to walk unsupported. My experience of spiritual awakening had deserted me. I stopped in the Centra on the way home, bought myself two packets of instant noodles and a boxed chocolate cake, and completed the walk slowly and carefully, one foot in front of the other.

At home I opened the lid of the cake box, took out a spoon, and dialled Melissa's mobile number. It rang, the ringing like a satisfied purr. Then her breath.

Hello? said Melissa.

Can we talk for a second? Or is it a bad time?

She laughed, or at least I think that's the noise she was making.

You mean generally or right now? she said. Generally it's a bad time, but right now is fine.

Why did you send Bobbi my story?

I don't know, Frances. Why did you fuck my husband?

Is that supposed to shock me? I said. You're the shocking person who uses bad language, okay. Now that we've established that, why did you send Bobbi my story?

She went quiet. I ran the tip of the spoon over the cake icing and licked it. It tasted sugary and flavourless.

You really do have these sudden bursts of aggression, don't you? she said. Like with Valerie. Are you threatened by other women?

I have a question for you, if you don't want to answer it then hang up.

What entitles you to an explanation of my behaviour?

You hated me, I said. Didn't you?

She sighed. I don't even know what that means, she said. I dug the spoon down into the cake, into the sponge part, and ate a mouthful.

You treated me with total contempt, said Melissa. And I don't mean because of Nick. The first time you came to our house you just looked around like: here's something bourgeois and embarrassing that I'm going to destroy. And I mean, you took such enjoyment in destroying it. Suddenly I'm looking around my own fucking house, thinking: is this sofa ugly? Is it kitsch to drink wine? And things I felt good about before started to make me feel pathetic. Having a husband instead of just fucking someone else's husband. Having a book deal instead of writing nasty short stories about people I know and selling them to prestigious magazines. I mean, you came into my house with your fucking nose piercing like: oh, I'll really enjoy eviscerating this whole set-up. She's so establishment.

I wedged the spoon into the cake so that it stood upright on its own. I then used my hand to massage my face.

I don't have a nose piercing, I said. That's Bobbi.

Okay. My deepest apologies.

I didn't realise you found me so subversive. In real life I didn't feel any contempt for your house. I wanted it to be my house. I wanted your whole life. Maybe I did shitty things to try and get it, but I'm poor and you're rich. I wasn't trying to trash your life, I was trying to steal it.

She made a kind of snorting noise, but I didn't believe she was really dismissing what I'd said. It was more a performance than a reaction.

You had an affair with my husband because you liked me so much, said Melissa.

No, I'm not saying I liked you.

Okay. I didn't like you either. But you weren't a very nice person.

We both paused then, like we had just raced each other up a set of stairs and we were out of breath and thinking about how foolish it was.

I regret that, I said. I regret not being nicer. I should have tried harder to be your friend. I'm sorry.

What?

I'm sorry, Melissa. I'm sorry for this aggressive phone call, it was stupid. I don't really know what I'm doing at the moment. I'm having a hard time maybe. I'm sorry I called you. And look, I'm sorry for everything.

Jesus, she said. What's wrong, are you okay?

I'm fine. I just feel like I haven't been the person that I should have been. I don't know what I'm saying now. I wish I had gotten to know you better and treated you with more kindness, I want to apologise for that. I'll hang up.

I hung up before she could say anything. I ate some cake, fast and hungrily, then wiped my mouth, opened up my laptop and wrote an email.

Dear Bobbi,

Tonight I fainted in a church, you would have found it pretty funny. I'm sorry my story hurt your feelings. I think the reason it hurt is because it showed I could be honest with someone else even when I wasn't honest with you. I hope that's the reason. I called Melissa on the phone tonight asking her why she sent the story to you. It took me some time to realise that what I was really asking was: why did I write the story? It was a very embarrassing and garbled phone call. Maybe I think of her as my mother. The truth is that I love you and I always have. Do I mean that Platonically? I don't object when you kiss me. The idea of us sleeping together again has always been exciting. When you broke up with me I felt you beat me at a game we were playing together, and I wanted to come back and beat you. Now I think I just want to sleep with you, without metaphors. That doesn't mean I don't have other desires. Right now for example, I'm eating chocolate cake out of the box with a teaspoon. To love someone under capitalism you have to love everyone. Is that theory or just theology? When I read the Bible I picture you as Jesus, so maybe fainting in a church was a metaphor after all. But I'm not trying to be intelligent now. I can't say sorry for writing that story or for taking the money. I can say sorry that it shocked you, when I should have told you before. You're not just an idea to me. If I've ever treated you like that I'm sorry. The night when you talked about monogamy I loved your intellect. I didn't understand what you were trying to tell me. Maybe I'm a lot more stupid than either of us thought. When there were four of us I always thought in terms of couples anyway, which threatened me, since all the possible couples that didn't involve me seemed so much more interesting than the ones that did. You and Nick, you and Melissa, even Nick and Melissa in their own way. But now I see that nothing consists of two people, or even three. My relationship with you is also produced by your relationship with Melissa, and with Nick, and with your childhood self, etc., etc. I wanted things for myself because I thought I existed. You're going to write back and explain what Lacan really meant. Or you might not write back at all. I did faint, if you object to my prose style. That wasn't a lie and I'm still shivering. Is it possible we could develop an alternative model of loving each other? I'm not drunk. Please write back. I love you.

Frances.

At some point the chocolate cake was gone. I looked into the box and saw crumbs and icing smeared around the paper rim which I had neglected to remove. I got up from the table, put the kettle on, and emptied two spoonfuls of coffee into the French press. I took some painkillers, I drank the coffee, I watched a murder mystery on Netflix. A certain peace had come to me and I wondered if it was God's doing after all. Not that God existed in any material way but as a shared cultural practice so widespread that it came to seem materially real, like language or gender.

At ten past eleven that night I heard her keys in the door. I went to the hall and she was unzipping her raincoat, the one she had brought to France that summer, and streams of water were trickling down her

314

sleeves and dripping with a light percussive sound onto the floorboards. Our eyes met.

That was a weird email, Bobbi said. But I love you too.

CHAPTER
THIRTY

We talked about our break-up for the first time that night. It felt like opening a door that's been inside your own house all along, a door that you walk past every day and try never to think about. Bobbi told me I had made her miserable. We were sitting on my bed, Bobbi against the headboard with the pillows propped behind her, me at the foot of the mattress sitting with crossed legs. She said that I'd laughed at her during arguments, like she was a moron. I told her what Melissa said, that I wasn't a very nice person. Bobbi laughed herself then. Melissa would know, she said. When has she ever been nice to anyone?

Maybe niceness is the wrong metric, I said.

Of course it's really about power, Bobbi agreed. But it's harder to work out who has the power, so instead we rely on "niceness" as a kind of stand-in. I mean this is an issue in public discourse. We end up asking like, is Israel "nicer" than Palestine. You know what I'm saying.

I do.

Jerry is certainly "nicer" than Eleanor.

Yes, I said.

I had made Bobbi a cup of tea, and she was holding it on her lap, between her thighs. She warmed her hands on either side of it while we were talking.

I don't resent you writing about me for profit, by the way, said Bobbi. I find it funny as long as I'm actually in on the joke.

I know. I could have told you and I didn't. But at some level I still see you as the person who broke my heart and left me unfit for normal relationships.

You underestimate your own power so you don't have to blame yourself for treating other people badly. You tell yourself stories about it. Oh well, Bobbi's rich, Nick's a man, I can't hurt these people. If anything they're out to hurt me and I'm defending myself.

I shrugged. I could think of nothing to say. She lifted the tea and sipped it, then settled the cup back between her thighs.

You could go to counselling, she said.

Do you think I should?

You're not above it. It might be good for you. It's not necessarily normal to go around collapsing in churches.

I didn't try to explain that the fainting wasn't psychological. Anyway, what did I know? If you think so, I said.

I think it would kill you, said Bobbi. To admit that you needed help from some touchy-feely psychology graduate. Probably a Labour voter. But maybe it would kill you in a good way.

Truly I say to you, unless one is born again.

Yeah. I came not to send peace, but a sword.

After that night, Bobbi started to walk with me from college to the sandwich shop in the evenings. She learned Linda's name and made small talk with her while I put my apron on. Linda's son was in the Irish army, Bobbi learned that. When I came home in the evening we ate dinner together. She moved some of her clothing into my room, some T-shirts and clean underwear. In bed we folded around each other like origami. It's possible to feel so grateful that you can't get to sleep at night.

Marianne saw us holding hands in college one day and said: you're back together! We shrugged. It was a relationship, and also not a relationship. Each of our gestures felt spontaneous, and if from the outside we resembled a couple, that was an interesting coincidence for us. We developed a joke about it, which was meaningless to everyone including ourselves: what *is* a friend? we would say humorously. What *is* a conversation?

In the mornings Bobbi liked to get out of bed before me, so she could use up all the hot water in the shower like she used to when she was staying in the other room. Then she would drink an entire pot of coffee with her hair dripping wet at the kitchen table. Sometimes I carried a towel from the hot press and draped it onto her head, but she'd just continue to ignore me and read about social housing online. She peeled oranges and left the soft, sweet-smelling peel wherever she dropped it, to turn dry and crinkly on the tabletop or an arm of the sofa. In the evenings we walked through Phoenix Park under an umbrella, linking arms and smoking at the foot of the Wellington monument.

In bed we talked for hours, conversations that spiralled out from observations into grand, abstract theories and back again. Bobbi talked about Ronald Reagan and the IMF. She had an unusual respect for conspiracy theorists. She was interested in the nature of things, but she was also generous. I didn't feel with her, like I did with many other people, that while I was talking she was just preparing the next thing she wanted to say. She was a great listener, an active listener. Sometimes while I spoke she would make a sudden noise, like the force of her interest in what I was saying just expressed itself from her mouth. Oh! she would say. Or: so true!

One night in December we went out to celebrate Marianne's birthday. Everyone was in a good mood, the Christmas lights were all lit up outside, and people were telling funny stories about things Marianne had done and said while drunk or sleepy. Bobbi did an impression of her, tipping her head down and glancing up sweetly through her eyelashes, lifting her shoulders in a feigned shrug. I laughed, it really was funny, and said: again! Marianne was wiping tears away. Stop it, she said. Oh my lord. Bobbi and I had bought Marianne a pair of gloves, a nice blue leather pair, one glove from each of us. Andrew called us cheap and Marianne said he lacked imagination. She put them on in front of us: the Frances glove, she said. And the Bobbi glove. Then she mimed them talking to each other like puppets. On and on and on, she said.

That night we talked about the war in Syria, and the invasion of Iraq. Andrew said Bobbi didn't understand history and she just blamed everything on the West. Everyone at the table made an "ooh" noise like we were all on a game show together. In the ensuing disagreement, Bobbi displayed a remorseless intelligence, seeming to have read everything on whatever topic Andrew mentioned, correcting him only when necessary for her broader argument, not even alluding to the fact that she'd almost completed a history degree. I knew it was the first thing I would have mentioned if someone belittled me. Bobbi was different. While she spoke, her eyes often pointed upward, at light fixtures or far-off windows, and she gesticulated with her hands. All I could do with my attention was use it on other people, watching them for signs of agreement or irritation, trying to invite them into the discussion when they fell silent.

Bobbi and Melissa were still in touch at the time, but it was clear that they'd drawn away from one another. Bobbi had formulated new theories about Melissa's personality and private life which were noticeably less flattering than those she had earlier advanced. I was striving to love everyone, which meant I tried to stay quiet.

We shouldn't have trusted them, Bobbi said.

We were eating Chinese food from paper boxes at the time, sitting on my sofa and half-watching a Greta Gerwig film.

We didn't know how codependent they were, Bobbi said. I mean, they were only ever in it for each other.

It's probably good for their relationship to have these dramatic affairs sometimes, it keeps things interesting for them.

Maybe.

I'm not saying Nick was intentionally trying to mess with you. Nick I actually like. But ultimately they were always going to go back to this fucked-up relationship they have because that's what they're used to. You know? I just feel so mad at them. They treated us like a resource.

You're disappointed we didn't get to break up their marriage, I said.

She laughed with a mouth full of noodles. On the television screen, Greta Gerwig was shoving her friend into some shrubbery as a game.

Who even gets married? said Bobbi. It's sinister. Who wants state apparatuses sustaining their relationship?

I don't know. What is ours sustained by?

That's it! That's exactly what I mean. Nothing. Do I call myself your girlfriend? No. Calling myself your girlfriend would be imposing some prefabricated cultural dynamic on us that's outside our control. You know?

I thought about this until the film was over. Then I said: wait, so does that mean you're not my girlfriend? She laughed. Are you serious? she said. No. I'm not your girlfriend.

Philip said he thought Bobbi was my girlfriend. We went out for coffee together during the week, and he told me that Sunny had offered him a part-time job, with real wages. I told him that I wasn't jealous, which disappointed him, though I was also worried it was a lie. I liked Sunny. I liked the idea of books and reading. I didn't know why I couldn't enjoy things like other people did.

I'm not asking you if she's my girlfriend, I said. I'm telling you she's not.

But she obviously is. I mean, you're doing some radical lesbian thing or whatever, but in basic vocabulary she is your girlfriend.

No. Again, this isn't a question, it's a statement.

He was crinkling up a sugar sachet in his fingers. We'd been talking for a while about his new job, a conversation that had left me feeling flat like a soft drink.

Well, I think she is, he said. I mean, in a good way. I think it's really good for you. Especially after all that unpleasantness with Melissa.

What unpleasantness?

You know, whatever weird sex thing was going on there. With the husband.

I stared at him and I was at a loss to say anything at all. I watched the blue ink of the sugar sachet rub off onto his fingers, etching his fingerprints in thin blue ridges. Finally I said "I" several times, which he didn't seem to notice. The husband? I thought. Philip, you know his name.

What weird thing? I said.

Weren't you sleeping with both of them? That's what people were saying.

322

No, I wasn't. Not that it would be wrong if I was, but I wasn't.

Oh, okay, he said. I heard all kinds of weird things were going on.

I don't really know why you're saying this to me.

At this, Philip looked up with a shocked expression, and he reddened visibly. The sugar sachet slipped and he had to pinch it quickly with his fingers.

Sorry, he said. I didn't mean to upset you.

You're just telling me about these rumours because you think, what, I'll laugh about it? Like it's funny to me that people say nasty things behind my back?

I'm sorry, I just assumed that you knew.

I breathed in deeply through my nose. I knew I could walk away from the table, but I didn't know where to walk to. I couldn't think of anywhere I would like to go. I stood up anyway and took my coat from the back of the chair. I could see Philip was uncomfortable, and that he even felt guilty for hurting me, but I didn't want to stay there any longer. I buttoned my coat up while he said weakly: where are you going?

It's okay, I said. Forget about it. I'm just getting some air.

I never told Bobbi about the ultrasound or the meeting with the consultant. By refusing to admit that I was sick, I felt I could keep the sickness outside time and space, something only in my own head. If other people knew about it, the sickness would become real and I would have to spend my life being a sick person. This could only interfere with my other ambitions, such as achieving enlightenment and being a fun girl. I used internet forums to assess if this was a problem for anyone else. I searched "can't tell people I'm" and Google suggested: "gay" and "pregnant".

Sometimes at night when Bobbi and I were in bed together, my father called me. I would take the phone into the bathroom quietly to answer it. He had become less and less coherent. At times he seemed to believe that he was being hunted. He said: I have these thoughts, bad thoughts, you know? My mother said his brothers and sisters had been getting the phone calls too, but what could anyone do about it? He was never in the house when they went over. Often I could hear cars passing in the background, so I knew he was outside. Occasionally he seemed concerned for my safety also. He told me not to let them find me. I said: I won't, Dad. They're not going to find me. I'm safe where I am.

I knew my pain could begin again at any time, so I started taking the maximum dose of ibuprofen every day just in case. I concealed my grey notebook along with the boxes of painkillers in the top drawer of my desk, and I only removed them when Bobbi was showering or gone to class. This top drawer seemed to signify everything that was wrong with me, everything bad I felt about myself, so whenever it caught my eye I started to feel sick again. Bobbi never asked about it. She never mentioned the ultrasound or asked who was calling me on the phone at night. I understood it was my fault but I didn't know what to do about it. I needed to feel normal again.

My mother came up to Dublin that weekend. We went shopping together, she bought me a new dress, and we went for lunch in a cafe on Wicklow Street. She seemed tired, and I was tired too. I ordered a smoked salmon bagel and picked at the slimy pieces of fish with my fork. The dress was in a paper bag under the table and I kept kicking it accidentally. I had suggested the cafe for lunch, and I could tell my mother was being polite about it, though in her presence I noticed that the sandwiches were outrageously expensive and served with side salads nobody ate. When she ordered tea, it came in a pot with a fiddly china teacup and saucer, which she smiled at gamely. Do you like this place? she said.

It's okay, I replied, realising I hated it.

I saw your father the other day.

I speared a piece of salmon with my fork and transferred it into my mouth. It tasted of lemon and salt. I swallowed, dabbed at my lips with a napkin and said: oh.

He's not well, she said. I can see that.

He's never been well.

I tried to have a word with him.

I looked up at her. She was staring down at her sandwich blankly, or maybe affecting a blank expression to conceal something else.

You have to understand, she said. He's not like you. You're tough, you can cope with things. Your father finds life very difficult.

I tried to assess these statements. Were they true? Did it matter if they were true? I put my fork down.

You're lucky, she said. I know you might not feel that way. You can go on hating him for the rest of your life if you want.

I don't hate him.

A waiter went past precariously holding three bowls of soup. My mother looked at me.

I love him, I said.

That's news to me.

Well, I'm not like you.

She laughed then, and I felt better. She reached for my hand across the table and I let her hold it.

CHAPTER
THIRTY-ONE

The following week my phone rang. I remember exactly where I was standing when it started: just in front of the New Fiction shelves in Hodges Figgis, and it was thirteen minutes past five. I was looking for a Christmas present for Bobbi, and when I fished the phone out of my coat pocket, the screen read: Nick. My neck and shoulders felt rigid and suddenly very exposed. I slid my fingertip across the screen, lifted the phone to my cheek and said: hello?

Hey, Nick's voice said. Listen, they don't have red peppers, but is yellow okay?

His voice seemed to hit me somewhere behind my knees and travel upward in a flood of warmth, so that I knew I was blushing.

Oh dear, I said. I think you have the wrong number.

For a second he said nothing. Don't hang up, I thought. Don't hang up. I started to walk around the New Fiction shelves trailing my finger along the spines as if I was still browsing.

Jesus Christ, said Nick slowly. Is this Frances?

Yes. It is me.

He made a sound which momentarily I mistook for laughter, though I realised then that he was coughing. I

327

started to laugh and had to hold the phone away from my face in case he thought I was crying. When he spoke he sounded measured, his confusion genuine.

I have no idea how this happened, he said. Did I just place this call to you?

Yes. You asked me a question about peppers.

Oh my God. I'm so sorry. I can't explain how I dialled your number. It really was an honest mistake, I'm sorry.

I moved over to the display near the front of the bookshop, which showcased a selection of new books from diverse genres. I picked up a science fiction novel and pretended to read the back.

Were you trying to get Melissa? I said.

I was. Yeah.

That's okay. I gather you're in the supermarket.

He did laugh then, like he was laughing at how absurd the situation was. I put down the science fiction and opened the cover of a historical romance. The words lay flat on the page, my eyes didn't try to read them.

I am in the supermarket, he said.

I'm in a bookshop.

Are you, really. Christmas shopping?

Yes, I said. I'm looking for something for Bobbi.

He made a noise like "hm" then, not quite laughing but still amused or pleased. I closed the cover of the book. Don't hang up, I thought.

They've reissued that Chris Kraus novel recently, he said. I read a review, it sounded like you might enjoy it.

Although I realise now you didn't actually ask for my advice.

Your advice is welcome, Nick. You have an enchanting voice.

He said nothing. I exited the bookshop, gripping the phone tightly to my face, so that the screen felt hot and a little oily. Outside it was cold. I was wearing a fake-fur hat.

Did I take our playful repartee too far there? I said.

Oh no, I'm sorry. I was just trying to come up with something nice to say to you, but everything I can think of sounds . . .

Insincere?

Too sincere, he said. Needy. I'm thinking, how do you flatter your ex-girlfriend, but in a kind of aloof way?

I laughed then and so did he. The relief of our mutual laughter was very sweet, and it dispelled the feeling that he would hang up on me, at least for the moment. Beside me a bus rattled through some standing water and wet my shins. I was walking away from college, toward St Stephen's Green.

You were never a big compliments guy, I said.

No, I know. It's something I regret.

Sometimes when drunk, you were nice.

Yeah, he said. Is that it, I was only nice to you when I was drunk?

I laughed again, on my own this time. The phone seemed to be transmitting some weird radioactive energy into my body, making me walk very fast and laugh about nothing.

You were always nice, I said. That's not what I meant.

You're feeling sorry for me, are you?

Nick, I haven't heard from you in a month, and we're only talking now because you got my name mixed up with your wife's. I don't feel sorry for you.

Well, I've been very strict with myself about not calling you, he said.

We were quiet then for a few seconds but neither of us hung up.

Are you still in the supermarket? I said.

Yeah, where are you? You're outside now.

Walking up the street.

The restaurants and bars all had miniature Christmas trees and fake sprigs of holly in the window. A woman went past holding the hand of a tiny blonde child who was complaining about the cold.

I waited for you to call me, I said.

Frances, you told me you didn't want to see me any more. I wasn't going to harass you after that.

I stopped randomly outside an off-licence, looking at the bottles of Cointreau and Disaronno stacked up in the window like jewels.

How's Melissa? I said.

She's okay. She's under a lot of pressure with deadlines. You know, which is why I'm calling to make sure I won't be in trouble for buying the wrong kind of vegetable.

Groceries seem to play a big role in how she responds to stress.

I've actually tried explaining that to her, he said. How's Bobbi?

I turned away from the window and went on walking up toward the top of the street. The hand holding the phone was getting cold, but my ear was hot.

Bobbi's good, I said.

I hear you're back together now.

Well, she's not my girlfriend as such. We're sleeping together, but I think that's a way of testing the limits of best friendship. I actually don't know what we're doing. It seems to be working okay.

That's very anarchist of you, he said.

Thanks, she'll be pleased with that.

I waited at the lights, to cross over to St Stephen's Green. The headlamps of cars flashed past and at the top of Grafton Street some buskers were singing "Fairytale of New York". An illuminated yellow billboard read THIS CHRISTMAS . . . EXPERIENCE TRUE LUXURY.

Can I ask your advice on something? I said.

Yeah, of course. I think I show consistently poor judgement in my own decision-making, but if you think it would help we can give it a shot.

You see, there's something I'm keeping from Bobbi, and I don't know how to tell her about it. I'm not being coy, it's nothing to do with you.

I've never suspected you of coyness, he said. Go on.

I told him I would cross the road first. It was dark then, and everything was gathered around points of light: shop windows, faces flushed with cold, a row of taxis idling along the kerb. I heard a shake of reins and the sound of hooves across the street. Entering the park through a side gate the noise of traffic seemed to turn itself down, like it caught in the bare branches and dissolved in air. My breath laid a white path in front of me.

Remember I had to go to the hospital for a consultation last month? I said. And I told you it went fine.

At first Nick said nothing. Then he said: I'm still in the shop now. Maybe I'll get back in my car and we can talk, okay? It's kind of noisy here, just give me ten seconds. I said sure. In my left ear I could hear the soft white sound of water, footsteps approaching and receding, and in my right ear I could hear the voice of the automated cashier as Nick walked past the tills. Then the automatic doors, and then the car park. I heard the beep that his car made when he unlocked it remotely, and then I could hear him get inside and shut the door. His breath was louder in the silence.

You were saying, he said.

Well, it turns out I have this condition where the cells in my uterus are growing in the wrong places. Endometriosis, you've probably heard of it, I hadn't. It's not dangerous or anything, but they can't cure it, so it's kind of a chronic pain issue. I faint pretty often, which is awkward. And I might not be able to have children. I mean, they don't know if I will or not. It's probably a stupid thing to be upset about since they don't even know yet.

I walked by a streetlight which cast my shadow long and witchy in front of me, so long that the tips of my body faded into nothing.

It's not stupid to be upset about that, he said.

Is it not?

No.

The last time I saw you, I said. When we got into bed together and then you told me you wanted to stop, I thought, you know. I don't feel good to you any more. Like, you can feel that there's something wrong with me. Which is crazy since I've had this disease the whole time anyway. But that was the first time we were together after you started sleeping with Melissa and maybe I was feeling vulnerable, I don't know.

He breathed in and out into the receiver. I didn't need him to say anything then, to explain what he was feeling. I stopped at a small damp bench beside a bronze bust and sat down.

And you haven't told Bobbi about the diagnosis, he said.

I haven't told anyone. Just you. I feel like talking about it will make people see me as a sick person.

A man walking a Yorkshire terrier went past, and the terrier noticed me and strained at its lead to get at my feet. It was wearing a quilted jacket. The man flashed me a quick smile, apologetic, and they moved on. Nick said nothing.

Well, what do you think? I said.

About Bobbi? I think you should tell her. You can't control what she thinks of you anyway. You know, sick or healthy, you're never going to be able to do that.

What you're doing now is deceiving her just for the illusion of control, which probably isn't worth it. I don't rate my own advice very highly, though.

It's good advice.

The cold of the bench had travelled through the wool of my coat and into my skin and bones. I didn't get up, I stayed sitting. Nick said how sorry he was to hear that I was ill, and I accepted that and thanked him. He asked a couple of questions about how to treat the symptoms and whether they might just get better with time. He knew another woman who had it, his cousin's wife, and he said they had children, just for whatever it was worth. I said IVF sounded scary to me and he said, yeah, they didn't use IVF I don't think. But are those treatments getting less invasive now? They're definitely improving. I said I didn't know.

He coughed. You know the last time we saw one another, he said, I wanted to stop because I was afraid I was hurting you. That's all.

Okay, I said. Thanks for telling me that. You weren't hurting me.

We paused.

I can't tell you how strict I've been with myself about not calling you, he said eventually.

I thought you'd forgotten all about me.

The idea of forgetting anything about you is kind of horrifying to me.

I smiled. I said: is it really? My feet were getting cold in their boots then.

Where are you now? he said. You're not walking any more, you're somewhere quiet.

I'm in Stephen's Green.

Oh, really? I'm in town too, I'm like ten minutes away from you. I won't come see you or anything, don't worry. It's just curious to think of you being so close by.

I imagined him sitting in his car somewhere, smiling to himself on the phone, how aggravatingly handsome he would look. I tucked my free hand up inside my coat to keep it warm.

When we were in France together, I said, do you remember we were in the sea one day and I asked you to tell me that you wanted me, and you splashed water on my face and told me to fuck off?

When Nick spoke, I could hear he was still smiling. You're making me sound like such a prick, he said. I was just kidding with you, I wasn't seriously telling you to fuck off.

But you couldn't just say that you wanted me, I said.

Well, everyone else was always talking about it. I thought you were being a little gratuitous.

I should have known it wouldn't work out between us.

Didn't we always know that? he said.

I paused for a second. Then I just said: I didn't.

Well, but what does it mean for a relationship to "work out"? he said. It was never going to be something conventional.

I got up from the bench. It was too cold to sit outside. I wanted to be warm again. Lit from below, empty branches scratched at the sky.

I didn't think it had to be, I said.

You know, you're saying that, but you obviously weren't happy that I loved someone else. It's okay, it doesn't make you a bad person.

But I loved someone else.

Yeah, I know, he said. But you didn't want me to.

I wouldn't have minded, if . . .

I tried to think of a way to finish this sentence without saying: if I were different, if I were the person I wanted to be. Instead I just let it fall off into silence. I was so cold.

I can't believe you're on the phone saying you waited for me to call you, he said quietly. You really don't know how devastating it is to hear that.

How do you think I feel? You didn't even want to speak to me, you just thought I was Melissa.

Of course I wanted to speak to you. How long have we been on the phone now?

I got to the gate I had come through, but it was locked. My eyes were starting to sting with cold. Outside the railing a line of people queued for the 145. I walked toward the main gate, where I could see the lights of the shopping centre. I thought of Nick and Melissa singing "Baby It's Cold Outside" in their warm kitchen with all their friends around them.

You said it yourself, I said. It never would have worked.

Well, is it working now? If I come and pick you up and we drive around talking and I say, oh, sorry for not calling you, I've been a fool, is that working then?

If two people make each other happy then it's working.

You could smile at a stranger on the street and make them happy, he said. We're talking about something more complicated.

As I got closer to the gate I heard the bell ringing. The noise of traffic opened up again, like a light getting brighter and brighter.

Does it have to be complicated? I said.

Yeah, I think so.

There's the thing with Bobbi, which is important to me.

You're telling me, he said. I'm married.

It's always going to be fucked up like this, isn't it?

But I'll compliment you more this time.

I was at the gate. I wanted to tell him about the church. That was a different conversation. I wanted things from him that would make everything else complicated.

Like what kind of compliment? I said.

I have one that's not really a compliment but I think you'll like it.

Okay, tell me.

Remember the first time we kissed? he said. At the party. And I said I didn't think the utility room was a good place to be kissing and we left. You know I went up to my room and waited for you, right? I mean for hours. And at first I really thought you would come. It was probably the most wretched I ever felt in my life, this kind of ecstatic wretchedness that in a way I was practically enjoying. Because even if you did come upstairs, what then? The house was full of people, it's not like anything was going to happen. But every time I thought of going back down again I would imagine hearing you on the stairs, and I couldn't leave, I mean I physically couldn't. Anyway, how I felt then, knowing that you were close by and feeling completely paralysed by it, this phone call is very similar. If I told you where my car is right now, I don't think I'd be able to leave, I think I would have to stay here just in case you changed your mind about everything. You know, I still have that impulse to be available to you. You'll notice I didn't buy anything in the supermarket.

I closed my eyes. Things and people moved around me, taking positions in obscure hierarchies, participating in systems I didn't know about and never would. A complex network of objects and concepts. You live through certain things before you understand them. You can't always take the analytical position.

Come and get me, I said.

Acknowledgements

In writing this book I drew a great deal from conversations with my own friends, in particular Kate Oliver and Aoife Comey; I'd like to thank them both very much. Thanks also to the friends who read early drafts of the manuscript: Michael Barton, Michael Nolan, Katie Rooney, Nicole Flattery, and most especially John Patrick McHugh, whose excellent feedback contributed so substantially to the book's development.

Special thanks to Thomas Morris for his early and unwavering advocacy of my work, and for many years of rewarding friendship. Thank you, Tom, sincerely.

I'm very grateful to Chris Rooke, in whose apartment much of this book was written, and to Joseph and Gisele Farrell, whose hospitality gave me the chance to work on parts of the novel in Brittany. Thanks are also due to the Arts Council of Ireland for their financial assistance in finishing this project.

Many, many thanks to my agent, Tracy Bohan, and to my editor, Mitzi Angel; their insight and help has been truly invaluable. Thanks also to the whole team at Faber, who have looked after me so well, and to Alexis Washam at Hogarth.

As ever, I'm immensely grateful to my parents.

Above all, at every stage in the writing and editing of this novel, I relied on John Prasifka for guidance, advice and support. Without him, there would be no book; all that's best in it is his.

A THOUSAND PAPER BIRDS

Tor Udall

Jonah sits on a bench in Kew Gardens, trying to reassemble the shattered pieces of his life following the sudden death of his wife, Audrey. Chloe, shaven-headed and abrasive, sits by the lake, finding solace in the origami she meticulously folds. But when she meets Jonah, her carefully constructed defences threaten to fall. Milly, a child quick to laugh, freely roams Kew. But where is her mother, and where does she go when the gardens are closed? Harry's purpose is to save Kew's plants from extinction. Quiet and enigmatic, he longs for something — or someone — who will root him firmly to the earth. Audrey links these lives together. As the mystery of her death unravels, the characters journey through the seasons to learn that stories, like paper, can be refolded and reformed.

FINDING ALISON

Deirdre Eustace

No one in Carniskey has ever truly understood what led Sean Delaney, a seasoned local fisherman, to risk his life in a high storm in the dead of night. Now, three years on from those tragic events, his wife Alison is still struggling with her unresolved grief and increasing financial worries. She has grown distant from her daughter and estranged from her friends and fellow villagers, particularly her best friend Kathleen, who harbours a deeply guarded secret. Isolated by its stunning yet often cruel surroundings, this is a community used to looking after its own. But the arrival of an outsider — artist and lifelong nomad William — offers Alison a new perspective on life and love that threatens to unearth the mysteries of the past.